COCAINE CONFIDENCE

Clifford Thurlow

YELLOWBAY BOOKS

Published by YellowBay Books Ltd 2012
www.yellowbay.co.uk

YellowBay Books Ltd
ISBN 9 7 8 1 9 0 8 5 3 0 5 2 3

Cover design by Emily Heaton

YellowBay Books is dedicated to edgy new writing.
Let us know what you think at **info@yellowbay.co.uk**,
Or visit Amazon and give the book a review

Act 1

The Spirit of the Times

......scene 1

Nothing beats a Tokarev.

You can take it down and put it back together in 12 seconds blindfolded.

You can do it in nine if you're Miro Stanislav.

What else are you going to do in the black hills of Pristina when you're ten years old and the big guns are booming, spitting death, echoing in your head. They echoed in his dreams and gave him nightmares. So you grow up. You forget the nightmares. People die. You live. It's not what you were, who you were, where you were. It's what you are.

I inglische.

Miro sits alone at the back of the restaurant chewing gum, turning the Tokarev in slow circles. His hands are magician's hands as he unsnaps the 7.62 mm clip, the slide from the barrel, freeing the springs, pin, hammer, catch, the long sensual curve of the trigger. He lays out the parts on the paper tablecloth, seven worn pieces of milled steel like the seven worn hills around the village where he was born.

The Tokarev reminds Miro of the past. It's a tough weapon and, like him, it has made the same kind of journey, slipping a crate at a time out of the back gate of the factory on the outskirts of Belgrade before being smuggled over the roads and rail tracks to the streets of London. You can buy anything in this city. Anyone.

But a gun's personal. It's a part of you. When you need a friend there's nothing like the Tokarev TT33. Just for old times' sake.

Miro is aware of Silvia's eyes watching him across the sea of tables with their salt and pepper pots and silver ashtrays stamped *Absolut* in blue. This is her place. Their place. A hole in the wall in Charlotte Street with three rooms upstairs and a basement hidden below their feet.

Silvia stands behind the glass counter with its display of baklava, the mobile phone in front of her silent as the grave. Kresimir and Teo drink tea, pouring it thick as glue from a silver pot with a long curling spout. Lech sits alone beside the door leading to the kitchen. He lights a fag from the fag he's smoking, turning the packet through fidgety fingers, the air thick with nicotine and some old tune, mandolins, a violin, an accordion - gypsy music the English call it.

Weaving through the cigarette fumes is the spicy smell of moussaka and sauerkraut simmering in iron pots. The big clock with a picture of Republic Square in Belgrade ticks away, counting time. The hands are about to join at midday, that sense of waiting, that sense of time being suspended reminding Miro of watching the sun come up over the hills, another day when you're still alive.

There's a photograph of Slobodan Milosevic fading on the wall, and a corkboard pinned with under-exposed snaps of people Miro can no longer remember. People he wants to forget. His father went to hell in flames when Miro was 12 years old. Even his face has burned from his memory.

Maybe Teo and Lech and his brother Kresimir would have been happier back in the village with the pigs and horse shit.

Not Miro. The past is dead. It belongs to the dead. This is the future. This is his city. There's an old story about the streets of London being paved with gold. It's true. Every word of it. There's money everywhere. You just have to know where to dig it up. And how.

The sound of the mobile vibrating on the counter is sudden, magnified. It snaps Miro from his reverie. Silvia delays a moment, sparks up a fag, then reaches for the machine. She listens, nodding her head slowly up and down, saying nothing.

Silvia doesn't smile, she never smiles, but Miro senses about her lips a look of satisfaction as she clicks off the mobile and places it back on the glass counter. She straightens up, the cigarette burning in the crook of her fingers, a hand on her wide hips like a hooker, a flash of gold glinting in the back of her mouth. Her eyes are as black as coal and there's a black stripe down the centre of her hair where it's growing through the blonde. Twenty-five years ago she could pop out kids in the morning and go back to work in the fields in the afternoon. Silvia can fight like a man. Better than most men.

She edges through the tables like a liner leaving port and stands peering down at Miro, at the ring of oiled steel, at his fine hands flat on the tabletop. She stubs out her fag, takes from the pocket of her skirt a folded square of brown paper which she opens and sprinkles out a rail of white dust along the gun's slide mechanism. She holds it for the boy. Their eyes meet and in their eyes is all the love they don't put into words. He takes the barrel from her and as he snorts back the line starbursts of dynamite explode in his brain.

Aghhhhhhhhhhhhh!

Miro throws back his shoulders, stretches his spine. Then his long slender fingers go to work, wiping the slide mechanism with the corner of an oil cloth, attaching the springs, pin, hammer, catch and trigger. He blows down the barrel, snaps it in place and connects the 7.62 mm clip with 8 cartridges, eight stories about to be told.

He takes six seconds.

Miro weighs the gun in his open palm. He looks at the weapon like you'd look at a painting. Or a woman. The Tokarev doesn't shine. It shimmers with an inner light. A life. He's given it life. It's a part of him. When he holds the hilt it's like holding his dick and sometimes when he's fucking he isn't thinking about who he's fucking, he's thinking about the Tokarev, how it feels when he squeezes the trigger and a slug explodes from the tip, the retort jerking in a wave of pleasure through his body.

He shuffles back the chair, tucks the gun down the back of his Levi's and pushes his arms into a brown buckskin jacket with tassels that sway when he walks. Miro is six something and towers over Silvia. Her eyes are pinpoints as she stares up at her son. She pulls him down by his lapels as if to kiss his cheeks, but no, she doesn't kiss him. In one swift movement she slaps him across both cheeks, forehand and backhand, hard slaps that ring out above the mandolins. He remains still, unflinching. Even as a kid his mother was tough. That's how you survive.

The hands on the big clock finally meet and the brass gong chimes 12 times.

Miro has 10 minutes.

Silvia speaks to him in Serbian, their own language, chopping at the vowels, and he brushes her words away.

'Speak English.'

'You come back straight,' she says.

Miro can see his reflection in her eyes. He has learned to trust no one, rely on no one. But if there is one person he would give his blood for, it is Silvia. She is his blood.

Miro strides across the restaurant, the heels of his boots ringing on the stone floor. The guys drinking tea come to their feet, Kresimir bursting out of his chef's jacket, five years older than Miro and already an old man. Teo, the neighbour's son, a friend from school, gut tumbling over his belt from too much baklava and strudel, a gold chain buried in the hair on his chest, the collar on his red shirt like the wings of some exotic bird. Lech, lean as a wolf in black-framed glasses like some German film director. His family had been wiped out while he was away at university studying medicine. Now he waits tables in NoHo. Better here than there. They can't take your brains from you. Even if they take everything else.

Lech crushes out his fag and watches, nursing his own thoughts. No one says anything. What is there to say? Every detail, every moment has been planned: in 10 minutes Miro will hold the future.

He looks at the faces around him. These are his people. The world outside could go to hell. It was going to hell. This was it. This was everything. *Silvia's* in Charlotte Street. His mother and brother, his two friends, survivors, the future moving like a bullet underground.

Miro and Kresimir high-five like Americans. Miro and Teo do the same. No one says good luck. It's bad luck to say good luck in Kosovo. Even in your own language. Miro makes his way towards the door and Lech calls.

'Hey, Miro...'

Lech has made a gun with his fingers and as Miro turns he shoots him twice. Head and heart.

Miro grins. Men enjoy doing the things they're good at. And Miro is good at what he does.

He grabs two garbage sacks and his helmet from under the counter and doesn't glance back as he hits the streets.

The black Harley Softail stands on the pavement outside, the chrome reflecting the shine on his cowboy boots. The bike fires first kick and he shoots through the traffic like a streak of sunshine, two blocks down, two left turns and he's parked in an alley beside Goodge Street station.

Don't shit on your own doorstep. That's what the English say. But the English don't know Kosovo.

They don't know the Albanians.

Miro spits out his gum.

He keeps the helmet on and the visor down as he slides a ticket in the automatic barrier. He avoids the square box lifts and takes the emergency stairs two at a time down to the platform. No one's waiting.

This must be his lucky day.

He moves below the CCTV camera, away from its prying eye, unbuckles the helmet and uses it to give himself an extra ten inches of height, reaching up to cover the camera with one of the garbage bags. He puts the helmet back on, strides the length of the platform and goes through the same process to cover the second camera. The security staff will finish their tea and roll another fag before they investigate. There's no hurry. Technology will always let you down.

Miro slips a fresh stick of gum between his teeth and makes his way back around the corner to the exit stairs where he leaves the helmet on the first turn.

He sweeps his hands through his hair. He's relaxed. Cocaine confident. He can feel the Tokarev pressed in the back of his waistband. For a moment it is still and silent except for the subterranean wind like the breath of someone dying. Then there's a rumble, soft at first, like thunder from far away, a sound that grows slowly like a fizzing bomb and detonates as the approaching train explodes into the station, the graffiti down the side of the silver carriages screaming messages in an unknown tongue.

Miro makes his way back down the stairs and reaches the platform as the doors are opening.

A handful of people step out: two women and three men: a young guy carrying a backpack, another in blue jeans and a black jacket, probably from one of the TV studios, and a guy in a turban and suit, a confident walk, a big moustache like some primitive warlord.

Something's not right.

He isn't carrying a bag.

And he's not a Turk. Miro's seen plenty of Turks and this guy isn't a Turk. He's from further East. He's sure of that. Miro's not sure why he's sure, you just get to feel these things.

He scopes the two women.

There's a girl in a red top, proud in her hard little body, chin high, head thrown back, tits pink as two ripe peaches. Someone'll be fucking her before the day's out.

He turns and concentrates on the woman: thirty-something in a fitted dark green and yellow checked suit, fingers white from gripping the attaché case in her left hand, right hand swinging free, stilettos tap,

tap, tapping along the platform. He studies her like you'd study a model on the catwalk. Neat figure. Good legs.

Miro glances briefly again at the kid with the backpack, the media guy, the turban, the tits. They stream by and disappear.

Now there's just the woman.

No one said the mule would come in a skirt. But why not? They're sending girls out to fight in wars.

Time finds a new routine, a new dimension, some place where everything stretches and goes slower. The platform's deserted like the streets of a town in a Western when the outlaws arrive. Miro gets into character, his long shadow stretching over the arched walls, the tassels on his jacket swaying with the rhythm, his dark hair swept back thick as a seam of coal. He ambles towards the woman, the tick of his Cuban heels and the drum of the woman's footsteps synchronizing like tango dancers. Like lovers.

The woman measures the distance between them. She glances across the lines to the opposite platform. The people waiting for the southbound train seem far away like figures across the width of a river. There's the wind rush of an approaching train.

Maybe she should skip across the live rail and join them. Go back to where she came from?

Their eyes meet. They don't know each other. But they know each other. Like a hare knows a fox, and a fox knows a fox.

Miro whistles the mandolin tune stuck in his head. He spits out his gum. The woman unbuttons her jacket. He notices the sweat beads breaking across her brow. Now they're close he can see her features, sharp cheekbones, a hook nose, almond eyes, her pallid skin like the pages of an old book.

She shakes her head and the drapes of her dark hair sweep about her shoulders. She's sliding her hand inside her jacket.

A train shoots like a rocket on to the opposite platform, brakes screeching, filling the air with the bite of locking steel.

Two shots ring out, loud as cymbals, fast as the speed of light.

Head and heart.

Neat and clean.

And the Tokarev is back in Miro's belt.

The woman's hand like an iron claw remains locked in a death grip on the attaché case. He pins her wrist flat beneath the sole of his boot and prises back her fingers, snapping them like chicken bones.

Passengers on the train stare through the grimy windows, seeing nothing. The tube pulls away and the only sound in the silence is the drum of Cuban heels and that crap tune Miro can't stop whistling.

He grabs his helmet as he climbs the emergency stairs and exits Goodge Street in under 10 minutes.

……scene 2

Global warming! Don't you just love it. The sky's blue. Colours are cardinal, primeval. This could be the Med, the sun doing its thing, bronzing bare skin, putting smiles on city faces, a shine on shop windows.

Bella can feel the heat on her back, a sheen of sweat below the tight top laced down her spine. Guy's got his arm draped around her shoulders, and they stand there like a couple out for the day, shading their eyes and peering at the display of Prada bags.

'Look, they're *adorable*,' he says. *'Half* price.'

'That's because they're, like, *so* last year.'

He groans theatrically. 'You're beginning to sound like my mother.'

'I didn't know you had a mother!'

Sharp as a snake bite, his pinch on the soft flesh under her arm reminds Bella that in the game they're playing she breaks the rules and Guy Bradwell makes them.

'Ouch, you bitch,' she says, but he's not listening, he's dragging her into the shop.

Now what?

The Pradas in the window get you through the door, but the stuff inside is mostly junk from China. A whiff of patchouli oil from a burning candle cloaks the flesh smell of cheap leather, and there's a mousy girl with beads plaited in her hair growing brain dead as she takes belts from a rack, dusts them and puts them back like some character in myth being punished for eternity.

'Morning,' Guy calls.

She turns away, fussed by the intrusion, and hangs a belt back on the rack.

This is her life. It will always be her life. The mousy girl lives out of town and gets the train into Paddington or Victoria. She wants to be a model or an actress or work in the media. She wants to do something, be something, get a cool tattoo, a piercing, a backstage pass, something, anything, and doesn't know she never will. There is a secret. The mousy girl with beads in her hair doesn't know the secret and how could she know you are either born knowing that secret, or you will live your life never knowing it.

Guy's study of the girl is brief and professional.

He turns to Bella with a bona fide look of affection, and is saddened when she gives him the evil. He kisses his fingertips and runs them over her skinny arm reddened by his pinch.

'You know I love you, darling,' he says.

'No you don't, Guy. You love yourself.'

'You have to love yourself to love others,' he fires back. 'That's what nanny always used to say.'

Guy Bradwell is the son of good Suffolk stock and as he sweeps his arm over the display of Prada bags he could be emulating one of his ancestors showing an heir all that would one day be his, all that the heir dissipated in the opium dens and gaming clubs of Victorian London before Guy was born.

Guy's still holding the pose. 'Your wish,' he whispers, 'is my command.'

'I wish I wasn't here.'

'Bella, you're such a drama queen. Come on, before I wet my pants.'

'Guy – '

'What colour?'

This is *sooo* Guy and it makes Bella smile.

The bags are *all* black.

It is at this moment that the mousy girl shuffles along behind the counter. Although there are lots of clues, she would not discern that Guy is the heir of good Suffolk stock, a fair to medium good-looking bloke passing thirty, his toff heritage evident in the lush sweep of his bronze hair, candy-striped shirt, blue blazer...

The thing is, until this moment, the mousy girl, hasn't seen Bella and, once she does, Guy becomes invisible. A cipher. Her eyes like a sculptor faced with a block of marble, or a pit pony in blinders, focuses on the girl in the tight black pencil skirt, the girl with long legs in pointy black ankle boots - *ankle boots and a short skirt, she must try it* - a corset top laced at the back with skinny straps, her breasts peeping over the cups, her fine bones defined below translucent skin, those big, green, wide-spaced eyes full of secrets. Is she a model, an actress, a celebrity?

The girl watches Bella's plump lips draw back in a disdainful smile and mouth a single word.

'Red.'

What does it mean?

Guy grabs the nearest black bag from the display and bolts for the door.

The electronic tag trips the alarm and the bells that ring out could be the bells calling the wicked to hell, bells to awaken the dead. They ring in Bella's ears and they ring in the mousy girl's ears, and for a moment, just a moment, they are sisters, they are twins, they connect...

These guys!

The mousy girl screams.

Bella legs it out into the street behind Guy and, out of the corner of her eye, she notices the cowboy sitting astride the Harley.

......*scene 3*

Of course, he notices her, seventeen maybe, legs smooth as a machine, dark hair streaming behind her in a black wave, features pulled into the elation of girls who haven't had their childhood stolen from them.

He kick starts the Harley and is about to pull across the traffic. But Miro is a slave to his senses. He likes girls. He likes them small and tight and young. And there's something about girls running. They touch a memory. A nerve. His sisters ran until they were caught, and after they were caught their eyes died and their tongues remained silent in their mouths. All he could do was what a man is programmed through his genes to do, he chased other men's sisters. Eye for an eye. Rape for rape. Blood for blood. The sun's beating on the black shell of his helmet and the girl's long legs have burned into his retina. Her smell's in his muzzle. She's the prey. He's the hunter. She's wild like a rabbit. Her wildness turns his mind like a drug and turns the wheel of the bike the wrong way.

Miro accelerates back down Goodge Street and around the corner into the NoHo maze that is home like a rat warren is home to the rats beneath their feet. This could be Istanbul, Sofia, Srebrenica, a bare square mile of London north of Oxford Street and south of nowhere, an imbroglio where the lost world meets the third world in a web of DHSS slums, mosques, Orthodox chapels, ethnic restaurants, film company offices, media bars...

He skids to a halt as the girl disappears into *Interface*.

The doors close. Cars shoot by. The sun gleams on the Harley chrome.

What is he thinking?

He just has to go back to Silvia's, deliver the package. But he wants to check out the girl. He wants to see what's going on behind that closed door. He wants another hit.

And fuck it...

He pulls the bike on the stand, sticks his helmet on the high back and unbuckles the pannier. He grabs the attaché case and walks out into the traffic confident that the cars will stop. They do.

......*scene 4*

Everyone takes drugs. Everyone. It's fun. And the good news is, you can get supplies anywhere. Same goes for sex. You'll get decent service in almost any pub in Kings Cross. You get the same in the champagne bars of Mayfair, but you pay a premium. If your needs are more refined, more complex, more 21st century, hit Charing Cross Road north from Soho, take a left off Tottenham Court Road, and follow your instincts to *Interface*.

It's not far from the place where the mousy girl without a name sells last year's Prada bags. She has never crossed the threshold on her lunchtime walks. She has never observed the italic typeface cut into a sheet of dull silver steel beside the double doors. She looks but she doesn't see. That's why she'll never learn the secret.

'Interface.'

Miro reads the word and shakes his head. There are so many words. Do you need that many?

He pushes through the double doors and stands in the triangle of sunlight like an actor on stage.

This is Miro's kind of place.

If he was going to describe it to Kresimir the first word that would spring to his mind is crazy. He likes this word. And he likes this bar with big blow-up nudes by Helmut Newton on grey walls that turn leaden as the doors close behind him. Oak planks from an old ship carpet the floor and art-deco chrome and leather chairs are gathered in nests around low tables. Vertical shutters are drawn over tall windows and through the gaps the sun projects stripes of light that give the domed interior the look of a bird-cage with golden bars and the clientele a burlesque, costume mask appearance.

The bird-cage effect is heightened by the trapeze swinging back and forth as a near naked girl in a crop top and thong goes languidly through her routine, her quizzical, faintly superior expression coupled by her long perfect body breathing life into the Helmut Newton photographs. Natalya Alexeyeva has white blonde hair, freckles across her nose and blue eyes that are about as deep and cold as the mountain lakes of Almaty in Kazakhstan.

That's where she's from, and she has every intention of returning once she has paid her way through school and qualified as an architect. She wants to see the blocks of Soviet apartments where she grew up pulled down and replaced with red-tiled houses with gardens at the back and trees lining wide avenues where children play on new bicycles. Her parents and two young brothers live in one of those vile apartments and she dreams of going home one day with her black cap and gown, her certificate rolled under her arm.

She may change her mind, people do, stay on, change her passport. Natalya Alexeyeva's only 18. She's got plenty of time. She doesn't know there's a secret, and doesn't know she knows the secret. She knows every man who sees her on the bird-swing wants to fuck her, ditto every man on the tube home to the one-bed flat she shares with two other girls in Hackney, the mini-cab drivers who speak her language, the weary web voyagers in their constant quest for new pornography. She doesn't know that when she paid £200 from her hard-earned savings for five portfolio shots to launch her modelling career, a short-cut to architecture school, and allowed the Danish photographer to talk her into stripping off her clothes because big agencies in their pursuit of perfection only study nudes before they employ models, that those shots went straight on the web. When you see Natalya Alexeyeva in the bars and on the street, the story you write for her is always different and is almost certainly wrong.

Now she swings to and fro, backwards and forwards, oiled limbs fluid as mercury, her shadow moving through the ghosts of silvery smoke that spiral around the bars of light, over the curved walls of the dome, over the polished round bar where Frenchie raps the countertop with a pair of drumsticks.

Tap. Tap. Tapper tap tap.

What is it with the drumming?

Does this guy want to be in a band? Is it Morse code? Is he sending signals to far away planets? Miro takes it all in.

You don't have to be on drugs. This place is a drug. This is multi-cultural, multi-ethnic, cross-gender, cross-dressing London, girls with boys' faces, boys in girls' clothes, the gimp head to toe in leather, a rubber mask stretched over his head, black eyes staring out as if from the bottom of two gun barrels, a zip across his teeth. Nice touch. But what's in it for him? There are old guys looking for action. Young guys and girls who provide it.

At a price.

There are blondes looking for jobs on television. Blokes with shoulder bags filled with film scripts. There's a writer in the penumbra behind the trapeze watching the girl, sucking on inspiration like a vampire. There's the smell of hash. And there's music, too, something indefinable, cellos and bass, the beat in tune with a pounding heart kiting on Charlie.

'You. Give me a Bud.'

Frenchie does a drum roll, tapping his way across the selection of beers, and pulls a Bud from the cooler. Miro percussions some change out on the bar and looks round like a kid at the zoo. He gazes at the gimp. The girl on the swing. He sees the running girl with green eyes with a bunch of lightweights and has half a mind to go over there, lift her out of the seat and stick her like a trophy on the back of his Harley.

'Is over there.'

That's Frenchie. He speaks like he's got his finger stuck up his ass.

Miro looks back. What the hell's he saying. The dude's got star-tattooed earlobes, a shiny scalped head like a moon, face hair in elaborate patterns, and English that doesn't sound like English. Miro stares into his eyes. The guy grins and points at the pale pink sign: La Toilette.

'What?' says Miro.

'You want, is over there,' he says in his high-pitched voice.

Miro swallows a mouthful of beer. Coke gives you a high. Shooting people gives you a different kind of high. Two kinds of high make you want to piss. The guy must be clairvoyant.

He leaves his change on the counter and pauses on his way to the loos to take a better look at the gimp. The guy – is it a guy? – sips his drink through a straw stuck in the zip over his mouth. He's alone, just doing what he's doing because that's what he wants to do. It's a free country. Miro's told Silvia a million times he doesn't care if they make enough money to buy the whole village from the Albanians, he's never going back. He loves this country. He gets free English lessons from the local council. Like Natalya Alexeyeva. Can you believe that?

There's a word in English that he tries to summon to his mind but it's lost somewhere in the haze and he falls back on the old standby.

'You crazy man,' he says to the gimp.

Miro isn't aware as he continues on his way that Guy Bradwell and every leathered-up queen in the bar is listening to the tango tap of his Cuban heeled boots.

La Toilette looks like a page torn from of a magazine. You could eat your lunch off the floor. Mirrors plate the walls on three sides, even above the urinals, and the pinprick lights set in the black ceiling look like the stars on clear nights in the hills when the motions of the universe seem to be saying you're so small and insignificant if you close your eyes, no one will see you.

Miro looks at his reflection multiplying to infinity, then takes in the rest of the show: the Chinese boy who looks about twelve standing still as a statue with hand towels over his arm, a silver dish with a pound coin at his side, his doppelganger motionless in the mirror. There's a guy studying the dotted blue line tattooed round his throat pissing in the urinal and, right beside him, a girl fixes her crimson lipstick. She's a dead ringer for Scarlett Johansson, not that Miro knows who Scarlett Johansson is. But he knows what he likes. He grins and she flutters her false eyelashes.

The handicapped cubicle's free. He slips in, bolts the door, and balances the attaché case across the curved sides of the sink. There's subdued lighting from the pair of sea shell light fixtures; the walls are solid, no gaps above or below. He's alone. Safe. No one in the world knows where he is. It's a good feeling.

He loosens his belt and, as he does so, the Tokarev falls from his waistband. He catches it before it hits the ground.

He places the gun on the chromium top of the swing bin and pisses needles. The coke does that. It's almost a pleasure.

That's that out of the way.

He lowers the toilet seat and places the case on the surface. He pauses before hitting the locks.

A booby trap?

No way.

He flicks the locks.

Fok!

The locks are doing what locks ought to be doing, like staying locked. He slides the switch-blade from his jacket, forces the steel tip deep in the locks and like torture victims the sheer force of pressure makes them open up. A spark of pleasure zips through his brain as he slowly lifts back the lid.

The plastic packages of sandy gold powder inside the case are tightly packed, five in a row, two rows in two layers: 20 half kilo bags that glitter with points of light. Perfekat. Tempting. Crazy.

Miro makes a nick in one of the bags, presses the plastic, and takes the overflow up his nose in one long snort that scorches the back of his eyeballs and erupts in a rush of scolding lava through his brain.

Aghhhhhhhhhhhhhhhhhhhhhhhhhhhhh!

The hit would kill some people. Stop their hearts. His body explodes into a million bright lights that rearrange in shifting patterns like chips of glass in a kaleidoscope.

Boom. Boom. Boom.

There's a pounding behind him like mortar fire, the retort magnified in the confined space.

He springs back, hits the swing bin with his elbow. His instincts are scrambled. His stomach lurches with nausea. He can't focus.

He hears a voice, deadened through the woodwork.

'You looking for company, Cowboy?'

What? What does it mean?

The voice is far away: You looking for company. And he hears Silvia's voice like an echo: You come back straight.

Always the voices...

You looking for company.

You come back straight.

His head's spinning. There's a bright light flaming behind his eyes. He hears the sound of screaming, screaming, pitiful, agonized, endless...

……*scene 5*

When men are tortured their screams are sporadic and controlled, flashes of pain that grow slowly, inevitably, into a sea of pain, a universe of pain, black and bottomless. As they lose control, their voices cease to sound human, the pitch rising as if reaching for something beyond their reach, something that isn't there. The sound travels through the hills and has the odd sonic effect of appearing louder along the high ridges than at the source in the wooden farmhouse just visible in the valley below. The echo rolls over the landscape and vanishes inside your head where it remains faintly and forever.

Miro sits on a can of gasoline, Russian army issue, a red star on the side, 20 kilos fully filled. He's 12. Big for his age. And fast. He's not afraid, but his senses are alert, as sharp as the wolves that survive among the rocky pastures above the tree line. He can feel the gun pressed into the back of his jeans, the weight of the jack-knife folded in his shirt pocket. He hasn't asked Silvia why she is sending him out at night alone with a can of gasoline. He knows why. Kresimir is 17, but clumsy. He scares easy. He's fat. He was born fat. There's been no food except the UN packages for three months and still he's fat.

There's a brief silence. Miro has a sense of waiting and the wait ends as the screams begin again with a new tone, another victim giving voice to his agony in his own way.

And another.

And another.

And what Miro is thinking is what every man thinks: how much pain could he stand? If he knew things that would lead to his own blood being captured and tortured, how many nails would they have to pull from his hands and feet before he told them what they wanted to know? How many blows from an iron bar across his kneecaps? How many times would they have to duck him into a drum of oil and hold him down before in his dying breath he blurted out everything? You hear other men in pain and what you can't help thinking is rather him than me.

Miro slips the gun from his waistband, unsnaps the clip. Fully charged, ready to go. He checks the lid of the jerry can, unscrews it, screws it tight again.

The scream grows in pitch, then peters out into a whine.

'He sounds like a pig in the slaughterhouse,' he says.

'Be silent.'

Silvia looks up at the sky, at the moon in its first quarter above their heads. It's past midnight, the trees losing definition and growing into a dark impenetrable mass. Clouds normally cling to the peaks but they have broken their ties and stars are appearing in misty clusters.

There's a fresh silence. It stretches. Torture is a gruelling business. The torturers are ready for a drink. They will drink themselves into oblivion. They will sleep with the satisfaction of men who have done a good job and they will return to their task in the morning. There is no hurry. There is no information that the men being tortured can give them. None that the torturers need to beat from their broken mouths. That is not the purpose of the exercise. These men or men like them have burned their farms and raped their sisters. It is their turn to have dead eyes and silent tongues. Spin the wheel.

Silvia takes out a cigarette lighter and gives it to him. He tests it several times and pushes it into his pocket with the knife.

'Don't lose it,' she says.

'I won't lose it,' he replies.

'Now go.'

Silvia is no friend to words. She stands. Looks down into the dark valley, then back at her son as he lifts the jerry can on to one shoulder. He supports it with one hand on the side, the other on the top. Atlas with the world on his back.

'You can do this?'

'Yes.'

'It is safer alone, Miro. It is always safer.'

'I know.'

'I will be waiting.'

The farmhouse is a blur deep between a cleft in the hills. The moon and stars give enough light for him to pick his way among the trees, but not enough to avoid the thorns from the wild blackberries that claw at his legs. His footfall is softened by the carpet of pine needles. He tries sliding the can over this carpet, but the sound magnifies in the still night and he steadies his arm as he lifts the thing back on to his shoulder and continues again, step by step.

There is no path down the hillside. He loses sight of the farmhouse as he moves from tree to tree, but he has fixed his eye on the moon and is reassured when the building appears again, the shape growing more defined until he can make out the clearing, the roof, the barn where the farmer would have kept a few cows, long gone into Albanian stews and Albanian stomachs.

He rests, and rests more often the further he descends. He has no doubt that he will reach his goal, complete his objective. This is more than just a youthful feeling of invulnerability. It is as if this journey down into the valley had been born in him like a gift for music waiting to develop.

It takes two hours to reach the fence around the farmhouse. His body is bathed in sweat. His arms are screaming from their sockets. He lays down, pulls the gun from his waistband, and stares up at the sky. He hears the song of the river singing over the stones. The breath of the night wind. A horse whinnies and grows quiet again. It sets the dogs off and he hears a voice shouting for them to be still.

He waits, motionless, regaining his strength, the Tokarev loosely in his hand, and what he's thinking is that he'll shoot anyone who comes close and he'll shoot himself rather than get caught and be put inside the farmhouse to be tortured.

The dogs grow quiet, his scent becoming a part of the palette of odours surrounding the farm. He gauges time by the arc of the moon and watches until it begins its descent into the hills. He leaves his place of safety and edges his way through a gap in the fence. As he draws closer, he observes the guard sleeping across the threshold outside the main door, a rag wrapped around his head, a Kalashnikov resting on his chest. The grey hairs in his moustache are lit by the moonlight. To Miro, everyone is old, even Kresimir is old, old and ground down by years of war.

He creeps slowly forward towards the first of the three windows on the side of the house carrying the jerry can in his two hands. Only when he gets close does he realise that the windows are above the height of his head. He doesn't have enough strength to lift the can up to the sill.

That's what Silvia told him. Make sure the windows are alight and the fire reaches inside the house.

Miro's first instinct is to run the can in a circle around the house emptying the gasoline as he goes, set it alight and hope for the best. But what if the liquid soaks into the ground? What if the guard and his comrades wake in time to put the fire out? He's biting his lips. He can feel the Tokarev coldly against his skin below his waistband. The moon's racing. He moves along the side of the house to the corner. The guard mumbles in his sleep, the tail of the turban across his mouth, and it occurs to Miro that if he wore a turban he'd be able to soak the cloth in gas and smear the sides of the building, cover the wooden planks...

He looks around for an old sack, but there's nothing, just the bare strip of dust edged by the dry grass running out to the fence.

Just a piece of rag...

Then it hits him and his bitten lips break into a smile. He transfers the cigarette lighter and jack-knife to his jeans, removes his shirt, unscrews the cap from the jerry can and soaks the worn fabric. He polishes the wooden walls in a sheen of gasoline, spreading it slow and even, coating the bottom half of the window frames, and reaching up along the top by standing on the jerry can. The windows are curtained from inside. No one can see him but he can see his own dim reflection in the glass and what he sees is a man not a boy. The boy has gone forever.

Miro moves to the next window and the next, along the back of the house and around the far side. He has to move fast so the gas doesn't evaporate, and he moves faster as the jerry can gets lighter. The moon grows heavy as it hurries into the hills. The last light disappears like a match burning out and he feels safer in the chilly glow of the starlight.

He shakes out the last drop of liquid, soaks his shirt, ignites it with the cigarette lighter, and runs back around the house, back the way he's come, the old wood bursting into flame with one touch from the blazing torch, the heat reaching his bare arms and chest, flaring in his eyes. The fire spreads over the walls, into the eaves, across the roof. He tosses the flaming remains of his shirt on the windowsill where he started and darts across the clearing, smoke billowing into the sky.

As he races for the fence, a burst of gunfire from a semi-automatic spits into the grass behind him. The trees in the distance are silhouetted by the firelight, the high leaves catching the reflection. Between the fence and the trees there's a clearing maybe fifty metres wide. Ten seconds.

He can't make it. He vaults the fence and throws himself to the ground. He scrambles backwards, crablike, away from where he jumped, moving by instinct. He slides the gun from the back of his jeans. The Tokarev has a fresh clip of 8 cartridges. It is old, well-used, a present from his father before he disappeared.

Time runs slow. He can smell gasoline on his hands. His ears pick out the sound of men screaming, dying in agony, and he can hear the beat of approaching boots, slow and heavy, getting closer. The guard reaches the fence, peers over into the trees beyond, and two bullets blow his skull apart like a flash of lightning.

He's the first Albanian Miro has killed. The first person. Hormones explode in his brain. His stomach churns with nausea. There's no time to stop and vomit. He runs. He runs uphill and he runs faster the further he goes, the steeper the ascent, his legs carrying him with some terrifying purpose, the fire lighting the night behind him.

There's white light in his head. Hammering on the door.

You looking for company...

You come back straight...

Miro's body is washed in sweat. Even his eyeballs are sweating. He pulls handfuls of paper from the roll, dries his face, and still he's drenched. He grabs more paper, dries his face again, his hair, the back of his neck, and flushes the paper away. He stares at the churning water, a spinning blue whirlpool drawing his eye to infinity.

OK. Concentrate. My name is Miro Stanislav. I'm in London. I'm safe. Someone is out there knocking at the door.

You looking for company...

He closes the attaché case and secures the locks. He checks. He looks at himself in the mirror and sees a version of himself he doesn't know. A stranger. His father. Miro takes swift breaths through his nose and unbolts the door.

The girl's standing there, hand on hips, yellow hair like a cartoon.

There's something not quite right about her. Or is it his eyes that aren't quite right?

'Your whole life shows in your face, Cowboy, and you should be proud of that.'

What does it mean?

He sees a ring of Chinese kids offering him hand-towels and swats at them like you swat flies. He's outta there.

He pushes by some dude in a white suit. He doesn't see him and doesn't know that from that moment on their lives are inextricably bound.

......scene 6

Who the fuck's that? Fucking Marlboro Man? People are just so fucking bad mannered.

Martin shakes with rage as he shoves the bolts in place, locking the door like he's locking a safe. Like he's rolling a stone over the mouth of a cave. He doesn't like public lavatories. And he doesn't like the idea of sharing the same seat as all those hairy-assed bastards at *Interface*. But his intestines are a coil of barbed wire. There's a rodent burrowing into his gut. He needs a hit. Like he really needs a hit.

Teeth grinding. Eyes shut. Elbows clasping his knees. Stomach in spasm. That last snort must have been laced with glass. With rat poison. With toilet cleaner...

O My God ...

...the barbed wire uncoils with a snatch of pain and with the relief comes the smell of something rotten, decaying, as if Martin's body is a microcosm of a dying planet. It's pasty, unpleasant. Drugs do that. They fuck with your insides. But is life through a clear lens worth getting up for?

He sits there panting, exhausted, damp brow, sweaty armpits, the tape in his head playing on a loop, crowding his thoughts. *People are just so fucking bad mannered.* And not just the cowboy swaggering out of the bog. Like everyone. Like everywhere.

Look around you. I mean really look around you. In every bar and street and airport they're there, they're everywhere: fat fuckers with bald heads, long shorts, sleeveless shirts. Chav slags with vacant faces, earrings, nose rings, cheap ugly clothes they don't know are cheap and ugly because if they had a gnat's idea of taste they wouldn't be hanging on the arms of these waddling beer guts with Chinese symbols tattooed into their flesh. Where did they come from? What do they want?

What are they so angry about?

What happened to those uncompromising Englishmen who fought at Agincourt, Waterloo, in Spitfires outnumbered ten to one? Gone. Vanished. Given this sceptred isle to the faceless paperless foreigner. Fuckers in turbans. Women dressed for the desert.

Look around you. I mean really look around you. Who told the working class to dress in flags and act like cunts? Who said we wanted to live in a multi-cultural society? Was there a debate in the Commons? A White Paper? A referendum? Did anyone ask *his* opinion? The opinion of anyone who's anyone?

It crept up on us like cancer. Like turning thirty. And what do you do? The only thing you can do. The only thing that's left. You take drugs. You observe the human condition through rose-tinted

Raybans and shop in Jermyn Street: a white linen suit for summer, Turnball & Asser cotton shirts on father's account, the only fucking thing he hasn't cancelled, hand-stitched brogues from Church.

Why do you bother? Why do you get the maid to polish your shoes and put a crease in your trousers? Why? To show you're a different species from the pitball scum with their tabloids and fucking chips. To show them class still matters. *Fuck me!*

Never again. Last night Martin went to a party. All fucking public schoolboys with good manners and bad dope cut with glass, rat poison, toilet cleaner. You've got to know your dealer. Keep your enemies close. Keep your dealer closer.

It isn't easy being Martin Campbell Gilchrist, not when you're 33, same age as Jesus when they topped him. Not when you've got a brother two years younger than you churning accounts in the City, buying property along the Thames Estuary knowing he'll treble his money when they drive the plebs out and build new luxury living apartment blocks for foreign investors terrified of the euro.

It isn't easy with a trust fund too modest to be worthy of the word, potential unrealised, opportunity lost, luminaries like bright lights shining on the family tree. Grandfather, a sculptor for fuck sake, half a ton of bronze in the Royal Academy, signed the Surrealist Manifesto in 1924 and got his name in the history books with André Breton, Salvador Dalí, Edward James and the rest of those effete assholes. Father won a *Souf Lunnen* seat from Labour and sat on Thatcher's front bench, red face, loud shirt, never in five years said a word worth reporting. More money than the UN aid budget for West Africa and he keeps Martin in poverty. Has he got to wait till the fucker dies before he can start living?

He unfolds a pressed white handkerchief, wipes his brow and stares at the shiny metal tube that holds the loo rolls. He looks and he keeps looking as if what he's looking at must be an optical illusion. A joke. A trick. A wind up. Martin can't believe his eyes. Pasty shit and no bog rolls!

'For fuck sake.'

No roller towel. No litter. What's he supposed to use, his fucking Calvin Klein's!

He pulls the lid off the swing bin, reaches in...and comes out with a prize.

A present.

A gift from the Gods.

Martin's the last kid in the game of pass the parcel and, boys and girls, just look what he's won, a lovely Tokarev TT33, solid, matt silver, no-frills.

Warm to the touch.

He looks at the weapon like you look at photographs from the past. Like you look at dead people at a road crash. It fits in his hand like it was meant to be there. Like a family heirloom. Like he's a puzzle with a missing part and the puzzle's complete. He sniffs the barrel.

'For fuck sake.'

He remembers the big bastard pushing by him. Foreign for sure. Dressed like a cowboy. What's that all about for fuck sake?

Martin cleans himself up with his handkerchief stitched with MCG in blue in one corner, a gift from some fucking relative at Christmas. Flushes it away. He lodges the gun in his waistband, readjusts the position. Feels good. Natural. He buttons his jacket, slides the Raybans up the shaft of his nose. Unbolts the door.

Pauses.

Locks it again. Martin's got a vivid imagination. He sees things. He sees a picture of the big cowboy standing outside with a big fist and that big fist like a comic strip fist is smashing his face to pulp.

Martin steps on the toilet seat and slips the gun into the light fixture. He takes a deep breath and unbolts the door...

......*scene 7*

Time's a funny thing. You wait for someone running late and it turns slow. You stand gazing at the carnival faces at *Interface* and it races. Miro can't tear his eyes away from the girl on the swing. She's a snowbird flying to and fro, backwards and forwards. He reaches for her foot and it slides from his fingers. Up she goes, then down again. Like a pendulum. He reaches again. And she's gone again like a white shadow.

His head's in two places at once. In the black hills of Pristina lit by orange flames. In the underground station at Goodge Street. The scream of a train. Two shots.

Head and heart.

Neat and clean.

He finishes his beer, leaves the change on the bar and makes his way to the exit. His heart's racing. He can feel sweat on his back, in the palm of his left hand that grips the attaché case. He can hear music. It's jazz. He likes jazz, and he's aware like you're aware when an itch needs scratching of the girl with green eyes watching him, studying him as he'd studied the snowbird, as he'd studied the girl with green eyes sprinting through the streets.

Is it the same girl? The same day?

He looks at her across the sea of faces and time and shadows climbing the wall and like pig iron is drawn to a magnet and a cocked gun is drawn to its target, he is drawn to her green eyes, sucked down the long tunnel of her casual scrutiny, his feet taking him on a detour to the chrome and leather chair where she sits with her legs crossed and her neck turned as if posing for a photograph. She'd look good on the back of his bike.

Miro stands there gazing at the girl. He wants to tell her things. He wants to tell her about that time when he shot the Albanian, an old man with white in his moustache. He wants to tell her about the flaming house. And the men burned alive in that house. He wants to tell her about the Albanians raping his sisters. Torching his village. And all these thoughts are like scraps of paper spinning around inside his head. He can't put them together. He doesn't have the words. The language. He looks into the girl's green eyes and she looks into the bottomless pit of his soul and they connect, they seem to connect.

She smiles. He smiles. Time is suspended. In another universe they live in a village surrounded by seven hills and they have seven sons. The music seems far away now. Like it's playing in another bar.

The same as he didn't see the dude in the white suit when he pushed his way out of the loo, Miro doesn't see Guy Bradwell working away at the tag on the Prada bag. Miro doesn't notice the boy with the twin earrings in his left ear. Or the girl with the boy's face who might be a boy with a girl's face.

They are faces without features. Marionettes. They see him, his long body looming over their table, but Miro only has eyes for Bella.

He gives her a perfect spread of white teeth and uses two fingers to indicate his eye sockets.

'I see everything.'

Her eyes glint below raised eyebrows. He's got half a notion to grab her like the Albanian girls he carried screaming and kicking over his shoulder from shattered cottages and burning barns. That's in his mind, and that's in the past. He's in London now. Be cool. Come back and find her another time.

He shoves a stick of gum between his white teeth, turns and his heels click over the floorboards. He swings open the double doors and as he steps into the sunlight he shimmers and disappears.

......*scene 8*

Martin washes his hands, slowly, fastidiously. He hates dirt, decay, his own smell. Brother Giles once said he hated himself but Giles for all his money has always envied Martin. He isn't naturally gifted. He has to work for everything he's got. If Martin wanted to go into the City and make a fortune he would. Life's too short for that. Life's meant for living. For fun.

He studies himself in the mirror, in the myriad mirrors, and is overcome by a sense of well-being, a feeling that something illusive, unnamed, just beyond reach, is coming into view, a ship on the horizon. Martin's therapist once told him that happiness creates a biological change that inhibits negative feelings and fosters an increase in energy.

Martin is happy.

He takes a hand-towel from the attendant and flicks a £1 coin in the air.

'Come on, boy, catch.'

And a multitude of little Chinamen do so with perfect timing.

There's a spring in Martin's step as he strolls into the bar. He is irritated, without being upset, when his vision is disturbed by the unwelcome diamond of sunlight entering through the open doors, disturbing the sense of harmony, his equilibrium – but not his buoyant mood.

He goes to close the doors.

He stands on the threshold, glances out into the heat haze and watches the big cowboy kick start the Harley Davidson.

Miro Stanislav looks back at Martin before taking off like a shooting star.

......*scene 9*

Guy Bradwell has wedged the screwdriver blade from the boy's Swiss army knife between the clamps of the security tag and is slowly levering it apart.

Why is life *always* so difficult?

He pauses in his labour and gazes around the bar. He needs a bevvy. He needs a holiday. Somewhere nice. On a boat. It wasn't meant to be like this. He gives the security tag another tug. It was silly stealing the bag in the first place. I mean, what's it worth: a tenner. A shot of vodka. Was he showing off? Pretending he was 17 again. Guy would give anything to turn back the clock and be a boy once more, a boy with soft skin, cheeks alien to the razor blade, skinny, giggly, gorgeous. He could mince into any bar from Piccadilly Circus to Walton Street and mince out with the fattest wallet in the place. If they were straight they learned how to bend. And if they were bent they learned how to remember. No one forgot a plating from Guy Bradwell. He was a legend. He *is* a legend.

Guy's restless eyes, as if informed by convention, roam the bar, settling on middle-aged men alone on bar stools, alone at small tables, settling as a butterfly settles on a fresh bloom, hovers for a moment and moves on. He has a butterfly sense of smell and can sniff them out a mile away: the stench of want. You can see it in their watery eyes, the way they sit, the way they hold a wine glass. It's all in the body language. Guy's language. He's fluent. The old perverts are sitting alone in *Interface* for any number of reasons, and the exact reason is something Guy will divine within moments of speaking to them. They trust Guy. He's well-spoken. He understands their needs. And he is accompanied by Arabella Channon. Brilliant, boyish, bedazzling Bella. What a find.

Martin appears back at the table inspecting his clean hands.

'Martin, has anyone ever told you, you look fantabuloso in white?'

'All the time. So, what is this, Darfur? A fucking drought?'

'Temporary. Cash flow,' Guy replies.

'Cash fweeze,' adds Bella, moving her arm beyond Guy's reach.

Jordan, the boy who carries a Swiss army knife, the boy with matching earrings, hears the softened *r* in her voice and it sounds like a little bell chiming *cash fweeze* and he replays the words in his head like a lyric in a song. He watches her move away from Guy and he knows they're together but not actually *together*. He could be in there.

Martin looks away from the table devoid of glasses and looks at Jordan like you'd look at a dog turd on the pavement.

Trilby looks at Martin looking at Jordan. Like Martin, Trilby is in white, her sleeveless, backless, A-line dress to the knees hinting at rather than revealing her exquisite figure, those long tapered legs, slender feet in spiky white heels. She has uncloudy blue eyes like flakes of sky, small, carved delicate features, pursed pink lips and a penis.

Guy glowers at Bella and continues. 'Martin, it's not a problem...'

'It is a problem. Your problem.'

'Do you want to buy a bag? It's Prada.'

'There you see, now you're making your problem my problem. Do I have cunt written across my head? No. And no, I don't want to buy a bag. I want a drink.' He glances at the boy. 'Jordan?'

'I don't have any money.'

'I don't have any money,' he apes. 'Not much of a playmate if you can't afford to play are you?'

Martin takes out his wallet and withdraws three £20 notes, which he gives to Jordan. He glances around the table.

'Vodka tonics?'

Trilby nods.

'Yes, please,' says Guy.

Bella nods.

'You old enough?' he asks her.

'I'm old enough for a lot of things.'

Martin glances back at Guy. 'Here they come,' he says. 'Generation Y. Echo Boomers. I want it all and I want it any way I can get it.'

Bella turns her head and gazes over her pale thin shoulder. She writhes in her seat, her movements like a leaf caught in a sudden breeze. Jordan's gaze is stuck to her like glue.

Martin watches like he's at Wimbledon. He snaps his fingers, waking Jordan from his fantasy.

'Jordan, listen: what you don't know you can't imagine. Don't try. Don't think about it. Don't even dream about it. Now,' he adds, holding up two fingers. 'Two pieces of lemon. Ice. Not slush. And do me a favour: tell that ass-wipe to shut the fuck up with the drumming.'

Jordan glances at Frenchie, tap tap tapping along the display of beers, at the rays of light like gold bars caging the girl on the trapeze, at the girl who looks like Scarlett Johansson, at Trilby, at Bella, at Martin pressing sixty quid into his sweaty palm.

Sixty quid for a round of drinks!

There's a great big world out there, a great big world beyond the council estates, the city academies, Thursday morning signing on, the old man telling him to get a job, mum telling him to go back to college. Yeah! Like for what? There's another life, and he wants some. He can feel it. Smell it. He was only up in the smoke buying a set of guitar strings in Tottenham Court Road, and here he is, in the centre of the universe with sixty quid in his hand. He could do a runner if he wanted. Out them doors, through the backstreets, just run and keep running.

Nah. That's what kids do. He's fucking 19. Do me a favour. His luck's in. Karma. That's what they call it. He's read about this stuff on the web and it works. It's like opportunity, or chance, or like knowing that what will be will be, and you'd better hang on to it before it's gone. He'd got lost looking for the tube. He could have asked anyone. But he'd asked directions from the people in white, and here he is, landing on his feet and getting the drinks in at sixty quid a pop.

Karma.

Karma = Money.

These people are rolling in it. Big Nobs his dad would have said. You can tell by the way they speak, the way they dress, the way they sit in these fancy chairs like they own the place. That Martin's a bit of a cunt. And there's something weird about Trilby, that deep voice like velvet, the way she looks at him with those baby blues, the way she took his arm when he asked the way, and when she led him into *Interface* it was like being in a video game and going from one level to another. From bad karma to good karma.

Jump in. Fill your boots. Dip your crust in the gravy. In for a penny...

'Right mate,' he says.

Martin watches the boy jerk his way to the bar. 'They all have that funny walk, like pigeons,' he says, and glances at Trilby. 'Whose idea was it to bring him here?'

'Yours.'

'Fucking all heart, that's my problem,' he says and shows her the gaping mouth of his empty wallet.

'Imagination,' she tells him.

'That's ten percent,' he responds and keys his mobile. 'I'm working on the rest.'

Martin holds the machine to Trilby's ear. It just keeps ringing. Then turns his concentration to the cigarette stub burning in the ashtray. He points without getting too close.

'What's this?' he says. 'Fucking stuff people smoke. You'd think we're living in Calcutta for Chrissakes.'

Trilby licks her fingers and extinguishes the fiery tip of the fag between them. Martin glances at his Omega.

'Where the fuck is he?'

'Inside the Circle Line it's quicker to walk,' says Guy.

'Not in these heels,' says Trilby.

Guy smiles and looks back at her with an affection spiced with vague resentment. Trilby is what Guy wants to be, what he could have been, what he should have been, and just looking at Trilby sets off a wave of testosterone that explodes through his system and gives him the last shot of strength that finally levers the security lock from the Prada bag.

'Et voilà,' he says and gives it to Bella. 'See, wasn't it worth it?'

'I thought it was for you.'

'Bella, you could try.'

'I am trying.'

Bella re-crosses her long legs. Guy's eyes sweep the room and settle with a little sparkle on a man on that long journey from fifty to sixty drinking alone at the bar.

'Hah huh,' he says, giving Bella a nudge.

She glances up from transferring her bits and pieces from her old bag to the new bag and as she crinkles her little nose she looks about 14 years old.

......*scene 10*

Trilby glances across the table at Bella, their eyes meet, and Bella's smile is genuine. In a world of make-believe, this is a real smile. People seldom surprise Trilby. They are banal, conventional, humdrum.

They ask her: *why do you, you know, why do you, you know...*

Because I can, she replies.

Because I want to.

Because girls have more fun.

Because women's clothes are nicer. Prettier. They feel good. They hang right. They are soft and sexy and suit me. They fit properly, and when I'm in costume, in camouflage, I feel thoroughly and completely alive; thoroughly and completely me. I am not one person - banal, conventional, humdrum. I am whatever I want to be, a spiralling helix of personalities and potentials, a whirling, swirling yin & yang of constantly changing dreams and desires.

I adore dressing and before dressing I submerge myself in an oily bath. I masturbate, usually twice, drawing the male jism from my body to prepare for transformation. I shave my legs, the fuzz from below my arms, and trim the neat triangle of my pubic hair. I pat myself dry with a towel, spread unguents over my skin, and on the bed I lay out my armour, small things, pretty things, freshly washed and smelling of sunshine.

I begin by sliding the straps up my arms and hooking myself into an uplift bra with pockets for silicone breasts. I shape the silicone with my palms, this act so completely feminine my back bows, my tummy tightens, my hip bones jut: even my expression changes. By altering your shape, even with artifice, you become a different person. I hold my chin high, pull back my shoulders, toss my short hair. I put on lacy panties. A drowsy erection sometimes stirs and only by concentration, by self will, does it fade into its feminine form, soft and obedient. A girl's penis. I snap into a garter belt, roll stockings over my silky legs, clip the stocking tops in their clasps and step into heels. I look at my reflection and wave goodbye to Thomas. I blink my blue eyes, and Trilby steps out of the glass.

Thomas swims on the surface of life. Trilby is a deep sea diver. Thomas wants to live. Trilby lives. Thomas wears suits. He's conventional. If you ask Thomas *what he does*, as crass people do, bankers, accountants, achievers, he will tell you he's an actor. *I'm not very good*, he says.

But he is good. He plays Trilby. He went to RADA. He does bit parts, commercials, short films. With his perfectly symmetrical face, startling blue eyes and small nose, it was hardly surprising that he was cast as a dancer in *Chicago* early in his career and, once he laced himself into the corset and stepped into black stockings and heels, he found his feminine self as few people do.

Thomas is a nice guy. Trilby is a bitch. When she wants to be. She is a thief. A liar. A predator. She is all the things that Thomas isn't, and when Trilby gets too full of herself, Thomas puts her back in the closet, removes his grey suit, and gets the train from

Liverpool Street to visit their cake baking parents in Goffs Oak. Nice people. Liberal Democrats.

But you are not interested in Thomas and his antecedents. It is Trilby who intrigues. Trilby who stirs the blood in your veins, the sleepy feeling between your legs. Trilby with blue eyes that see into the future.

But what, you know, what makes her tick?

I mean: *why do you, you know, why do you, you know...*

Because I can.

Because I want to.

Because girls have more fun.

Try it. *I dare you.* Take a hot bath, jerk off, shave your legs and step into a pair of panties, a padded bra, a garter belt, silk stockings. Don't be tempted by tights. Garters are sexy. The clasps show through soft fabrics. Your bum looks cute. Run the razor over your cheeks, then lay out your make-up: foundation, eye-liner, mascara, lipstick, powder. Less is more. Drag queens don't know that. Girls do.

Take a breath, look at your reflection and mouth the secret word:

HAIR.

Hair is dead. You have to play Jesus and bring it back to life. Give your hair lots of time. Lots and lots of time. If it doesn't work, do it again. Your hair is the frame that flatters the masterpiece. That's what you are. That's what you have become. You are the bug remade as a butterfly, and your hair, *au naturel*, with extensions or a wig, is *everything*, the thick sweep of ash blonde curls caressing my shoulders and complementing my blue eyes that gaze back from the mirror where I see a beautiful creature appearing like a negative turning positive in the dark room.

I am a slave to beauty. Beautiful men. Beautiful women. I am a beautiful object and, as I step into a white dress that clings discreetly to my curves, I am all that is forbidden, desirable, sublime.

Martin grabs his phone from the table and presses the redial button. He glances at Trilby with a look of relief as she moves to sit beside Bella.

'Finally...'

......*scene 11*

Krishna's machine pulses in his trouser pocket, his leg quivers, he feels like he's having a seizure.

MARTIN pops up on the screen.

'Can't talk, man. Catch you later.'

Martin! That's just what he needs.

He stirs his coffee, grainy and sweet, it takes the roof off your mouth and keeps the buzz going during downtime.

Martin!

Krishna hates himself for doing what he does. But what are you going to do? You start dealing to a few friends to finance the lifestyle and wind up at one o'clock in the afternoon in *Kosta's* waiting for product. You glance around at the chipped gold paint on the plaster friezes, the greasy stains on the red plush chairs, at Kosta Ali Pasha striding up and down like a caged bear, like a prisoner waiting for the verdict at a war crimes tribunal.

You slip the mobile in your jacket; sip your coffee.

'You *awlright*, son?'

You've forgotten that Dixie Dean's on the stool beside you at the bar. You turn and catch in the mirror a flash of the eyebrow ring decorating your face. You stare into Dixie's dead fish eyes, you turn back to the mirror, and a question runs through your head:

Are you out of your fucking skull?

And for a moment, just a moment, you see in the corner of your mind the silver frame on the mantelpiece with the 10x8 photograph of Baba in scarlet robes, his round face below a barrister's wig with plump lips that can't resist smiling, and you recall like you recall random dates, 1066, 1492, 1972 – the year Baba fled with his young bride from Uganda because Idi Amin was a moron who drove out the Asians. You recall with unutterable pride how Baba got a job driving a London Transport double decker while he retook the bar exams he'd already taken in Kampala, and how he never complained that this was bureaucracy gone loco, unfair, racist, or how he wore out his shoes and kept on smiling while he begged for pupillage at the Inns of Court. And you can visualize that unwavering smile withering like a lemon left in the bowl if he knew you were sitting in *Kosta's* with an eyebrow ring, with a companion who butchers the English language, with a bunch of broody gangsters dealing cards, killing time, with anonymous, paperless girls cleaning up the detritus and vomit from the previous night's drinking and drug abuse.

Krishna licks the tips of his fingers.

They drink their coffee from small glasses hotter than hell.

Dixie slams his down in the saucer and taps the face of his watch.

'People to see. Fings to do. Ain't got all day,' he says.

He speaks to Alya behind the bar as if what she did or felt or might reply mattered or meant anything to anyone anywhere in the world, as if Alya was a human being with rights and responsibilities, with feelings, hopes, desires, as if Alya could finish placing the glasses on the shelf, climb the stairs from the basement and leave *Kosta's* of her own free will. It confirmed to Krishna Guru Singh that Dixie Dean had something in common with Idi Amin, he was a fucking moron.

Alya doesn't glance back at Dixie, but stares at Krishna with hard, empty eyes, a look of contempt.

'Wassat all about, then?'

'Nuffin',' says Krishna.

Dixie lights a fag and leans closer to whisper. 'You know summink, I'm beginning to miss the Italians.'

'Good ice cream.'

'Good liars,' says Dixie and looks lost. 'Where'd they all go?'

'Property. They saw the future.'

'Smart, see. They're like us. Not like this lot. Fingers in everything. Up their own asses. Building, trucking – '

'Fucking.'

'That's the future. I'm going to say one word,' he says, the light angling down into the basement putting a glow on his pasty features: 'The Innernet.'

'The World Wide Wank?'

'Exactly, my son,' Dixie says and taps the side of his nose. 'You get 'old of a camera for a couple of grand, chat up a bunch of schoolgirls, give 'em twenty quid apiece and make videos. Lot of perverts out there. Gotta 'ave summink to wave their dicks at.'

The glint in Dixie's eyes fades as the light from outside turns to shadow, the space filled with the silhouette of a broad Albanian who looks grim and grows grimmer as he stamps down the stairs and approaches Kosta. Krishna recognizes Yilly, Kosta's boy, his brother, his son, something, big as a barn, almost as big as Kosta. Krishna can't hear what they say, but as Yilly makes a gun from his fingers and points at his head and heart it looks like someone's been snuffed.

Kosta's chest inflates and he seems to grow taller as he sucks air through his teeth. Krishna can sense the vapour coming from his ears. He's like an old steam train straining on a steep incline.

'So, Kosta, whassa story?' shouts Dixie. 'I've got punters out there waiting for therapy.'

Kosta's expression doesn't change. He slowly approaches Dixie, nodding his head, like he's going to reply, and in one swift movement punches his hand where it lays like a white fish on the bar top, crunching and cracking the bones.

Dixie screams like a man being tortured, his pale skin turning translucent, icy, spectral.

'You come. You buy. You go,' says Kosta. 'Is good. You stay in my house, you say nothing.'

'You fucking broke my hand. Fuck me, Kosta.'

Tears flow from Dixie's dead eyes. Kosta steps around the bar and pours a brandy. He slides it across the counter.

'Iz my house.'

'OK, man. I didn't mean nuffin'.'

'You, I like. I like you say nothing.'

Kosta glances at Krishna, including him in the warning, then paces back across the dance floor to

Yilly. He speaks loud and fast, his voice booming as he beats Yilly on the chest with a finger broad as a gun barrel, the words like opera, alien to Krishna's ear.

Yilly's head bobs up and down like one of those nodding dogs in the back of a car. He buttons his jacket over his big chest and as he vanishes through the sunlight on the stairs, Krishna feels a stab of envy. It's like out there life is moving, growing, progressing, and down in the subterranean vault they're submerged in *maya*, in illusion, in *avidya*, ignorance of the true self.

Fucking nonsense.

Kosta drops down in a chair at the table where his countrymen turn the cards with listless repetition, slapping pound coins on the table top, shuffling, dealing, waiting.

Dixie sips his brandy, face wet like washed marble, and Krishna glances back at Alya. She has watched Kosta's outburst without emotion from the circular stage, and now goes back to work, her right hand clasping a yellow duster going up and down the brass pole, and like the sculptor who carves gods by day and bends to pray to them at night, Alya that night will strip off her clothes and fuck the pole and fuck the clients, Alya and other girls, new girls, young girls with shaved pussies, breasts bouncing, the stage lit by revolving lights that turn their moist bodies steel blue, fluorescent green, rose and alabaster.

Chameleons.

Like him.

And for a moment, just a moment, he thinks he might go back to the LSE and finish his law degree. Baba can fix it. Dealing was fun once. Now it's not fun. It's business.

His phone vibrates again. He doesn't look at the screen. He continues to look at Alya and has a sudden and absurd urge to take her by the hand and lead her out of the cellar into the fiery light of day, away from Kosta with his war crimes past and big hands that once they've been laid on a girl the girl will do anything rather than feel their weight again.

Who are these girls? Where do they come from?

Krishna knows.

He knows Alya's story.

And he should do something about it.

But what? What can he do? Alya's property. Merchandise. An asset. And there's more than one Alya.

There're hundreds.

There're thousands.

They just keep coming.

More every day.

……*scene 12*

They come on the bus from Bucharest, Budapest, Prague, Krakow, Vilnius, Tallinn, from Istanbul and Madrid. They step out at the coach station in Victoria with their modest bags and bright eyes and there's a nice woman from Russia or Romania or Albania there to offer a bed for the night, a job as a waitress, a room in a basement flat with four other girls. They're teenagers, just out of school, runaways looking for a bit of life. A taste of London. That's globalization. You can fuck the whole world without straying beyond the route of the 19 bus and that's due in no small part to Kosta Ali Pasha.

The girls work at *Kosta's* for a week, waitresses, cleaners. It's a bit of fun. They find it strange that the other girls in the flat are always floating about in their underwear. They find it strange that men come at all hours of the day and night. They know, deep down they know, exacltly what the girls are doing, and they know in their hearts and their souls that that's something they will never do.

Never.

Ever.

Never.

It takes a week. Just a week. At the end of seven days, you owe Mr Ali Pasha £500 in rent. That's how much it costs to live in a flat in London. Your own room. Completely safe. How are you going to pay? Your papers, if you had any, have disappeared. Mr Ali Pasha is looking after them until you pay the rent.

How are you going to pay?

Kosta Ali Pasha doesn't mind getting his own hands dirty. When a job has to be done, you do it yourself. That's how you leave Tirana with refugee status, EU assistance and a new red British passport. That's how you arrive with nothing but your big hands and with those big hands you shape the world in your own image. You build a kingdom.

'You come,' he says.

And you go. You don't say anything. You stop stacking glasses, polishing the brass pole, and you follow him through the back room where they weigh and package white powder, out the heavy door, which he holds open, and into the black Mercedes parked in the alleyway. He turns the key and the locks snap into place. You remember that sound, the rasp of metal against metal, and when you tell your story it sounds dramatic, embellished, theatrical. That's the trouble with truth, it's always a cliché.

The seats in the car are big with wide arms. The engine hums. You sit with your hands in your lap, your legs long and pale below your short skirt. He drives carelessly, one hand on the wheel like he's steering a boat, and through the tinted glass you stare at the shop windows and the hurrying crowds all busy and going somewhere.

The girls at the flat are running about half naked. Men are coming and going. Mr Ali Pasha takes you to your room and closes the door. Through the net curtains the light makes snowflake patterns on the wall. His shadow is huge. You know what's going to happen. Of course you know. But still it seems unreal. A dream. A movie. You know what's going to happen but knowing doesn't make it seem real.

Take off your clothes.

Your heart's pounding. Your throat's dry. You're panting for breath. You grin. That grin has nothing to do with happiness. It's because it's so strange. So absurd. Two weeks ago you were at school.

Take off your clothes.

The voice of Kosta Ali Pasha is deep, unyielding, a growl like thunder, and in the tone of that voice that rattles your bones you hear not the barest hint of compassion, a quaver of pity, of humanity. It is the voice of bad dreams, the voice you heard in your subconscious and dismissed when you climbed on the bus at home in Bucharest.

Your eyes stare. Your teeth are locked tight. You can smell sweat under your arms as your fingers run tensely down the buttons of your blouse. You look round, unsure where to put your blouse, and drop it on the floor. You unzip your denim skirt with the yellow flowers embroidered around the pockets. You unhook your bra. You pause for a second, just a second, then run your knickers down your legs. You do as you're told. And once you do as you're told without a fight, without feeling the weight of those big hands on your bare skin, once you do as you're told the first time, it isn't so hard to do as you're told the second time, the third time. And it's not you who took off your clothes, the inner you, the you you were when you got on the bus.

That person is back in Bucharest, Budapest, Prague, Krakow, Vilnius. You are far from home. Alone. No one can see you. It doesn't matter. Not really. Not that much. And there's nothing you can do. Nothing. You're just a skinny girl with ribs and hips that stick out, your breasts betraying you as they swell and shudder with the beat of your heart. You have stood in front of the mirror admiring your breasts with pink nipples that grow taut when you take them in your fingertips, and when you squeeze down hard warm shivers run down your spine. It is vanity that has brought you here standing naked before Kosta Ali Pasha, your shoulders hunched, your hands cupped over your pussy.

He pushes you down on the bed as you would push a door closed behind you and you lay there watching through the veil of your long dark hair. He removes his clothes and sets them down over a chair, his movements slow and deliberate as if the task is fatiguing. He turns and stands staring down at you, his cock bobbing up and down like a restless animal, his enormous chest covered in hair, broad as a tree. You are small and thin and white. He is big and dark, and you can't imagine how that animal between his legs will find its way inside your tiny body.

'Please...'

He doesn't hear you.

Of course he doesn't.

He takes your legs like they're wish bones on a chicken, pulls them apart, and it hurts when he fucks you. You're dust dry and frightened, and it hurts, it really hurts, his big cock slicing you in two, and everything you ever feared is coming to pass, and it is not worse than you imagined but worse than you could have imagined. You've only ever done it a few times with boys at home. They come quickly, and you wait for Kosta Ali Pasha to come. But he doesn't. He stops and you feel grateful as he pulls himself out of your broken pussy.

You think it's over. But it's not over. It will never be over. He rolls you on to your front. You are a feather in his hands, inanimate. He levers your thighs apart. He pushes at the crook of your legs until you're balanced on your knees. Your bottom's in the air. Your back's at an angle. Your face is forced down into the pillow. You hear him spit. Once. Twice. You feel his spittle being wiped across the cheeks of your bottom, into your back passage, and he fucks you again, in your bottom, in that private, secret place.

This is what hell must be like. Dark and painful. An animal burrowing inside you, chomping at your insides, tearing you apart.

Tears flow from your eyes. You can't believe this is happening. Even in your subconscious you never imagined anything like this would ever happen.

You're drenched in sweat, your own sweat, his sweat. He heaves at your hipbones and pushes himself into you, deeper and deeper, and the pain is relentless, a pain like torture, a pain so vast and consuming you never want to feel such pain again. Your face is wet with weeping, your throat is parched and your body grows numb as his big cock drills into your bottom, fucking you, changing you, reshaping you, breaking you as a horse is broken, moulding your body and your mind, and it won't be as bad next time. It won't be as painful next time. Next time it will be better.

He erupts inside you and you feel the hot gush of his semen scolding your raw innards. Your knees collapse. You are crushed as if beneath a building in an earthquake. You can't move. You can barely breathe and he lies there panting like a big hairy dog.

'You good girl,' he says.

You will remember him saying this. You good girl. Your father always said you were a good girl because you were tall and pretty and worked hard at school. Your mother said it, too. You helped in the house without having to be told. You looked after your little sister. You knew, you always knew, you knew deep down that when you saved the money and bought the bus ticket for London something terrible was going to happen. That's what happens to girls like you.

He pushes himself up. Dresses. You're not sure what you're supposed to do, so you just stay there, hugging your knees, your face hidden. He pulls the chair closer to the bed and sits. You look up as he takes from his pocket your papers, a photo of your sister on her way home from school, your mother hanging washing. He lays them down one at a time in front of you and as you stare at those photographs you can no longer feel the pain in your bottom, in your pussy, on your hipbones fingerprinted in pale blue bruises. It feels as if a steel hand has taken hold of your heart.

You look up into his face with its big proud moustache and you look back at the photographs of your sister and mother. You look up again and, as you do so, Kosta Ali Pasha runs his finger over his throat.

'Is good. They safe. No problem.'

You summon up the English you learned at school and practised on the bus. 'I want to go home...'

He lays his big hand flat in front of you on the bed. He taps his hand with a finger. 'My money. You pay.'

'But...'

'You pay.'

His voice as he says these words grows deeper, louder, and in his voice is that tone, that echo, like a distant bell, and just as you took off your clothes without a struggle when you heard that tone the first time, you know there is nothing you can say, nothing you can do. Nothing. You have nothing to offer. Nothing to give. Nothing. You will pay and keep paying, and as you sit there staring at the photographs of your sister and mother, you blame yourself for being there on that big bed with the leopard skin sheets, a wooden dresser with drawers you will fill with cheap lurid underwear, the oatmeal carpet, the light through net curtains making patterns on the wall, the wardrobe where you will hang little dresses that are quick to put on and take off, where you will place high-heeled shoes that make you taller, stretch your waist, push out your breasts for men to reach for.

It's my own fault. All my own fault.

That's what goes through your mind. And you don't know and how could you know that it's not your fault. It's not bad luck. It's not random. Nothing's random. People in Bucharest have been watching you, as people in Prague and Krakow and Almaty in Kazakhstan are watching other girls, the young ones, the pretty ones who want a taste of life. The gangs know they are coming before they know themselves. They are a commodity. They will fuck ten men a day on a good day, £40 for a blow job, £60 for straight sex, £100 for anal, £200 for lesbian shows, £300 for the night.

A girl on her back can earn £5,000 a week, and she'll pay and keep paying and she’ll be grateful for the small sums she is given and the small sums she steals. You will buy underwear and clothes that tell the men who visit that basement flat what you are, what you have become, and you will send small sums of money home to your mother, and she will know, somehow she'll know, deep down she'll know just what her little girl is doing in London.

Kosta Ali Pasha slides the photographs back in his pocket, stands and pauses at the door.

'You good girl.'

And now you understand what he means. He means: you be a good girl. You do as you're told.

You hear the door close. You roll on to your side, you bury your head and you weep big salty tears that soak the pillow. You feel his sperm oozing out of your bottom. You can smell it. Like farm animals in rut. There's a fire blazing deep inside you. Your bones have turned to dust. The spiral of your DNA has been altered.

You cry and keep crying. The light outside dims. The pattern on the wall begins to change. Then Lule comes with ointment, some cotton pads, a bowl of soapy warm water. She tells you to turn over, to go up on your knees, and you do as you're told. You do as you're told and you feel so thankful as she wipes away the sticky mess with a cloth, you cry even more, this fragment of human kindness in the dim room with the patches of shadow deepening on the wall like a reprieve, like hearing that a loved one is still alive after an air crash, after an earthquake. Lule coats the cotton pads in ointment. It stings when she spreads the ointment inside your bottom. It will make it better, she says. She is businesslike, efficient, like a nurse. She's done this before.

Eva enters with a toilet bag in one hand, her free hand concealed behind her. She's smiling. She's always smiling. And the girls burst into laughter as Eva pulls a pink plastic prick from behind her back. At first you're not sure what it is. You don't laugh. But you smile. You want to tell the girls that you're not going to go with the men who come to the flat. But you are. You know you are. You want to say you're not like that. But you are like that. You are now.

You are about to begin a new life. These are your friends. You want them to like you. You look back into their faces. Tears roll down your cheeks and Lule rubs them away with her fingertips.

'Iz OK,' she says.

You start to cry again. You cry a lake of tears. A sea of tears, as if those tears will wash away the pain in your heart, and of course no amount of tears ever will. You try to speak but your words of English have gone from your mind. You want to be at home with your sister. You want to be back at school with the people you know. People like you.

Lule dries your tears with a cotton pad. She takes you in her arms and somehow, somehow, it's terrible, but not quite as terrible. Someone cares. You're not dead. You are not alone. Other girls like you have been lured to this basement room with the leopard skin sheets and oatmeal carpet. You saw this room in your dreams and dreaming of the room has made it real. It was always waiting for you in your future. You sensed it as the bus pulled out of the station in Bucharest.

Lule brushes the hair from your eyes.

'Thank you.'

Eva takes from the toilet bag a razor, a tube of cream, a pair of nail scissors.

'Snip, snip, snip,' she says, and smiles.

Lule taps the pillow. You make yourself comfortable, legs spread like a woman in labour, and you don't think about it, and you don't know why, but you don't feel embarrassed as you lay there naked, Eva snipping at the dark patch of your pubic hair. She spreads cream over the stubble and shows you how to shave, running the razor against the grain. It stings when she uses tweezers to pull out the stubborn hairs from inside the lips of your vagina. But it has to be done. It's better, they say. Easier to keep clean. It doesn't smell. And young girls with shaved pussies look like children. That's what you are. A child. An object. A commodity. You have no rights. No responsibilities.

It will also occur to you later that no one before Lule and Eva had ever seen you naked except Kosta Ali Pasha, not since you were a child, but the girls are always running about in nothing but their knickers, it's normal, and what's normal quickly becomes accepted, natural, routine. You are in this together. And being together makes it easier.

Lule runs baby oil between your legs, into the crease of your bottom, over your tummy. You look down on the shiny seashell of your bare white mount and think of Kamila, your sister, 13 now. You don't know how Kosta Ali Pasha got the photograph of her coming home from school. Who took it? Why? Who took the photograph of your mother hanging washing? You don't know. You will never know. You just know you have to protect them. Nothing else matters. There is nothing else. You wanted to learn English. You wanted to be a teacher. Now what you have to do is more important.

Eva uses the dildo to show you how to unroll a condom over a man's cock. You practise. The girls laugh. You're not very good at it. You'll get better.

'Never do it without one,' Lule says, and waves a warning finger.

You understand. And you understand without having to be told that only Kosta Ali Pasha doesn't need a rubber. He knows the girls are clean when they get to London and he fucks them up the ass so they don't get pregnant, because kings in their kingdom like apes in the jungle like to know they're the first.

In Lule's room you try on clothes, black underwear, black stockings with elastic tops, a see-through dress, red shoes with tall heels. You drink tea from a white mug with a canon and the word Arsenal in big letters. There's food in the kitchen, but you can't eat. Your stomach's in knots. You can't imagine ever eating again. The girls talk, they never stop talking, and you don't understand everything they're saying. Eva misses Prague. It's the prettiest city in Europe, she says. Lule comes from Tirana, the same as Kosta Ali Pasha. She's been in London three years, on my back, she says, and Eva laughs, and you try to imagine what it must be like, how many men have passed through that basement flat in three years. In three years you'll be old. You'll be twenty.

Eva paints your eyes, your lips, your nails. You look at your reflection in the mirror and the girl standing there in the sheer dress with red lips doesn't look like you, and that night when Lule sends a man to your room, it's the girl in the mirror who parrots the price list she has taught you. You're frightened, but the man is old with grey hair and grey eyes and in his eyes you see that he is nervous, he too is frightened. He counts out £60 from his wallet.

'I just want it to be nice, you know, nothing, nothing, you know...'

You can't understand what he's saying. You reply with nods and shrugs, with eyes.

'OK.'

You take the money, open the door and give it to Lule, who is waiting outside. She gives you a warm smile, touches your cheek.

'Five minutes,' she says.

You return to the room, remove the see-through dress. He reaches for you. He holds on to you as a man thrown overboard from a boat would hold on to flotsam in a choppy sea. He kisses your neck. He tries to kiss your lips, and you move your mouth away. You're not sure why, but you don't want to be kissed. Kisses will have to be paid for. Like everything else.

He takes off his shoes and trousers, his pants, his jacket. He leaves his shirt on. You slip out of your panties and bra, the black stockings up to you thighs accentuating your nakedness as you lay on the bed, knees bent, legs spread. Your freshly shaved mount shines in the dim light, the lips of your vagina are a piece of fruit, moist with oil, and after being raped by Kosta Ali Pasha the old man rocking on top of you isn't as bad as you thought it was going to be. He comes and he goes, and you wash and stand at the window that has the view of people's feet passing on the pavement above.

Another man comes that night. And a third.

They come next day and the day after. Young and old. Black and white. Fat men. Bullies with tattoos. Skinny restless men who had needed courage to make the call and now they are there in that basement room they are not sure what to do, the procedure, and you show them.

The weather grows warmer, the days become weeks. You heal. You heal quickly. You learn quickly. You learn how to constrict your pussy around their cocks, you tighten your thighs, you gasp as if in pleasure and you slide from beneath them the moment they shoot their load. You pull tissues from the box and ease the wet rubber from their softening cock, you drop it in the bin, and look back at their empty faces. You smile. Make compliments. You're a lovely girl. They'd love to meet a girl like you in the pub, in the park, at work. They'd leave their wife for a girl like you. You pull the dress that's quick to put on over your head, step into your shoes and ask for a tip, for the maid, you say, and when they leave a banknote on the chest of drawers you send the money home to your mother in Romania.

You have your regulars. They come once a week. Twice a week. After they fuck, they want to talk. They talk about their wives and their work. And you listen. You give them time. You learn English. You are good at what you do. And sometimes, just sometimes, when you lay there with a man between your legs, you close out the shadows patterning the ceiling above, you close your eyes, and pretend that you are in the woods outside Bucharest with a boy from school, and if you hold your breath, if you relax, if you shut off the flow of your thoughts you get a moist feeling between your legs, your gasps of pleasure are real, and you hate your calm, your poise, the confidence that grows in a girl with nothing, and nothing to lose.

Lule takes the phone calls from clients and, when business is slow, she parades you with the other girls, and you can't reconcile in your mind why, when you compete in this way, you want to win. You want to be chosen. It makes no sense but in small things there are small satisfactions. You have come to accept what you are and forget who you once were.

Sometimes, not often, but sometimes you wonder what kind of man is it who goes into telephone boxes and reads the cards and calls the numbers that guide him to this place where he can fuck a girl for sixty quid and fuck off home with a hollow feeling in his gut. These men are not Kosta Ali Pasha. They are not evil. They are just ordinary men. Married men. Men without love. Men who see naked girls in the newspapers and on the Internet and just want a fuck. They are, like you, a commodity, a cliché, prey to the spirit of the times.

......*scene 13*

One morning Lule hurries to your room. She's excited about something. You don't react. You have learned not to trust Lule. Not to trust anyone. Like the distant drip of a tap, you have at all times the uneasy feeling that you are being watched, as they watched you back in Bucharest, as they are watching your sister. Lule tells you to get ready, wear something *smart*, and she takes you back to the club where you were taken by an old Romanian woman when you first arrived on the bus. You're not sure what to expect. How you will feel, and it doesn't matter because you will hide your feelings.

Kosta and other big men play cards. It's noisy. They toss coins across the table. You wait. You watch until the hand is over, and Kosta Ali Pasha pushes back his chair. He looks you up and down as country people look at horses and dogs. A long time has gone by, six months, nine months, it's hard to remember. He doesn't seem to recognize you.

'You dance.'

There's music in the background. Someone turns up the volume. Lule tells you to take off your clothes and you do so without hesitation. You tune into to the music and recall, straining for the memory, that you like dancing, you are good at dancing, and when you dance that day for Kosta Ali Pasha you close your eyes, you swivel your hips and you shake your breasts as you lean forward over the circular stage. You dance faster, wilder, and it seems at that moment as if this is what you were born to do. It seems natural to be there naked, shaved, your long body coiling like a serpent around the slippery pole. Sweat coats your skin, the lips of your sex are slicked with juice, pink as a sea creature, an object men crave, and if Kosta Ali Pasha sends you to the back room with the black sofa and a man follows it will seem as natural as drawing breath when you open the zip of his fly. You will take his cock in your mouth and make it moist. You will slide a rubber over its length and in your eyes he will see desire as you lay back on the sofa and draw his cock into your oily wet body.

These thoughts run through your mind as Kosta Ali Pasha watches you dance, his head bobbing up and down as if he's into the beat.

The music ends and he takes out a roll of red £50 notes which he tosses at your feet on the circular stage.

'Take,' he says, and flutters his hand, dismissing you.

You don't go back to the flat that day. You don't collect your clothes. You don't get the chance to say goodbye to Eva, to Safaa, the Moroccan girl, to Biata, the little plump blonde from Poland. After Lule drops you off in a taxi in a new flat in a place called Knightsbridge, you will never see her or any of the girls again.

You join Madalena; tall, Brazilian, self-assured, beautiful. She takes you shopping. You spend the roll of £50 notes, peeling them off like sheets from a notepad. You buy new things, strange things: a bikini, sports clothes, jogging shoes. The flat where you live is big and airy with a view over the trees of Hyde Park. You drink tea from china cups. You have lunch in Japanese restaurants with men who speak many languages and those men return with you to the flat. They are a different sort of men. You're a different sort of girl. You're not a prostitute, a sex worker. You are a natural resource, the gift for a contract signed, the perk, the bribe, the favour returned, the unspecified special services on the expense account.

You get used to having nice clothes, a driver, a masseuse to rub precious oils into your precious flesh fresh from jogging around the Serpentine.

When you run, the wind in your hair, your mind grows empty and there is nothing but the movement of your limbs, the sound of your breath, the beat of your heart. When you dance at the club you see in the spinning lights the lust in every stranger's eyes. You close your eyes and imagine you are running in the park, the wind in your hair, the trees above your head. You squeeze your nipples, you run your pussy up and down the shiny brass pole, and you fuck those unknown men in the back room just as you imagined you would that first day when you danced for Kosta Ali Pasha. These aren't sad fuckers from telephone boxes. They are the men who matter. Men in grey suits, councillors, lawyers, dealers, celebrities, sportsmen, politicians, a judge, a Cabinet Minister, a Saudi prince. You recognize faces from the newspapers, powerful men with loud voices, Russians, Americans, oil men, arms suppliers, advisers, envoys, the men with their hands on the wheels of the free market.

Sometimes when the chauffeur comes it's not to take you to the club, but to take you and Madalena to houses in the country and you watch from the tinted window as the long black limousine slides through tunnels of trees and sleepy villages, cottages, gardens, flowers. It seemed once that the life you were living was not your life. Now it is your life. You wear beautiful things. You visit beautiful places. But you want your own life back. Your home outside Bucharest is fading from your memory and you must return before it fades forever.

You arrive at houses with long drives and lots of windows. Inside you find wide corridors and big rooms where the men waiting for you have different needs. Special needs. They want to tie you up. Or dress you up. They want to piss on you. They want you to piss on them. If they want to beat you or spank you, you squirm as if in ecstasy and say that will be divine, delicious, delightful. You are a thesaurus of pleasure. Someone is nearby. It won't go too far. And if it does, it doesn't matter. There are always more girls, young girls, pretty girls setting off across Europe, a self-replenishing commodity, the oldest profession.

It was at one of these country house parties where you met Krishna Guru Singh and you're not sure why you told him your story. You have never told anyone anything about yourself. And you tell him everything. Everything. How you left Bucharest on the bus. How Kosta Ali Pasha raped you. How you come to be there that night in a silver evening dress, a £300 pair of high heels, in silky clouds of pale cream underwear.

You tell him because he has kind eyes, an open face, because like you he is only there in that country house in a place they call Buckinghamshire to provide a service: he brings the cocaine rich men tap from small squares of paper into your pussy to lick out and sniff out. It's what the men who matter want to do. You tell Krishna Guru Singh these things, and then you cry. It is the first time you have cried since that day when you wept those tears in the basement flat long, long ago, and when Krishna Guru Singh puts his arms around you it is the first time that a man has taken you into his arms out of pity. Not lust. And the lust you can tolerate. Pity will kill you.

Act 2

The Tokarev Story

......*scene 14*

Life is a cliché. That's what Martin says.

Bella's end of term reports are a good example:

Bella is a daydreamer.

Bella doesn't try.

Bella could do better.

The thing is, Bella decided *not* to do better.

The nuns didn't understand. She didn't really understand herself. But after topping the class during those first two years at the convent, Bella began to see all those As on the report card as shards of glass, the spikes for traitor's heads at the Tower of London, like blunt nails crucifying Simon.

Just thinking about Simon gives Bella that weird feeling that a strangler's hands are around her throat, hands with dirty nails, pressing, pressing...

The feeling started at school when she sat beside the window at the back of the class on windy afternoons with an ache in her tummy, the leaves falling from the elms and skipping across the field where the groundsman marked lines on the hockey pitch, the low clouds scurrying out to sea from the Kent coast. She sat watching summer turn to autumn and set her sights further down the alphabet: Bs, Cs, Ds, until finally she escaped before her A levels.

Bella didn't want to fail. She didn't want to succeed. She didn't know what she wanted. All she did know was that learning Latin verbs came easily, the same as clearing the bar with a back flop in high jump, or turning into a boy to play the lead in the school's production of *Romeo and Juliet*. Learning lines was as effortless as swallowing poison, and when she lay prone at Juliet's side Bella could understand at fifteen the allure of suicide. The local *Gazette* was effusive, *Shakespearean drama adroitly interpreted, Arabella Channon is a girl with prodigious gifts and was totally persuasive in the difficult role playing a young lad.*

It wasn't difficult at all. She played Simon.

She should have been Simon. He should have been her. When the egg split something got scrambled. She got too much of something and Simon didn't get enough. Bella ran before Simon could walk. She was talking while he still babbled. He was just like her, but not like her, not so *adroit*, so eager, so impatient.

Bella's no longer clear what belongs to memory and what belongs to family folklore. But if she closes her eyes and concentrates, she can recall floating with Simon in a balmy sea, two little fish, a mirror image. Then the waters vanished, erupted in a tsunami. She glided along on the tide and left her little brother tangled in knots behind her. He emerged five minutes later, blue faced and breathless, the umbilical chord like a noose around his neck, and it seemed from that day on whatever she did Simon would do it five minutes later.

Simon is Bella's second self, her avatar. He is always there like a shadow and when she gets that ache in her tummy and senses the strangler's hands at her throat, the only way to get rid of those feelings is to concentrate really hard on something else, conjugating Latin verbs, running really fast, dancing until the sweat runs down her back, role playing in the silly games invented by Guy.

Then, she can block out the past.

She can block out the sound of the music.

The sound of Martin grabbing his mobile, stabbing the buttons and slamming it back down on the table.

The sound of Guy seeking trade, a noisy affair as he sucks air through pursed lips, his elbow nudging her ribs, his spirit coddled by the prospects of the day.

Bella has a switch in her head and when she flicks the switch she enters a private world where there is no past and the future is just around the bend, on the tip of your tongue, beyond the horizon.

Maybe tomorrow?

Maybe Trilby'll find it?

She's looking. Right now she's looking, and Bella feels cosy and cared for with her long white hands in Trilby's left hand, palms upwards like an open book. Trilby slowly, carefully, studies the pattern of lines, a map of hidden treasure, she says, head tilted forward, a curtain of silvery blonde hair hiding her face.

'The left hand's the past,' she adds, pointing, and it sounds as if her voice comes from the past, deep and far away like an echo. 'The left hand is who you were. What you were. Where you come from. The right hand is constantly changing - '

'Weally?'

Trilby looks up and Bella sinks into her bottomless blue eyes.

'Really,' says Trilby. 'We don't only get one life. We get one life after another. Endless endings and new beginnings.'

It's what Bella wants to hear and it makes her wriggle in her seat. Trilby's chocolaty voice puts her into a swoon. Her imagination races. Her heart beats faster. A flush runs over her neck and colours her breasts as they rise and fall over the cups of her corset.

Trilby looks down again at Bella's hands, reads the lines, the pearly nail of her index finger – the exact shade as her lips – striking out on a journey from her wrist to the space between her first and second finger.

'Now let's see...'

'If I have a future?' asks Bella.

Trilby returns a smile so rare it's a pity the Danish photographer who cons girls out of their kit and on to the web isn't there to record it.

'You're like one of those little batteries,' she replies. 'The ones with the gold tops and *lo-ng* life.'

Bella glances up. 'What about the near future?'

'This is it, babe,' says Guy, interrupting.

The moment of still dissolves, and the sound of the music and the sound of Martin punching his mobile flood back across Bella's consciousness.

Scarlett Johansson drifts by, a burst of red like a Sale sign, and slides on to the stool beside the silver-haired man Guy's been ogling. Frenchie drums the bottles. The girl on the swing carves arabesques from the smoky blue air, the arc of the trapeze breaking the line of golden bars on the upward swing, the balance of light returning as it retreats, back and forth like a pendulum. Bella has watched Natalya Alexeyeva many times and envies that sense of freedom you would have floating through the air.

Jordan stands at the bar in his Che Guevara tee-shirt, hands in his back pockets, trying to look cool, and Bella has a feeling that before the day is done he'll be doing things he doesn't want to be doing. There are no classes they say for beginners in life.

She looks back at Trilby and Trilby sees the shadow douse the light in her green eyes.

'This is it?' asks Bella.

'I'll do it properly one day,' Trilby answers.

'When?'

'Whenever. You know where to find me.'

'I think so...'

'Number 22. Fourth floor. Above the fruit and veg.'

'Oh, yes, I wemember.'

Martin slams the phone back down again.

'Why do people have mobiles if they only switch them on when they're in the fucking cinema?'

Trilby closes Bella's hand like she's folding away a love letter. She sits back, the diffusion of light giving her features the carved look of a mask.

'Can you *weally* see the future?' Bella asks her.

Trilby raises her shoulders in modesty, her gaze moving from Guy, to Martin, to Jordan as he pays for the drinks.

She looks back at Guy.

'Now, his luck's about to change...'

'I am his luck,' says Bella.

'Then his luck's running out and your luck's about to change.'

'Oh, goodie!' Bella wriggles again.

Trilby turns towards Martin and lowers her voice.

'Martin has something up his sleeve. A surprise.'

'A nice surprise?'

'Martin's surprises are always nice. For Martin.'

Like an addict, Martin's mobile is glued again to his ear.

'I'm going to kill somebody before the day's out,' he says.

'You see,' adds Trilby. 'Martin reads the future as well.'

Trilby's glance shifts from Martin to Jordan. He's on his way back from the bar carrying a tray containing four vodkas, four bottles of tonic and a pint.

'Now he's about to set off on a *lo-ng* journey.'

'He must have new batteries,' says Bella, watching the boy, and Trilby's perfect lips flicker with the hint of another smile.

……scene 15

Jordan places the tray on the table. Martin checks there are two quarters of lemon in his glass. He scoops up the change and takes a long hard look at the pint.

'What's that?' he demands.

'Pint of lager,' says Jordan.

'Lager. A pint. Why?'

'I like it.'

'He likes it. Look at yourself, fucking fourteen years old and you've got a gut already.'

'No I haven't.'

'You will have: fat gut, no hair. Tattoos. Fucking chips,' says Martin and pauses. He's writing a script, spinning out the dead time, crossing one white trouser leg over the other and straightening the crease. 'Let me ask you something: why is it the rich stay thin and the poor get fat? Have you ever thought about that?'

'No.'

'Exactly,' says Martin, turning to Guy. 'You can always tell the under-class, you just can't tell them much.'

Guy sips his vodka and enjoys Martin's outbreak of cruelty. Even at school he admired his gift for knowing exactly how to be cruel and who it was safe to be cruel to, the young boys during their first term boarding, the elderly masters adrift in a changing world.

Martin turns back to the boy.

'Got any fags?'

Jordan pushes his chin forward. 'Here,' he says. 'You taking the piss?'

'I beg your pardon. I said, you got any fags?'

Jordan does his rat impression, eyes narrowed, teeth clamped, lips pulled back.

Fuckin' tosser. What he's saying is: who are you? What do you want? Where do you come from? You're six feet in your socks and he's five seven and you can feel him looking down on you. How do they do that? Looking down their noses as if to say you're not one of us. You're nothing. Fuck off back to where you come from.

Jordan thinks about throwing his pint in the cunt's face and walking out. Going home. Putting new strings on his Fender. Hit some chords. Fucking sitting there in his white suit, hair swept back like a cunt. Vodka and tonic. Two quarters of lemon. Ice not slush. Fucking homo. His ol' man's got their number. La-de-da voice comes out of their trap and next fing you know their mitts are down your pants.

He's staring down at the bubbles dying on his pint and as he lifts his chin, Jordan becomes aware of the girl looking at him across the table with green eyes like green stars. He looks back and it's like looking at an angel, at a goddess from a Black Sabbath cover, her lips turning into a fleeting smile...

There is a long still moment while he stares at Bella.

This is the moment, one of life's big moments: the moment to leave the pint on the table and walk out.

The moment passes.

Jordan loosens his grip on the glass and looks back at Martin.

'Here,' he says, dumping a packet of Benson & Hedges *gold* on the table.

Martin glances at Guy, then stares back at the Bensons like he's found a dead rodent between his bed sheets.

He looks back at Guy, shaking his head.

'See what I mean. Now the oceans are boiling, the ice caps are melting, the dolphins are dying and time is ion fucking freefall, how the fuck do people end up buying this stuff. Or Lambert & Butler. I mean why?'

'Cos they're cheap.'

Martin stares back at Jordan. 'Cheap? Are you taking the piss? If you want to save money, don't fucking smoke. If you are going to smoke, buy a proper brand.'

'They are proper. A lot of people smoke 'em.'

'A lot of people. Who? Come on, who? I want names.'

'I know people.'

'He knows people. They wouldn't happen to be very common people, would they?'

Jordan takes a long swig from his pint, settles the glass down on the table, steady as she goes, and leans forward, chin first.

'As a matter of fact, they happen to be nice people.'

See, that's the way to do it. That shut the cunt up.

Jordan watches Martin take a fag from the packet and light up. He inhales, exhales, pulls a face.

'Listen...' he says and gazes up like a poet looking for a word.

'Jordan,' says Trilby.

'... in these health conscious times we smoke Marlboro Lights or Camel Lights. Buy them. Otherwise, *Jordan*, you can't play.'

Martin takes another drag, grabs his phone, presses redial and holds the machine to Trilby's ear like a piece of evidence.

'Must be at the movies,' he says.

And Trilby's thinking: *it was funny the first time.*

......scene 16

Man's pituitary gland produces endorphins. They are natural pain killers. They flow through the body to the brain and give you a mild high, fresh energy, a feeling of euphoria.

You can mimic and enhance this natural phenomenon with a chemical called diacetylmorphine, a drug synthesized from the opium poppy.

H. Smack. Brown. Scag. Heroin.

Good gear is like an orgasm. If you have an orgasm on heroin you see the face of God.

Trust me.

The good news is, H has never been cheaper or more plentiful and, while Afghanistan remains the playground for the War on Terror, it'll stay that way. Like it's meant to be that way. Across the length of the Golden Crescent, the inaccessible valleys stretching from the frontiers of Iran to Pakistan transform in springtime into seas of white poppy the farmers of Nimruz, Helmand and Khandahar turn into crystalline powder. Horses carry the powder in sacks out of the valleys and, just as goods have travelled the silk routes from east to west since the time of the Han Dynasty, Japanese 4x4s take the raw material over invisible borders and unmarked trails to factories in Turkey where it is refined and sent on to the consumer in the west.

It makes sense that Turkey joins the EU, trades in euros, opens the borders. That's what the free market is all about.

Dollars and cents. Supply and demand. Profit.

Take the black, brass-studded attaché case Miro Stanislav lays on the preparing table in the kitchen at *Silvia's*.

It's amazing that something so small can be worth so much. Like gemstones. Like secrets. Like contacts.

They gather round as if Jesus is about to do tricks with loaves and fishes, raise the dead. Kresimir lowers the flame below the big pot of cooking apples and dries his hands on his apron. There are clients in the restaurant listening to crap music and waiting for their lunch.

They can wait.

Miro pops the locks and they stare down at those plastic bags of gold-flecked brown stuff as if at a row of well-stuffed bratwursts during the hungry days, as if at a curl of smoke on the horizon, the first glimpse of home after a long journey: 20 bags of brown, two tightly packed rows above, two below.

Kresimir grabs one of the bags and weighs it in his palm – a good cook keeps the weights in his head.

'Half a kilo.'

Lech does the maths in his head and checks on his watch calculator: a half kilo bag is 500 grams; at £50 a gram on the street, that's £25,000. Twenty bags is £500,000. He shows the figure on his watch to Silvia, his eyes magnified behind black-framed glasses.

Kresimir whistles.

'We stamp on it two times,' says Teo.

'Two million,' says Kresimir in a hushed voice.

'And people to pay in every place.' Silvia looks at the men like they're boys and counts on her fingers. 'Kandahar, Tehran, Istanbul, Paris, Calais, Dover, people, people.'

Miro's still wearing his crash helmet and as he takes it off and places it on the shelf beside a stack of white plates his expression changes. Fine lines like rails of H cross his smooth brow. His lips shrink. His eyes twist on their stalks. The knots in his brain are loosening.

Silvia doesn't notice this Jekyll and Hyde impression. Her eyes are fixed on one of the half kilo bags. She takes it out of the case and like blood rising from a cut, the powder rises to the plastic surface of the bag.

She stares at her son as he stands back, searching the waistband on his Levi's, the pockets of his buckskin jacket. The colour drains from his face. The whites of his eyes are a palette in shades of pink, pupils small as pinpoints.

'Fok. Fok. Fok,' he bursts. 'I fuck up.'

'What you say?'

Silvia grabs his jacket, pulls him closer.

'I lose it. I lose the gun.'

She slaps him across the face. Front hand and backhand. 'You fuck up if you don't find it,' she says, and lets go of Miro to run her finger over the split in the bag of heroin.

'Just a hit,' he says. 'To check...'

Lech closes the attaché case and seals the locks. 'The cocaine makes you quick. It gives you an edge. Heroin twists your brain,' he says. He stares up at Miro, lips curled. 'To mix you would have to be a fool...'

As the word leaves Lech's mouth, Miro lifts him off his feet and slams him against the wall. The shelf breaks. The crockery tumbles, smashing like it's a Greek wedding. Miro pulls Lech back up and head butts him, shattering his glasses and the fine bones across the bridge of his nose. Blood erupts from his face and rains over the place where Kresimir rolls pastry.

The outburst lasts two seconds.

Silvia drags Miro off. Lech slips down to the floor, holding his head back. Kresimir grabs some ice.

Miro stares at his mother.

'It was a woman.'

'What? What are you saying?'

'A woman. It was a woman. She bring.'

'They change, the Turks change many times,' says Lech, looking up from the floor. 'When they know what gun it is that kill the woman they will come looking for us.'

'When they come, I will be waiting,' Miro replies.

'With no gun,' says Lech.

Miro snaps his fingers. 'I get another.'

Silvia grabs Kresimir's carving knife and holds it to Miro's throat. He doesn't flinch. She's not going to use it.

'No, Miro. No. You go. Go now. You find your gun.'

......*scene 17*

There's a big clock on the wall and it's ticking.

People wait for their moussaka and sauerkraut, their strudel and baklava, their coffee and a shot of slivovitz. They sit in pairs and groups and extended families around paper tablecloths with Slobodan Milosovic staring down from the wall, the tinny cassette playing a *valtz*, the smell of home in the air. They are in no hurry. They listen and they wait and they watch as Miro Stanislav strides through the restaurant like Lucifer casting darkness about him.

......*cut*

There's a Tokarev TT33 with 6 caps in the light fixture in the handicapped cubicle at *Interface*. If you look close, you can make out it's shadow on the ceiling.

......*cut*

Costumed for cabaret, Bella shows less reluctance than you want to imagine as she leaves Martin's table beside the door at *Interface* and follows Guy to a table closer to the bar.

Guy looks back at Martin and raises his glass.

'I'll pay you back,' he says

'I know you will.'

Jordan watches Bella. He can't take his eyes off her. He studies her arms and shoulders glowing white as candlewax in a beam of sunlight. They don't make 'em like this where he comes from. They're all fat slags with hair pulled back and earrings like bike wheels. They don't smile. They've forgotten how to smile. No one smiles where he comes from. If you smile they think you're a cunt. If you smile they want to know what's so fucking funny all of a sudden.

'Who's that?' he asks, the words slipping out, and the cunt looks horrified.

'I beg your pardon?' Martin replies.

'Just asking.'

'It is assumed that people know who people are and if people don't know who people are they have the courtesy to wait until they are introduced.'

'Right.'

'This could be your lucky day, *Jordan*.'

'Why's that then?'

Martin adjusts the creases in his trousers and sits back in the chrome and leather chair. 'You've got a lot to learn,' he replies, 'and I might just teach you a thing or two.'

'Right.'

Jordan finishes his pint, opening his gullet like some extinct sea bird and gulping the stuff down in one.

Martin watches and the image that comes to mind is an organ grinder's monkey and he can't recall ever having seen an organ grinder, or his monkey come to think of it, but this picture is burned in his memory, perhaps from a film, perhaps from the novel he'll write one day. Where did these people go? These characters? These Londoners? The Pearly Kings. The costermongers. The Great Train Robbers. The Cockney villains stringing rivals up on meat hooks. Now it's all accordion players and gypsies sticking pins in their babies to make them cry. It's little turds in red tee-shirts with crass accents.

Trilby's been to the loo and is crossing the bar with Scarlett. Martin indicates with his chin.

'So, Jordan, what do you think of Trilby, fancy her?'

'She's all right.'

He switches to Scarlett. 'What about her?'

'Marks out of two, I'd give her one.'

This isn't Jordan speaking.

It's Krishna, standing at his shoulder. Martin clocks the eyebrow ring.

'Sorry, got held up. Fucking traffic,' Martin says.

That's one of the few things Krishna appreciates about Martin, his gift of irony. 'It's quicker to walk inside the Circle Line,' he replies.

Trilby presents herself for kissing. Krishna obliges, air brushing both powdered and chiselled cheeks.

'Looking good,' she says, and glances at Jordan. 'This is Jordan. Jordan, Krishna. He's a God.'

'Yeah right.'

'Listen,' says Martin, bored with the formalities, 'before I go completely ape, you got any smokes?'

Krishna conjures up a pack of Marlboro Lights and tosses them to Martin. As he does so, he notices the pack of B&H *gold*.

'Who's smoking them?'

Martin nods at Jordan.

'Aren't they chav fags?' he asks.

It raises a smile from Martin, the muttering of the four-letter c word from Jordan and a change of topic. Krishna looks serious.

'The Turk didn't show,' he says.

'What?'

'That's it. No show. No snow.'

'You holding?'

'Emergency rations.'

Martin sniffs the back of his hand.

'Follow me, my man. To La Toilette.'

Jordan watches them sidestep their way through the growing crowd, through the seams of light and shadow, Martin in white, Krishna in black, two knights in a game of chess, and it seems as if everyone at *Interface* has a mission, a purpose, a role. Everyone is constantly coming and going. Like they're doing something. Changing tables, partners, an elaborate dance set to the beat of the barman's drumsticks.

Trilby pulls her skirt straight beneath her as she sits. She takes his hands and, as she leans forward to study his palms Jordan feels a heady complicity, a sense of belonging. There is a superior way to live. These people know that. They know how to talk and dress and behave without feeling self-conscious or embarrassed, without caring what other people think or believe or might say or do. They've all got good karma.

He glances across the shifting sea of bodies trying to get a glimpse of Bella.

......scene 18

Bella's focus drifts along the bar where lone men perch on stools like giant dwarfs on mushrooms, and younger men and girls and blondes circle them like fish feeding around a coral reef.

She sips her vodka tonic. Jazz, a piano and bass, washes over her, moody and familiar. The flesh of her arms and shoulders is lambent against the black laced top. She can feel Jordan's eyes on her like two points pinning her to the wall of his imagination. She is a precious object, coveted and desired. She is completely aware of this. This is not vanity. Just a detail.

It's her birthday today, Simon's birthday, and she remembered when she woke up and she remembers again now. She hasn't told anyone, not even Guy.

She glances at him sitting across the table nursing an empty glass, the heel of his right foot resting on his left knee, his neck swivelling on its axis as he turns hissing *polari,* and if she cared she'd look it up in the dictionary to find out what it means. Guy likes to think of himself as a big fish who knows where the little fish go when they don't have anywhere else to go. He prides himself on knowing how girls should dress and undress, how they think, what they think, and would like to be a girl so that he could put all this theory into practise.

He found Bella in a watery moment in Duke of York Square watching the fountains that rise straight as candles from the paving stones, the crest of the jets exploding in crystal flowers, splashing her skirt and shoes.

Her eyes were glossy with tears, and he said, I'm going to bottle those tears and sell them to the highest bidder at Sotheby's.

He pulled a handkerchief from his top pocket.

That's how things begin.

Two tears and a clean white handkerchief.

Pigeons chase around their feet. The late sun stretches the shadows and makes rainbows through the water jets.

He has a nice voice.

'Hi. I'm Guy,' he says and gasps. 'Oh my God, that rhymes.'

'Bella,' she murmurs.

He looks concerned as he studies her teary eyes.

'It can't be that bad,' he says.

'Yes it can.'

She dries her eyes on the handkerchief and when she tries to give it back to him he makes a little bouquet and shoves it in the top pocket of her blazer.

'Look, there's a seat,' he says, as if his discovered something rare and extraordinary.

Her legs are tired. Her feet are hot. She's been walking forever.

They cross the square, it's like crossing the threshold from something into something else. Their words mesh naturally, spontaneously. He takes her two hands as they sit, and his features grow tense as he listens to her story. When her words run out, he takes the handkerchief back out of her blazer pocket and dabs at her eyes. He dabs at his own eyes. He seems choked up. It's real. It seems real.

He can't speak. And when he does speak he tells her his story, a version of his story, a new draft that draws her into his world of drama and charm. His eyes are brown, soft as a girl's, alert, watchful, and when he says he's going to get a bottle of vodka and the best caviar money can't buy his expression grows brighter and, in that instant, she forgets why she is in Duke of York Square in her school uniform reluctant to go home and unsure where she'll go if she doesn't.

Guy *adores* caviar. He lives for caviar. Champagne for my real friends, real pain for my sham friends. That's what Francis Bacon said, and *he* should know. He gasps. 'Those paintings!'

Bella follows him around *Partridge's* pushing a trolley, reading the labels and rearranging the jars. He asks the Spanish staff if they would recommend the California Golden Osetra for a midnight feast, and doesn't listen as they try to reply.

She leaves the shop carrying the bag and when they wave down a taxi in the Kings Road it seems as if they've known each other forever. Guy listens. He makes her laugh. He says rude things that wouldn't be funny if anyone else said them but they are funny when Guy says them. He will teach Bella new things. Not all at once. Slowly. A step at a time. You don't have to see the whole staircase. That's what Martin Luther King said. Just the first step, and the first step is to climb into that black cab to punish her father for what he has done.

Guy has bought a bottle of vodka, buckwheat blini, quails eggs, a tub of sour cream. Bella is wondering about the best caviar money can't buy when, with a flourish, he produces a tin of Iranian Special Reserve from *her* pocket like a magician pulling a rabbit from his hat.

'Voilà.'

'But...'

'It's £200 a tin you know...'

'...you stole it.'

'No I didn't.'

'You did.'

'You did you mean.'

'Oh my God!'

Guy's grinning. 'It's fun, isn't it?' he asks.

And it is fun. It's awful. Dishonest. Wicked. But it's just one little tin. They can afford it.

Guy takes her hands, looks into her eyes. 'In life you should do *everything* once.'

It's not a question. It doesn't need an answer. But she speaks without thinking, 'Yes,' she says, and then she does think. She nods her head. 'Yes,' she says again, a contract signed in invisible ink.

Guy releases her hands.

She sits back in the big leather seat. Bella likes riding in taxis, she doesn't like taxi drivers very much, the way they always go on about the foreigners and the price of everything, but she enjoys that feeling in a taxi that time is suspended, the past gone, the future unknown. She gets a taxi from Victoria when she comes home for the holidays with Daisy. Mummy has her tennis, the sales, tea at Peter Jones, she's much too busy to meet them, and Father is manacled eternally to his computer. You don't get ahead by getting behind.

The shop windows flash by like memories, the mannequins with the eyes of lost girls, perfume ads, Jamaican rum. Bella likes the rhythm of taxis, the sense that she is in a boat rising and falling with the waves and would have liked this journey to last until the sun went down and London dressed in its suit of lights. It has been a long day, a long week since

Sister Gilbert appeared in the biology lab wrapped in black with lips pursed in holy concern. Bella knew before their eyes met across the sea of girls in bottle green why the sister was there. The strangler's hands froze around her heart, she felt herself slipping beneath the surface of time.

The future for Bella had always seemed remote, abstract, something she didn't quite believe in or would ever come to pass. Death is a glimpse of your own future. Death makes you grow up. It is like a bridge. It takes you by the hand and leads you across the bridge to some new place where you can forget your frozen heart, where you can forget everything and just be and say and do nothing. I mean, what's the point in cramming for Oxbridge? It's too late for that. She doesn't want to dig wells in Somalia, massage her CV showing she cares for the starving millions. It's all lies. All spin. Everyone is always trying to be something, do something, and she doesn't want to be or do anything except turn back time just five short minutes.

The taxi circles Sloane Square and pushes into the stream of steel melting into Sloane Street. She tucks her legs beneath her, straightens her skirt. She had been walking for hours. Down Brompton Road. Fulham Road. Shops and houses. More shops. Right and left. People outside cafés talking and laughing. People hurrying by with packages and bouquets of flowers. The sun silvering the trees.

It was when she stopped to stare at the new fountains that the jets of water finally coaxed the tears from her eyes. She had left Daisy behind at the crematorium. Bella needed to be on her own. And, in the end, that's what we are. What we all are. Alone. Totally alone. Alone and it doesn't matter. Nothing matters. She looks at Guy, neat in a pale brown suit, a blue shirt open at the neck, polished brown shoes. Who is this man? What does he want? What is she doing here with him in this taxi? What does it matter?

Her back is damp in the wool blazer. The vehicle accelerates, sweeping into the curves. Guy takes her hand and she sees in his eyes something gentle and lost, herself perhaps.

Guy's flat is above a shop in Notting Hill with busts on pedestals, wine red curtains and speckled mirrors in gilt frames. Orchids turning rancid droop over the rims of vases, the prints and mirrors and sculptures lit by the last light of day.

He takes the carrier bag to the kitchen and Bella like a visitor at a gallery remains in the centre of the room until the print of Dalì's *Metamorphosis of Narcissus* draws her to look closer. She recalls the painting from art classes at school and, as she stares into the landscape she feels as if she is entering that mysterious and irrational space, that she is a flower and a rock, a boy like Romeo and a girl like Juliet, that she will become a part of the scenery, the furnishings that are all a bit worn, a bit frayed, but warm and inviting.

She crosses the room to look at the prints on the opposite wall, and what she sees at first seems to be a trick of the fading light. She draws closer. Her heart races. A flush burns her neck and, for a moment, just a moment, she forgets about the funeral, the embarrassed look on the curate's face, Daisy holding her hand. She forgets everything as her gaze shifts from one print to the next, the scenes in black and white strange and surreal, people posed in masks, in costume, in nothing at all. Girls in leather. People hanging in chains and fixated on bottoms and whips. She is shocked and fascinated. She looks away and looks back again. She can leave, right now if she wants to. But she doesn't want to leave. You give up grief, as you give up an addiction, by leaving one world and entering another. Bella wants to drink vodka and eat caviar at £200 a tin. She wants to forget this day and see what a new day brings.

She deposits her straw hat on the crown of a marble figure who might be Napoleon. She throws her blazer over a chair and herself across an old sofa.

She calls Daisy.

'Bells, where are you? You just vanished.'

'I couldn't stand it another second.'

'He'll kill you when you get home.'

It's the wrong thing to say and they both fall quiet. Daisy's fourteen and is trying to be brave. Bella is three months from eighteen, a bird flying the nest, casting off the chains of childhood.

'I'm not coming home,' she says.

'I wish you would.'

'Will you be all right, Daze?'

'It's you I'm worried about.'

'Don't.'

'It's worse for you, Bells.'

She loves Daze. She's smart. And she's clever. Both things.

'I'll call you every day.'

'Pwomise.'

'Pwomise.'

There's old fashioned music leaking from the kitchen. The beat of a knife on a wooden chopping block.

'Gotta go,' says Bella.

They blow kisses down their phones.

Guy appears in a chef's hat and apron. You should always dress for the occasion, he says, depositing the hat on another sculpture.

They sit in big wingback thrones at opposite ends of the coffee table surrounded by Narcissus and the naked girls. They eat Iranian caviar with toasted blini and drink vodka so cold it scolds her tongue. The music is German. Marlene Dietrich, he says.

They dance. Guy wears her straw bonnet. Bella glimpses her reflection in the mirrors, a schoolgirl in uniform, hair tousled, features glazed. Beauty doesn't see itself and when it does something is lost. They drink more vodka. They get giggly and silly. Bella is being seduced. She is aware of that, she knows while it's happening, and lets it happen. You have to try everything once.

She grows solemn and watchful as Guy runs through the buttons and zips and helps her out of her school uniform. He turns her round, unsnaps her bra, runs her panties down her legs, kisses her bottom. He's like an old friend. A girlfriend. Guy doesn't want to sleep with her. He wants something, everyone wants something, and it might be amusing finding out just what.

Bella sleeps in the big bed with the black quilt and awakes with a clear head and no clothes. Guy has sent them to the laundry. They were smelly. Like the graveyard. He lies. He always lies. She will learn that, but she doesn't know that yet. He has something fantabulosa she can wear, a black pleated dress like Marlene Dietrich, a string of pearls, stockings clipped to a corset, high heels that are too big, Guy's size she imagines, and she slip slops her way among the marble busts and candelabra eating yoghurt from the tub.

Guy dresses in a frilly shirt and waistcoat, a green visor. He places the chairs together at one end of the coffee table and sits with a pack of playing cards that he spreads in a line, flicking them one way and the other like a wave. He shuffles and cuts, the cards slipping through his fingers like silk, then deals two hands. Everyone, he says, should know how to play poker. Poker is like life. You have to know when to bet and when to bluff, when to withdraw and when to up the stakes.

That's what he's doing, upping the stakes, from black underwear to the mysteries of poker to her first visit to what Guy calls the torture garden, a cupboard arrayed in whips and canes, costumes and masks like those in the prints on the wall. She's barefoot in the Marlene Dietrich dress and steps into black boots with high spiky heels. Guy tells her the whips and canes are not to hurt people, they're just for fun. Fun has many moods and many faces.

Bella will learn that pain can turn to pleasure just as pleasure turns to pain, opposites and compliments, and sometimes on long afternoons as she watches the dust motes dancing in the afternoon sunshine it feels as if her soul has slipped the chains of her body. She remembers floating with Simon in a satin sea like two bubbles and the details seem stronger, more real and poignant than the events of the day.

......*scene 19*

Bella finishes her vodka tonic.

'Happy Birthday,' she says.

Guy looks at her as if she's mad, glances back at the bar, and back at her again.

'Have you seen that? Look. It's not hair, it's a rug,' he says.

Bella isn't paying attention and wonders who tells these men that of all the bars in NoHo, it's at *Interface* where they'll find relief for their particular weirdness.

Guy on these occasions has the same furious tone as Martin, but reserves his malevolence for people who can't hear him. He shields his mouth with the flat of his hand.

'He's wearing enough slap to coat a wall.'

'It's cheaper by the yard.'

'Just cheap, darling.'

Guy grips her arm suddenly as his gaze settles on another victim. 'Look. Oh my God. Look. Who let him in here? It's a gorilla, an ape. It's an orang-utan in a monkey suit.'

'They're extinct.'

'Excuse me: there's the living proof. Where do they find these people? Who are they? What do they want?'

'That's your job.'

He turns with a plotter's smile like they're members of a secret society.

'I love you,' he says, and she swats at the lie with her long white hand.

'He must be a bouncer,' Bella adds, playing the game.

'You think?' He strokes the side of his face, considering. 'Close together eyes. No neck. Forehead like a dinner plate. Those long arms and short legs are proof of a well-known scientific fact...'

Guy pauses for her to join in.

'Small willy.'

They burst out laughing as Martin and Krishna pass the table. Krishna kisses his fingers and runs them over Bella's neck.

Guy grips her arm with sudden urgency.

'Now, there's a contender.'

His restless quest settles on the far end of the bar where a blonde with the calm desperation of girls who have been nurtured by the small screen and dream of passing through the glass is vacating her place with a treasure: a business card.

She sashays across the bar to the loo where, behind closed doors, she will write in block capitals the date, where she met this face known by millions and what he may be able to do for her. It is important to write these things down immediately, record the details: knowledge is power. At home she will slide the card into a plastic envelope in the directory bought at *Ryman's* and, as people once went to the Bible for inspiration, on nights when she isn't out networking she leafs through the little black book and reads these names to herself like a prayer.

Guy, of course, has had his eye on the silver-haired celebrity for some time and is feigning this sudden discovery.

Bella turns up her nose.

'He's sort of   '

'Cute?' Guy suggests.

'Old.'

'He's the one on that quiz show, you know: *And now this is your last and final chance,* and the audience all scream: *It's All or Nothing*.'

Bella shakes her head.

'In the afternoon?'

Bella doesn't watch TV in the afternoon. She watches the dust travelling through the sunbeams and imagines they are flecks of long gone dinosaurs, the secret particles of ghosts.

The blonde passes, wiggling her bony hips, tossing her hair, the business card in her hand like a winning lottery ticket.

'Thank God, the slapper's gone,' adds Guy. 'He looks lonely.'

'He doesn't look lonely.

'He looks lonely, sweetie.'

'He's old.'

'No older than your dad.'

......*scene 20*

He stands opposite, hands clasped together in front of him. Mummy at his side. Like a model. A portrait of grief in a fitted black suit. A veil. Who wears a veil to a crematorium? The sun's hot. The trees are motionless. Her hand is damp gripping Daisy's hand.

There's just the four of them. No friends. No family. Even the curate has left them alone in the memorial garden staring down at the solitary wreath, white flowers with Simon in red.

Bella looks up from the shade of her straw hat. Her lips shape the same word through closed teeth. It would seem from the distance that she is chanting a prayer, but close up, Daisy can hear her sister's mantra: Killer. Killer. Killer. Killer. Killer.

Father looks up. Their eyes meet.

'Killer. Killer. Killer.'

He shakes his head. Looks down.

Bella turns and walks away, through the gate and out on to the Brompton Road. She doesn't know where she's going. She just wants to go. She just wants to walk and walk and keeps on walking and doesn't stop until she reaches the crystal flowers in Duke of York Square.

......*scene 21*

Krishna uses a silver spoon scorched black on the underside to dig out a gram of brown from a plastic bag on to a square of white paper. He is on his haunches in the handicapped loo using the flat surface of the toilet seat as a base. He starts with a level spoonful, then adds a bit extra a few grains at a time.

Martin's got his back against the door. He stares up at the ceiling where he can just make out the blunt, L-shaped shadow of the gun lying in the light fixture. He looks back down at Krishna.

'How much do I owe you? he asks.

'Must be £300.'

'I'll have it for you tonight.'

'Nice one.'

'A lender nor a borrower be. Fair's fair. Got to settle up before I find a new dealer.'

'Yeah, well good luck to you.'

'If you can't get the gear.'

Krishna looks up. 'Martin, there's a fucking war going on out there. The Turks are buying up everything they can lay their hands on and selling it to anyone with the readies, Russians, Albanians, Serbs. They're all at it...'

'And they're all over here. What happened to our own villains? You drive through the East End to buy bagels and it's full of mosques and blokes in blankets. You're not a Moslem, are you?'

'Like you don't know?'

'I'm serious.'

'Hindu.'

'What's the difference?'

'About three thousand years,' says Krishna. 'This look all right for you?'

'Why the fuck do we let them in?' Martin studies the little pile of powder. 'Is it a gram?'

'Give or take.'

'Which?'

'If anything, it's a bit over.'

'Do for me.'

Martin watches Krishna shuffle the brown into the centre of the square of paper. He folds the square corner to corner, folds the ends to the centre and the apex over the base in such a way that it fastens the small package in a neat rectangle.

'They're asylum seekers,' says Krishna.

'Nothing to do with free schools, then? Health care?'

Martin removes two antique snuff boxes liberated from Father's collection, opens the package and empties the brown powder into one of them. He licks the residue from the paper, rubbing the granules into his gums.

Krishna measures out the coke.

'Want to do a couple of lines?' he says.

'Yours or mine? So, how come you got in?'

'Very funny. Take the overage on yours.'

Martin shrugs magnanimously. 'Yeah, fuck it.'

Krishna takes a small pinch of coke and chops it up on the toilet seat with the edge of his Oyster card. He divides the result into two lines and Martin carefully pours the bulk of the coke into the second snuff box. He licks the paper. Drugs secure in his pocket, Martin turns his attention to Krishna's eyebrow ring. Krishna's been waiting for it.

'Do me a favour, be original,' says Krishna. 'Don't ask if it hurt. First thing everyone says.'

'People are so predictable. So?'

'Nah, not really. Stung a bit.'

Krishna completes the preparations.

'Merci,' says Martin.

Martin scoops his line on to the back of his hand and takes it like snuff, half up each nostril. Throwing back his head. Sucking air through his teeth. Savouring the rush. There's nothing like coke. It's like money. It lets you be who you are.

Krishna takes out a thin, customized pipe shaft to work on his. As he reseals the two ziplock bags he's thinking: what the fuck now as he watches Martin climb up on the toilet seat. Krishna pushes the sealed bags in his jacket pocket.

Martin stands down with a fucking great grin that fades into a snarl as he presses the barrel of the gun against Krishna's throat.

'Holy fucking Ganesh...'

'Give me the gear and you walk out on two legs.'

'Do what?'

'You gone deaf?'

'Have you gone fucking mad?'

'Hand over those bags before I spray your fucking brains all over these bogs.'

'Martin. It's me...'

'You. Who the fuck are you? Fucking rentboy.'

Martin forces the gun up under Krishna's throat, in the soft flesh, where it hurts. Krishna can't believe this is happening. His knees are shaking. His body breaks into a sweat, the coke streaming through his veins like broken glass, and he sees in Martin's wild eyes not Martin but a vision of himself stretched out in the morgue with Baba standing there, hands gripped behind his back, a look of genuine bewilderment on his shiny brown face. He can hear him say, as Baba would say, that it can't possibly be his son because he doesn't recognize the eyebrow ring.

'Martin...'

'Give me the bags or they'll be scraping you off the wall.'

'Jesus. OK. OK.'

Krishna takes out the bags of drugs and places them on the toilet seat.

'Take them, man,' he says. 'Just be careful with that thing.'

Martin slides his shades up his nose, then leans close to Krishna's ear.

'BANG!' he says.

He lowers the gun and cracks up laughing, reeling back into the corner of the cubicle.

'What the fuck,' says Krishna, and Martin gets back in position.

'Stick 'em up.'

Krishna does so, and Martin cracks up again.

'Your face,' he says. 'Did you shit yourself?'

Krishna glances at his face in the mirror and what he sees is that fucking ring of gold piercing his right eyebrow. It's tribal. It's so fucking English. You get it done to give yourself a sense of belonging, and here's the rub, here's the irony, the stupidity, it's to belong to something you don't want to belong to. In the reflection he watches Martin tossing the weapon from hand to hand. He then turns the gun handle first to Krishna.

'You want it? Pay for the gear?' he asks.

'No.'

'You know what it's worth?'

'About eight years.'

Martin caresses the gun before shoving it down his belt.

'You've got a screw loose, Martin, you know that...'

And the shades are down. And the gun's back under Krishna's nose.

'What did you say?'

'Holy fuck, not again.'

'Apologise.'

'Martin...'

'Fucking apologise.'

'All right, Martin. Sorry.'

Martin looks thoughtful as he lowers the gun. This is a Road to Damascus moment. This is Siddartha sitting under the bodhi tree.

'You sure you don't want it? Pay off what I owe you.'

Martin presses the gun in Krishna's hand and Krishna takes it just to keep Martin from keeping it.

'OK.'

Martin, bowing like a gent, opens the door and Krishna leaves the loo with the Tokarev in his inside jacket pocket. He doesn't know there are six live ones in the tank and one of them belongs to him.

......*scene 22*

You try them all, you mix them all, but in the end, nothing beats coke. Coke is a window on life and through that window you see the landscape like it's painted by David Hockney, strong lines; primary colours.

Just a few crystals lighting up the grey stuff and the exchange with Greta May the previous night runs through Martin's head like it was etched on his hard drive, filed there for him to return to and examine in all its embryonic promise.

Corruption in Brussels.

- Who gives a shit?

Snouts in the trough.

- Interesting.

Hands in the till. All that waste. All that money.

- What is this girl going on about?

Can't trust anyone these days, he says.

They're all at it.

Even Daddy?

Oh, no, of course not Daddy.

Of course not Daddy my ass.

They want to force Europe down our throats, force us into the throat of Europe: one currency, one market, no borders, gypos flogging heather, and why not? You don't have to buy up properties along the Thames and wait ten years. You just have to keep your eye on the open window.

Martin smiles at his reflection lit by the pinprick lights in the black ceiling, takes a towel from the Chinese chappie and watches Scarlett fixing her lips.

'How many times you done that today?' he asks.

'Who's counting?' she counters, and flutters her inch-long lashes for his benefit.

'You know, when a butterfly flaps its wings over the Amazon there's a hurricane in Alabama.'

'You want to see me wag my tongue?'

'Can't wait.'

They smile. They belong to the same club.

Martin moves in close and whispers to the Chinese boy. Krishna leans over from the adjoining sink to listen.

'There are two rules in this life,' Martin says, 'Rule Number One: there are no rules...'

Martin tosses a £1 coin above his head and, quick as a snake, Scarlett snatches it out of the air.

They bowl out of the bogs and Martin takes in the scene as you would on arriving home after the holidays. In a world of change, *Interface* for Martin is a constant, something to rely on, the moody jazz, the soft reassuring sound of promises and lies, Guy getting acquainted with the mark at the circular bar, his girl sitting there like she's doing a cover shoot for *Bondage Weekly*. Where does he find these little tarts? How does he turn them into such foxes? How come he's always broke?

Who gives a shit?

The gimp's hunched over his table. He always brings a smile to Martin's lips.

'Can I get you anything?' he says. 'Walnut Whip? Set of handcuffs.' The gimp closes the zip over his mouth and Martin speaks over his shoulder to Krishna. 'I love that guy. Don't you just love that guy?'

He doesn't need a response. He's talking for the sake of talking.

'...fucking ice caps are vanishing and what do they do, stop filling the air with shit and carbon? No, the Russians and the Americans and the fucking Danes and the rest of them are all making claims on the land that used to be under the ice so they can pump up more oil and more gas and turn it into more pollution. Are we fucking loco or what?'

Krishna isn't listening.

He's thinking about the gold ring in his eyebrow. He can't see it, he can see its shadow, feel it. Like he can feel the lump of metal in his jacket. Like he feels a lump in his chest like nausea. For some reason Alya keeps dropping into his head like a regret, like an exposed nerve in a dying tooth, the way she watched Kosta Ali Pasha breaking Dixie Dean's hand, the way she turned to him with a look of loathing, a look that said you're just like the rest of them and you're worse because you think you're better.

Is he projecting?

Krishna keeps moving, straight for the door, straight out into the hazy light of NoHo, straight into a cab.

......*scene 23*

Martin collects his party.

'It's playtime. Let's have some fun.' He scrolls down his mobile, presses, listens and shakes his head at Trilby. 'She's doing that modelling gig, right?' he says.

'It's on our way.'

Martin looks with deadly earnest at Jordan.

'Jordan.'

'What?'

'Leave the fags.'

He does so.

In for a penny.

Martin holds the door and Jordan follows Trilby out.

Early afternoon. Traffic light. Not a cloud in the sky. Martin loves London. The buildings are cleaner. Parks are greener. Bars are open 24/7. Sling all the foreigners out and it would be paradise – he glances down at his shiny shoes – not his maid, good Catholic girl, not the ones that are useful, just all the scroungers and asylum seekers, fucking gangsters and beggars. The scum.

He turns to Jordan.

'So, dear boy, what is it you do?' he asks.

Jordan sniffs, shrugs, rolls his shoulders. 'Not a lot. Play a bit of guitar.'

'He plays guitar. Lead?'

'Yeah thas right.'

'You didn't want to be a striker for Chelsea, then? Or be on Big Brother? Or be a disc jockey?'

'Nah.'

Martin loses concentration as the two women wrapped in black from head to foot cast their shadow in his direction.

'Fucking blue eyes and burkas,' he says, shaking his head. 'If they're not footballers they're fucking fashion victims. Do you know how many guitarists there are for every band that makes it? Like fuck all.

Like, did you ever think about doing some A levels? Like getting an education? Like getting a job? Fuck me – '

Jordan breaks into a grin.

Karma.

They've come to a halt at a red BMW convertible parked on a meter and there's a fine stuck on the windscreen.

Martin shakes with rage. 'Five minutes. Fucking five minutes. If I find the asswipe who did this I'll rip his fucking tongue out.'

Martin's got the fine in his hand but he's concentrating now on the grey Audi edging in and out of the space in front of his car, the back bumper air kissing his front bumper.

'Can't fucking drive for traffic. Can't park without some zombie from the jungle rearing up out of the dead with a fucking stop watch.'

The Audi settles. The engine dies. Martin watches the shaven-headed driver step out.

'Oi you.'

The bald guy looks back.

'Yeah, you. I'll tell you something, my fucking dog can park better than that.'

The world pauses for a moment. Coke's confidence is a veneer. Baldy hits the locks, stands straight in pointed size 11 shoes, and scratches his cheek. His accent belongs 5 miles south of the river.

'You got a problem?'

Trilby steps between them. 'No, he just got a fine is all.'

Baldy takes in the curves shaping her white dress, blonde tresses, eyes of fire. She smiles.

'Cos I sort out problems. For a living,' he adds.

Martin's tapping his pockets like there's something missing, something vital, like an internal organ. He waves the fine about.

'It's nothing,' he says. 'It's these fucking tribesmen...'

The bald guy looks again at Trilby, he'd like to fuck her, at Martin, like some music hall act in his white suit, at the kid in the tee-shirt. He turns away, then turns back again to Martin.

'Careful when you come out, less that dog of yours is driving.'

He strolls jauntily down the street and looks back again.

'Oi, you. Yeah, you.'

He's nodding in Martin's direction as he holds his finger and thumb an inch apart. Then he strolls off again, back straight, six feet of muscle in a black suit. Martin hisses through his teeth.

'I sort out problems for a living. Works out twice a week and thinks he's Arnold fucking Schwarzenegger.'

Trilby rips the fine in two pieces and drops the trash in the gutter.

A convoy of police cars, sprayed up and plain clothes, shoot by with flashing lights and wailing sirens.

No one even looks.

......*scene 24*

The ninth floor in the Gyroscope Building.

It revolves like a clock. If you stand in one spot and focus on the London Eye, an hour later it will be back in view. Glass from floor to ceiling, inside the curved walls, sixty girls undressing or getting dressed, naked and not giving a shit, sitting and standing about, bored and starving, staring blankly out at the changing view, at the arc of the sun, and it can be sad the sun through glass on warm afternoons.

That's what Greta May's thinking. She's thinking: What am I doing here? I don't need this. I'm too old for this. I'm better than this. She turns her back on the Eye, the Tate Modern, the Oxo Building. She can smell sweat on tee-shirts, angst on bare flesh; it really is a cattle market, pedigree livestock, pert bottoms, breasts swinging like udders, de rigueur shaved mounts, sullen eyes that could be a reflection of her own eyes.

God, she needs a hit. Greta needs a hit a lot more than she needs to be the face of *Shameless*, and deep down somewhere vague she's preoccupied by the thought that doesn't want to be the face of *Shameless*, that to be the face of *Shameless* would be shameful, fraudulent, a fabrication, that she'll be a part of something she doesn't want to be a part of. She doesn't need to be a part of.

Greta can do anything. Anything. And what people can't understand is that when you can do anything it's hard to know what to do. Be a model. Be an actress. Work on the telly. Work on a magazine. Call friends for favours. She's been too coddled, too cared for, too privileged, she's had too much and the problem is you can't help but get used to it, you can't imagine not having it, having everything. When all those unknown grubby people look at Greta she sees hostility in their eyes, the girls want to be her, the boys want to sleep with her, and what they don't know and will never know is the perfect life, perfection itself, can be so stressful, so empty, so pointless, so boring.

She sighs as she reties her bathrobe and watches a girl of about sixteen doing her thing in the bright lights of tall lamps, each movement punctuated by the click of a camera, an instruction, an expletive. The girl is naked except for the solitary black glove that reaches above her elbow and the heart-shaped black bag she holds over her pubis. Her arm in the glove conceals her breasts and she gazes coldly over one shoulder as if her youth and nudity is a serious matter, and it is: one of these sixty girls will become the face of *Shameless*, a new anti-aging cream designed for women in their fifties and sixties, for women like her mother trying to hold back the clock and they have as much chance of doing that as putting a brake on the slow grinding turn of the Gyroscope, the spin of the earth, the turning of the days.

On the walls are pale pink posters picturing a black box illustrated with an artist's impression of Botticelli's *The Birth of Venus* rising, not from a shell, but from a pink orchid that imitates the female vulva. Above the box is the word *Shameless* in black and, below, the strapline *Forever Young* in a jaunty red loop. To complete the design they need a long thin flawless girl with inexplicably abundant breasts and pink nipples that match the painted orchid. There's a soundtrack, too; the photographer likes to work to his own music, and the evocative chords of Pink Floyd provide a retro, fractured, melancholy feel like the sun hitting the panels of glass.

The photographer is famous. Famous for being an asshole. Angus McTee. A squat Scot with a barrel chest and short legs designed for balance. He holds his camera in two hands like a phallus, like a gun that shoots in rapid spurts. He has a swarm of assistants, girls almost tall enough, almost thin enough, almost voluptuous enough to be models. But not quite. Boys who aren't sure what they are, who they are, where they're going, and for now they are in the reflected glow of West End glam as they raise the 1000 watt Kleig light half a centimetre, adjust the white umbrellas, the shadow area lit by two 75 watt fill lamps, shifting the 100 watt rim light behind the subject and out of the firing line of McTee's field of focus and vitriol. On a glass table McTee's book *Peep Show* is piled up with a sign £20.

The PA could be thirty. She could be forty. She could be forty-five. She has red hair out of a bottle, carmine lips, more vampire than vamp, big teeth faintly lipsticked as if with blood, black clothes, sharp bones and half-moon glasses over the rims of which she is suddenly staring at Greta.

'Which one are you?' she demands.

'Greta May.'

She casts her eyes over her list. 'May. May. Maybe not,' she says, she's witty too, and looks up again. 'How old are you?'

'Twenty-three.'

'Who sent you for God's sake.'

'Not *him*. My agent.'

'Same thing, dear. Can't live with them. Can't kill the fuckers.'

'So what would you like me to do?'

'Let's have a look...'

The vampire pulls the tie on Greta's bathrobe and flicks the garment over her shoulders. She gazes at her naked body as you would looking at yourself in a new dress in the changing room when you feel, well, it's pretty good but maybe, just maybe, I'll find something better.

'You may as well carry on, now you're here,' she says, and gives Greta a long black glove.

'Oh, thank you.'

The PA makes a note and looks back again at Greta, registering her face now she's registered her voice, cut glass, clipped, courteous, faintly antique, faintly condescending. The PA has spent her life mastering the intonation, the lilt, the tempo, and still feels vaguely ill at ease when she hears the real thing. Accent is everything.

The session with the child model has come to an end. The photographer throws his camera at one of the effete lighting boys and he catches it, barely, bruising his chest. The tears streaking the child's cheeks betray the 'who gives a shit' heroin chic of her blacked up eyes and gelled up hair. Across that sea of sixty young faces thirty are identical, like those figures you make by folding a sheet of paper like a concertina, cutting a silhouette, then unfolding a line of soldiers or a line of little girls joined at the toes and fingertips, the faces of *Shameless*, ditto, ditto, ditto.

'Bastard,' she whispers, and gives the triangular black bag to Greta.

'Focking time wasters,' says Angus McTee.

He prowls around, adjusting the lighting set up. He has bare feet, which Greta finds oddly intimate and intimidating as she stands there, back arched in a perfect bow, shoulders straight, breasts pushed forward. A goddess. Men get erections in front of their computer screen and jerk off into their handkerchief when they see girls like Greta May.

Angus McTee looks bored.

'For fock's sake. Are we going to be here all day?'

'I'm waiting for you.'

'Don't. Just get on with it.'

I don't need this.

I really don't need this.

She steps into the ring of lights. Pulls the long black glove over her hand, up her arm. McTee takes his camera from the injured spark, adjusts the lens, moves the big light stand back a centimetre.

Greta gets into a pose, legs together, the triangular-shaped bag modestly over the triangular patch of her pubic hair, arms propping up the domes of her breasts, nipples just hidden, lips curled in utter disdain.

'Are you shivering? Stop shivering for fock sake.'

'I'm not shivering.

'You're focking shivering.'

'Oh fuck orf.'

McTee is looking through the lens at her. 'I can see it. This is body cream, not ice cream for fock sake.'

'Oh fuck orf.'

Click. Click. Click.

She twists and turns in furious poses, thrusting out her chin, her breasts, her heart-shaped bottom that once covered a 1000 bus shelters, bending her knees one way and the other, slipping and sliding on the spot, the click, click, click of the camera recording every move, every gesture, the bitter taste of bile rising to her throat injecting scorn in her flawless features. It's weird, but she comes to life in front of the camera. She wants to do something else but what? This is who she is.

'Yeah, baby, give it to me.'

'Fuck orf.'

Click. Click. Click.

The door opens and closes. She catches a glimpse of Krishna and the fact that he's there sweetens her sour mood. She feels relieved, relaxed, totally at ease in a black glove being painted by light, damp with perspiration, knowing that Krishna will be carrying a little something. He always has something. And *he* has something.

Click. Click. Click.

The photographer moves one way, then the other. They are dancing in bare feet...

We're just two lost souls swimming in a fish bowl

Year after year

'Yeah better. Go for it, baby. You're smeared with toffee nut fudge, with Belgian chocolate. Covered from head to toe. A dog's licking it off – '

Running over the same old ground

And now we've found

'Fuck you.'

'Fock you.'

'Fuck you.'

The same old fear

Wish you were here

'Licking, licking. A big black hairy dog with a big fat tongue, licking your legs, your face, your pussy.'

'You *arse...*'

'Nice. Nice. You're getting moist between the legs.'

And the terrible thing is she is getting wet. She can feel it. Smell it. Her nude body aflame in the heat of the lights. The guitar wailing like some extinct animal. The stream of filth in the Scotsman's mouth. The mesmerising click, click, click of the camera.

'Feel that tongue, baby. Feel that tongue.'

'You piece of shit.'

'Yeah, baby. Give it to me. Give it to me baby.'

She tosses her hair, moves her arm up to her shoulder, exposes her right breast, rubs the pussy-shaped bag between her legs, slicks the shiny black leather with a smear of girl juice.

Click. Click. Click.

These shots aren't right for *Shameless*. She knows that. Angus McTee knows that. These are shots that he'll put in a book or up on the web for all those sad fuckers wanking over YouPorn.

God, she needs a hit.

......*scene 25*

Martin steps out of the car and leans back through the open window.

'Five minutes.'

Trilby and Jordan get out of the vehicle and watch as Martin makes his way towards the revolving door at the front of the Gyroscope Building.

'He's a right bastard,' says Jordan.

'If you follow him through that door he'll try and come out first.'

'That's what I mean.'

Jordan shoves his hands in his back pockets and feels the package of new guitar strings. He still has half a mind to bugger off home, cut his losses.

'So, where we going?' he says.

'Where would you like to go?'

'Dunno. Nowhere.'

'That's a possibility.'

Trilby leans against the side of the BMW, left leg bent at the knee, the sole of her shoe resting on the paintwork. Jordan looks back and he's sure he's seen her somewhere before, maybe on the telly.

'Someone's going to have him one of these days,' he says

'Undoubtedly,' she replies in her velvety voice and he really hasn't ever seen anyone with such amazingly blue eyes.

Cars and vans swish by, a river of molten steel, their reflection elongated in the curved glass walls of the building, their image captured by one or more of the four million cameras watching our every move.

......scene 26

On the ninth floor a blonde with bubbles of curly hair pouts for Angus McTee, absorbs the abuse, wiggles her bum. The music beats against the walls, a storm of sound. The Vampire struts on stick legs.

Greta May pushes her arms into her bathrobe and joins Krishna in the doorway.

'I, like, really don't want to do this any more,' she whispers.

'You were great,' Krishna says.

A faint smile crosses her delicate features. When you're up there, doing your thing, naked in the spotlight, even if you hate it, it gives you a high and when you step down you feel like a balloon deflating as the energy runs out of you. She's hot, breathless, her body below the bathrobe sticky with sweat.

'Have you got anything?'

Krishna gives her a wrap.

'Short supply,' he says.

Greta holds the wrap inside her pocket as latchkey kids hold keys and black miners cling on to blood diamonds.

'Can you, you know, pay...'

'Course,' she says. 'Sorry...'

'It's a bad moment.'

They both look back as the door swings open.

Martin.

Grinning. All in white. Surprised to see Krishna. And pleased. He kisses Greta's hand.

'Hello, you old tart, I've been calling you for, like, hours,' he says and smiles at Krishna. 'Serendipity, man. It really is my lucky day.'

'I've been waiting for, like, hours,' says Greta.

Martin waves his mobile at her.

'It upsets the photographer.'

'Don't explain, he's just a jumped up little oik.,' Martin declares. 'Do you want to come for a ride? Do something? Forget everything.'

'I can't,' she says, and Martin's look of disappointment is total: total ham. He leans closer.

'Word of warning, ducks, never date your dealer. Always ends in tears.'

'I've got to see someone in a play. I promised.'

'And I've got to get hold of some money,' says Krishna.

'Well, we all know how you do that,' says Martin, and turns again to Greta. 'Your people back?'

'Daddy should be in later.'

'And Mummy always goes to collect him? That's so sweet.'

'Only if she's been naughty while he's away.'

'Has she been naughty?'

'I suppose...'

'That's why I adore your mother,' says Martin and focuses again on Krishna. 'Listen, just a word outside.'

He kisses Greta's cheeks and holds the door open for Krishna. 'You're looking fabulous,' he says. If you don't get the gig I'll kill whoever does. Love you...'

He's about to go, then remembers. 'Greta, darling, do me a favour, turn your sodding machine on.'

......scene 27

Martin follows Krishna into the circular corridor. All the love's gone.

'What's going on, dude?'

'Change of plan,' says Martin. 'I need the piece.'

'You what?'

'I need it. Business.'

'Aren't you stepping out of your league?'

'Just give me the fucking gun.'

'Don't you owe me money?'

'You'll have it tonight. Now, hand over.'

Krishna looks about him. The lift's are still. The corridor's empty. The wide spiral of white marble stairs is silent. He whips the gun out of his jacket and drives the barrel into Martin's throat.

'Hand over my fucking money – '

' – what?'

'Before I spray your fucking brains all over these walls.'

Martin stares into Krishna's eyes. He takes hold of his wrist and pulls his hand slowly down.

'Krishna. Gun.'

They pull away from their clinch. Martin's sticks his hand out. Krishna lays the Tokarev in his palm.

'Don't ever pull a stunt like that again.'

'You did it – '

'Now shut the fuck up.'

Martin conceals the weapon in his waistband.

'Martin, what's going on, man?'

Martin waves a warning finger. 'I said, shut the fuck up,' he repeats and buttons his jacket.

Krishna watches Martin descend through the bars of light crisscrossing the stairwell. He looks back, makes a gun from his fingers.

'Bang.'

'Wait,' Krishna says, 'you didn't say what Rule Two is.'

Martin stops. There are lines across his brow.

'You said there are two rules...'

'Yeah: Rule Two, don't forget Rule One.'

He's gone. Death Descending A Spiral Staircase.

......*scene 28*

Circa 1952: a game of cricket on a village green.

All eyes are on Arjun Patel.

Except for those of the elderly lady who rides by on a bicycle with a basket containing a Yorkshire terrier with a bandaged foot. She has grey hair in a bun and is probably solving a dastardly crime.

The local Bobby, plump cheeks, hands behind his back, stands at the church gate with the curate, young with thinning red hair and blue eyes like an Apostle.

Men in tweeds smoking pipes push out of the *Duke of York* clutching pints of warm bitter.

A chap in a deerstalker pulls up in a green MG.

The postman pauses after opening the red pillar box situated behind a row of striped deck chairs where assorted matrons and majors with handlebar moustaches watch Patel marking his crease with the tip of his linseed-oiled willow.

The umpire wears a straw boater and has several v-necked jumpers tied about his waist. The day is balmy, a mild south-easterly rustling the leaves on mature trees where thrushes and blackbirds return year after year to build their nests. There are no pigeons.

Intense fielders in starched whites man the boundary.

A man whispers to his son. 'Watch this, my lad.'

Horatio Marley, a tall West Indian with a long stride, polishes the leather ball against his crotch. He takes a 40 yard run up, delivers a worthy leg spin and Arjun Patel tucks the ball behind the wicket for a four.

There's a polite round of applause.

......*scene 29*

Arjun Patel opens his eyes.

Shakes his head.

Watches the forensics team in white jump suits crawling on hands and knees around the body of a dead woman.

'Issa fuckin Balkans out there, innit,' he says. 'What you supposed to fucking do? Can't even speak to these fuckers without a terpreta.'

Detective Inspector Patel has a straight from central casting plod accent and stands below a CCTV camera hooded in a black sack while he leafs through a Turkish passport. Arc lamps that look as if they've been nicked from a fashion shoot light the tunnel walls at Goodge Street, closed for the day and causing havoc on the Northern Line. What with the points failure at Covent Garden and the suicide at Embankment, this isn't a good day for London Transport. Or London commuters.

'You sure it's drugs?' says Marley.

'Look at 'er arm, son, covered in bruises. Fingers snapped. What do you fink she was 'anging on to, her fuckin virginity?'

'Didn't know the Turks used women.'

'Equal rights, son.'

'Bastards.'

'Who, the Turks or the ovver lot?'

'All of them, Inspector. All of them.'

Patel takes a long look at his colleague.

'You're right there son,' he says.

Detective Sergeant Marley looks down at the woman, her body twisted at an angle, her skull blasted open, her brains spread across the platform like sick. He'd like to have ten minutes in a locked cell with whoever it was who killed her and another ten with whoever it was who sent her to London. Throw the regulations out the window and just give him ten minutes.

One thing Marley can't stand is women being abused. His mother was beaten senseless by his rotten-to-the-core father and the old man was gone before Marley left primary school. He hates being a statistic, a cliché: another black kid from South London being brought up by a lone mother, even if he was one of the lucky ones.

Mum worked ten hours a day as a hospital cleaner. She studied administration skills at night and he was eighteen and doing A levels when she finally hung up her mop and apron to take up a position behind the information desk at the Chelsea & Westminster.

Long journeys, she told her son, start with the first step, and he never forgot it.

It had taken Marley's mother ten years to get the job she wanted and in those ten years he never once saw her without a smile. She took him to the Baptist Church in the Old Kent Road every Sunday. She sat at night doing her homework as he did his own, and she taught him you get where you want to go by hard work, by trusting in God and playing by His rules. That's why he joined the force.

Tall, 28, a first in law from Durham, everything he is and everything he might become he owes to his mother. He doesn't remember his father. His mother never knew her father. There's a whole chain of Marleys without fathers going back four centuries to Africa. Horatio Marley is going to break that chain.

He crushes his latte cup and looks round for a bin. Course, there isn't one.

Steve Zimmer from forensics pitches up with a grin and a pair of tweezers that holds a mangled slug sticky with blood.

'Came out the back of her head, Arthur,' he says and Patel throws up his hands.

'How many times do I have to tell you...'

'Eastern Europe if you ask me.'

'I am asking you,' Patel says.

Zimmer drops the bullet head in a plastic bag, opens the velcro on his jacket and slips it safely inside the pocket. He glances at his watch.

'Should know by tea time,' he says.

......*scene 30*

'Daze...'

'Can't talk, Bells, I'm just going into biology.'

Kiss.

Kiss.

'...wait, Bells, I forgot...happy birthday...'

Bella closes her machine.

Guy gives her a little wave as he slides from the stool he's been keeping warm for her and, like Pavlov's dog, she vacates the leather chair where she's been sitting with an empty glass trying to imagine what she would have been doing today if Simon were there to share their birthday. It's on days like this that she can't help remembering all those awful fights in Father's office, the way he would point his finger at Simon like a gun and how the words were like bullets that made her brother burst into tears. Bella likes to recreate the fantasy and casts Simon with his own gun, shooting his own bullets, and she recalls reading that if you can see something in your mind you will hold it in your hand.

Bella seems almost surprised to find clutched in her fingers a mobile phone that she slips into the Prada bag. She walks unhurriedly, spine straight, chin high, eyes a little misty. She is aware of what she is, what Guy has made her, what she has become.

There's a drum roll from behind the bar.

'Henry Fox,' says Guy, lowering his voice to a whisper, 'Bella.'

'How nice to meet you.' Henry's whispering, too, like they're members of an ear-whispered communion.

She doesn't reply. She focuses on Henry Fox, her head turned to one side, pink lips faintly parted. This isn't an act. The clothes are an act. The girl's a natural. One shot from Angus McTee and she'd be the face of *Shameless*.

They shake hands. It's all very formal. Guy finishes the vodka tonic Henry must have bought him. As he places the glass on the bar, he appears to be struck suddenly by a revelation and gasps in wonderment.

'Oh my God, I just noticed, that's gorgeous. I love the colours. It must be Ferragamo?'

Henry's tie is a pattern of reds like a painting by Mark Rothko. He turns it over and reveals the label.

'I knew it.' Guy does the gasping thing again, then lowers his voice. 'Henry has refined tastes.'

Henry smiles sheepishly as he studies Bella perched on the stool. 'Would you like another drink?' he asks, turning from Bella to Guy, including him in the invitation.

'Love to, but I have to dash,' Guy answers. 'Maybe later.'

Guy taps his jacket pocket, smiles that self-satisfied, self-congratulatory smile Bella is beginning to find tiresome, and they watch him go.

There's a moment's still. Just the background chatter, the music, the clink of glasses. Bella's not sure how long she's been sitting beneath the domed roof at *Interface* but it seems like an eternity, like she's a part of the décor, a Helmut Newton nude flat against the wall; even the trapeze artiste has gone, and it feels as if the bars of light are power flows sucking out her energy and leaving her empty, bereft, a blank canvas. She considers telling Henry it's her birthday, but what's the point? He is not interested in her as a human being, he is interested in her as a man would be interested in a bus that can convey him from one place to another.

Well, not exactly.

Henry is quietly, coyly, fascinated. He looks into Bella's eyes but he doesn't see two sparkling fields of green. No, he sees a picture from the past, the picture he always sees on these occasions, a photograph in black and white, not faded but sharpened by time, embellished by imagination, a boy of six or so in a country house, darkness beyond the leaded windows, the bed sheets pulled back to reveal a shameful stain of urine.

Nanny's intake of breath is sharp, almost a hiss. She snaps at his pyjama cord, folds him over her knees and plays the drum of his bottom, toes and fingertips skimming the ground, the sound of her hand tolling like thunder. The little boy weeps, snot running from his nose, pyjama bottoms around his ankles, and no one comes to comfort him.

There will be other nights while mother slumbers in her sleeping-pill-two cocktails-before- dinner sleep of the dead when his bottom is displayed for nanny's cruel hand and, when he goes to boarding school at thirteen, Henry will be prepared for the intrinsic eroticism of the bullying, the cold showers, running barefoot around the top field on frosty mornings, memories purged of malice and made humorous for consumption on *Desert Island Discs*.

Now with his silver hair, pale eyes, carved cheekbones that look good on the TV screen, Henry Fox knows every time a stranger sits at his side at the bar in *Interface* that the stranger posing as a fan could as easily be a tabloid journalist and, in his imagination, it is not Nanny's skeletal hand that he sees but a pack of wolves circling his house in Belgravia, the probing lenses of the paparazzi, the headline splash: *Whatever Gives You Pleasure Gives You Power*, his catch phrase from *All Or Nothing*. Any day, at any second, he could be exposed, shamed, humiliated. He knows the risks. But risk is what makes you what you are.

Bella.

Worth every penny. He can't stand these little tarts who don't know what they're doing. And the older he gets, the better the ratings, the more money he earns, the more he looks back into the past and makes a paper chain to link the present. He gazes into the girl's green eyes and smiles.

'What about that drink?' he asks.

'A vodka tonic would be nice,' she says and taps the rim of his half empty glass. 'The wine matches your tie,' she adds.

'Red's more to my taste, I suppose.'

'You're not sure?'

He shakes his head, looks boyish, girlish.

'You know, I like it when someone else chooses.'

'Decisions R Us,' she says, grabbing the tail of Henry's tie to pull him closer. 'You, Henry,' she adds, 'are a naughty boy.'

He rolls his eyes but the sizzle of anticipation is cruelly shattered.

A tall cowboy swings through the double doors and marches up to the bar across from where they're sitting. Miro Stanislav takes Frenchie by the wrists, slides the drumsticks from his fingers and breaks them, one in each hand like matchsticks.

About time someone did that.

'Vhere is he?'

'Que faites-vous? What the fuck...'

Miro screams. 'Vhere? Vhere? I want the man in white.'

Miro points at his clothes. Frenchie isn't responding.

Miro grabs him by the collar, heaves him over the bar and shakes him like a piece of rag.

......cut

'We should go.'

'You finish your wine and wait a minute, Henry.'

Miro drags Frenchie through the bar towards *La Toilette,* the leathered-up gays, the trannies and drama queens half wishing it were them.

'Vhere is he? You find.'

'I don't know, man. I'm just the fucking barman.'

The Chinese boy remains still as a figurine from the First Emperor's terracotta army. It looks like he's been practicing for 2000 years.

There are three cubicles. Miro pushes the doors open, one after the other. One's locked and the wood shatters with one kick from his Cuban-heeled boot.

The scene's worth a moment's pause.

The orang-utan in the monkey suit last seen being mocked by Guy Bradwell sits with his trousers around his feet, while Scarlett exercises the skills of her hurricane tongue. She's a real worker, dedicated, and continues in her task until Miro drags her off the guy's lap.

'Vhere is he? The one in white.'

The monkey tries to stand, but Miro's hand on the top of his skull holds him just where he is.

Scarlett Johansson doesn't miss a beat.

'They come. They go. Just think of me as part of the furniture.'

Miro has no idea what she's saying. She looks into his eyes, she sees the pain, and he sees the stain of lipstick on her top lip. He rubs it off.

'You crazy girl.'

'That's me.'

Miro looks back at the orang-utan. His erection has transmogrified into a sea creature coiled in a fuzzy nest of orange pubic hair.

Frenchie has remained obediently watching the interlude and now follows Miro into the handicapped loo. He sticks his hand down the tube of the waste bin but Miro expects a more thorough search and tips out the balls of paper, the empty fag packets, the condoms, the needles, sweeping the stuff across the floor with the side of his boot.

'Look. Look.'

'I'm looking, man. *Que faites-vous!*'

'I kill him. I kill him.'

Frenchie rummages through the rubbish, finds an ear-ring, the heel from a shoe, crawls on his knees into the corners, explores the space behind the waste pipes.

'I kill him. I kill him.'

Miro pulls the shell-shaped lighting fixtures from the wall and they smash into millions of little shells as they hit the floor.

'Vhere is my gun?' he cries, a wounded animal, voice magnified in the confined space. 'I fuck you. I fuck you all.'

He drags Frenchie back out of the cubicle and stops at the Chinese boy. He looks at his own reflection on the long mirrors, then back at the boy, back at Frenchie.

There's silence in the bar when Miro returns, a ring of faces like a circus audience. The swing is motionless. Only the gimp carries on doing his thing. Like nothing. Just sitting, head to foot in leather and rubber, a fizzing glass with a straw. He's like a black hole. A crack in the universe. A mass of matter that adds up to nothing.

Miro takes him by the back of the neck like you'd hold a cat, lifts him to his feet and rips the hood from his head. There's a collective intake of breath. Everyone leans forward and what they see is some poor old fuck, man or woman, it's uncertain, shrunken cheeks, dead eyes, woolly white hair. Miro drops the creature back in its seat and it slips the hood back over its head, the mystery gone.

The audience remains silent. The faces are all similar, lacking definition, androgynous, moribund, watchful.

Only the girl seems alive, the running girl, skin glowing, eyes amused. Miro glances at the man with her as he circles the bar. Is it her father? Her grandfather? He likes this place, but he doesn't understand it, he doesn't understand the dynamics, the connections. He takes a pack of gum from his jacket and shuffles out a stick for Bella.

'Thank you.'

'That man,' he says, 'vhere is that man in the white clothes?'

'He's gone,' says Bella.

His anger seems to fade. He lowers his voice.

'He come back?'

'He's like a bad memory. They always come back.'

'And me. I come back,' he says.

He folds a stick of gum between his white teeth, strides back through the bar and out the double doors.

......*scene 31*

Martin often says he hates driving. And it's not that he hates driving. He just hates other people driving. I mean, just look for chrissake: there's a bus up ahead pulling over, there's enough space for a Humvee to drive through the gap and the ass-wipe in front just sits there like a fucking blind man.

If you can't fucking drive don't fucking drive.

He sits on the horn. Throws up his hands. Points his pistol fingers at his temple.

Martin has this fantasy of shooting the brain-deads who clog up the roads and it's soothing sitting there in the traffic with the cold bulk of steel pressing against his groin. He's not going to slot the fuckers. It's like Ascot and Henley. He doesn't want to go, but it's nice to know he can.

It occurs to him that you need a gun like you need the right suit. They're a fashion accessory. Everyone's got a gun these days. Gangsters. Yardies. Terrorists. Mullahs. Rappers. Bent Filth. Guns are cool. It's not a precaution to arm yourself. It's common sense. Fifteen year olds know that. Learn from the young. Get a weapon. It feels right. It gives Martin that sense of zen serenity that comes to people who have found a purpose, a calling, and he sees before him a future unrolling like a red carpet leading to palaces of ever greater joy and pleasure.

Life begins today.

Now.

This moment.

With a gun.

The sun pulses in a static sky of the purest blue, the otherworldly blue of Trilby's eyes, and he wonders what the hell he's doing hanging out with this freak, with this kid sitting in the back of his car with features arranged in a complex puzzle of empty spaces and ignorance. He studies the boy in the rear-view mirror.

'You drive?' he asks.

'Nah.'

'Thank Christ for that, at least that's one less wanker on the road.'

'Who are you calling a wanker?'

'I beg your pardon?'

'You heard what I said, you calling me a wanker?'

'Are you getting uppity, Jordan?'

'You're fucking lucky that bald bastard didn't have you...'

'Let me ask you a question, smart ass: if you were in a room with a pit bull terrier slavering at the mouth, with its jaws pulled back over its teeth, what would you do, wait for the beast to attack, or slip quietly out the door?'

'Just don't call me a wanker, awright.'

'They're all so touchy,' Martin says, and sees his chance, rocketing around the ass-wipe and pulling behind the bus.

The engine throbs. The hood's down. Martin rides the clutch, waiting for his moment.

The black kid driving the bus takes off without indicating, grinds through the gears and picks up speed along Park Lane. This is the widest stretch of road in Central London: eight lanes separated by a river of flower beds, Hyde Park to the left, the best hotels on the planet housed in the Regency buildings to the right. Martin's digital chronometer touches 75 as he slices through the traffic, lost tourists with foreign plates, black-windowed limos full of oligarchs, the flotilla of taxis. He circles Marble Arch on two wheels and slots into the line slowing to turn left into Edgware Road.

'Fucking look. Jesus Christ. I mean...'

The south end of Edgware could be a prosperous part of some unbombed city in the Middle East, men in jalabiyas and shalwar kameez, women in jibabs and hijabs, leather masks, the spicy perfume of mint tea and roasting lamb around shops open on to the pavement, more signs in Arabic than English.

'Sharia compliant! What the fuck does that mean?'

Trilby brushes the creases from her skirt and ignores him. She's heard it before. She doesn't object to girls wearing veils. Why should she? When you tuck your cock between the crease of her backside you're in a veil. Martin's white suit is a veil.

Jordan is veiled as Che in his red tee-shirt. We've all got something to hide.

Martin fiddles with the radio.

No fucking reception.

'I mean, if they're going to come over here they ought to dress like us, live like us.'

'No one lives like us,' she says.

'I don't mean us, I mean them,' says Martin, brushing his arm across the world. 'Look, it's a fucking heat wave out there and they're buried behind masks and black curtains.'

'That's what they wear in the desert,' Jordan adds.

'Oh, do they now, thank god you're here to enlighten me.'

'Well, it's true...'

'Well, it's true...nya nya nya na na. Wanker.'

Jordan grins.

He's just a cunt. A bully. A verbal bully. You just have to stick up for yourself, stand up to the cunt.

The traffic's coiled like Rasta hair, hot and sticky. There's a white van in front pumping out diesel, an arm riddled in tattoos hanging down the side of the door, slapping the metal. Some fucking builder from Essex, and he thought the congestion charge was supposed to keep these bastards out of London during the day.

The flotilla of taxis left behind in Park Lane floats by in the bus lane and Martin feels aggrieved that these white supremacists are allowed in the bus lane anyway. I mean, they're all private businessmen, like the builder in the white van; why is it that cabbies are allowed to go about their business while all the plumbers and repairmen have to sit in the strawberry jam? It doesn't make sense. Things have to make sense.

We're going to bomb the bollocks out of Iraq and take their oil. Fine. It makes sense. We're going to bomb the bollocks out of Iraq to bring them democracy. Why? There isn't a single Moslem country in the world that has what we call democracy. When are they going to bomb the fuck out of the rest of them? It's got to make sense. There's got to be a logic. There is no logic letting cabbies use the bus lane, and he'd use it himself if there weren't so many fucking cameras everywhere.

The van peels off towards Paddington Station and a cacophony of horn blasts accompany the BMW as Martin shoots over the crossing on a red.

The Westway flyover's up ahead. It's like a frontier. Londonistan on one side, the ruins of Beirut or Baghdad on the other, halal lamb fading into the fetid miasma of piss and grime. Women with fags gripped in thin lips hurry by in anoraks and trainers with children and plastic bags. Unshaven men with red eyes move broken things in and out of second-hand shops in buildings that all look as if they are in the middle of being built or pulled down, a stasis, everything dusty and scratched, third world.

'Where do you live, Jordan?'

'Why'd you wanna know?'

'Jordan, I thought you were going to be fun. Because you're not fun. You're a fucking pain in the ass.'

'Just asking why you're asking.'

'Isn't that rhetorical?'

'What?'

'I envy your bliss, you know that?' says Martin.

'Yeah, right, Walthamstow,' says Jordan.

'Does it look like this?'

'Nah, not really, Walthamstow's more multi-ethnic.'

'Multi what?'

'More Pakis, Bangladeshis, more foreigners, you know, a melting pot.'

Martin tries the radio. Dead.

The steel snake slithers to a halt. Martin taps out *William Tell* on the steering wheel. To his right there's a gang of boys sucking on bottles of *Strongbow*, spitting through their teeth, skinning up joints. They wear blue jogging trousers tucked into their socks, sleeves rolled up to reveal the Union Jacks etched into their flesh, Burberry baseball caps with long peaks. They all have the same narrow drawn faces, pinched and terrifying, and what is it with Burberry? His mother wears Burberry for chrissake. They are hovering about like vultures outside an off-licence with mesh for windows like a cage.

He inches forward. Smoke from a fire smouldering in a tip curls languidly into the air, fat pigeons stamp about in the gutters among cars without wheels, small children with shaved heads carry sticks. Two girls of about fourteen in little clothes like little prostitutes walk by with big hoop earrings and angry faces.

'Whatchu fuckin' lookin' at?'

'Fuck you.'

'Fuck you, you fucking perv.'

It would be funny if it wasn't so fucking sad. I mean, who are these people? How did they turn out like this? Do they ever stop and look inside themselves? And if they do, what's there? What do they see? Do we see ourselves as we are, or do we see the version of ourselves that we would like to be?

Martin isn't troubled by introspection: there's just this moment, but sometimes a scene from the past pops into his head, always the same scene: the classics class had just ended, he was about to leave when Dr Owen, a Welshman with a sour tongue, loomed over him and quoted some Chinese sage: Ordinary people often fail at the point of succeeding, he said, and marched out of the room.

He can't recollect the context, he's not sure what point Dr Owen was trying to make, but now in down moments, on melancholic mornings after druggy nights, those words come back like an itch on an old scar. He should have challenged the Welsh git. He should have told him what he thought of him: what all the boys thought of him.

If there is one thing that Martin is not it's *ordinary*. There's never been a Campbell Gilchrist who's ordinary. They are all special in their own way, and you find the way by being what you are, by being yourself, not a replicate in a Burberry cap, a clone in a Sharia compliant hijab, a city cipher like Giles in his pinstripes and Harrow tie. Is he still at school for chrissake?

Martin's watching the little slags in the side mirror. They have the instincts of rodents and look back to give him the finger.

He turns again to Jordan.

'You got a gun?'

'Do what?'

'Do we speak the same language? I said have you got a gun?'

'Only cunts have guns.'

'Do they now.'

The road widens.

The traffic thins.

There's a sign: St John's Wood, and the BMW roars as Martin lurches into a right turn and hammers it down the backroads to Hampstead.

......*scene 32*

Dick's.

Another bar, it's a city of bars, and if you were placing bets you'd take odds on that Krishna's talking to his reflection in the mirror.

Widows. Divorcees. Or their husbands just don't give a toss. You can see it in the body-language. No hurry. Nothing to go home for. Too much money. Too little time. Ripe.

Just out of view, bending over, a strained look on his features, Ozzie eases a cork from a bottle of red.

Easy as she goes. Easy as she goes.

Snap.

Half the cork comes away with the corkscrew leaving the other half embedded in the bottle.

'Fucking thing,' he says.

'Any danger of a drink?'

Ozzie seems surprised to see Krishna sitting at the bar.

'You took your time.'

'Traffic,' says Krishna.

'Know anything about wine?'

'You're the barman.'

'Yeah, right, and what a shit job it is an'all. Third fucking bottle this has happened to today.'

'Must be your technique.'

'Must be the wanker I work for buying antifreeze and marking it up as house red.'

'Not a recommendation, then?'

'I wouldn't use it to clean the toilet.'

Krishna's eyes stray from his reflection to the two women along the bar. This is what *Dick's* is all about: mid-fifties, bright-eyed, buzzing, impeccable. Ripe.

'What are they drinking?'

'I wonder,' says Ozzie, 'in a champagne bar.'

'Better give them another bottle and bung a glass my way.'

'Aren't they out of your price range?'

Krishna conjures up a wrap as if from behind Ozzie's ear.

'Depends on what you're paying with.'

Ozzie snaps the wrap from Krishna's fingers.

'Bolivian Express? Would you like to play with my tits, Sir.'

If it all sounds rehearsed it kind of is.

Dick's is one of Krishna's hang-outs. You get a nice class of people. It's a classy place, no zinc and stainless steel here. The bar's pale mahogany, the stools have padded backs, Andy Warhol's print of Marilyn is from the first run, the music's Mozart. It's the kind of place where he could take Greta May. Not that he ever will. It's best not to mix business with pleasure. Not in his business.

Ozzie looks more lively now the wrap's in his pocket. You don't always have to take drugs to feel good, just the promise can do it.

He flips three tulip flutes on the bar, opens a frosty bottle of *Cristal*, fills the glasses and rams the bottle in a tub of ice. He slides one of the glasses to Krishna and delivers the other two along the bar. They are women for whom men have been buying champagne all their lives, but still their response is one of polite surprise. Ozzie nods along the bar to Krishna.

Krishna raises his glass.

So do they.

'Won't you come and join us?'

He does so, dropping the streetwise tones of the dealer and switching to the clipped, classless timbre of his secondary trade. It's all multi-tasking now. Everyone's a chameleon.

'I didn't want to intrude,' he says.

'You won't be.'

'Thank you.'

He moves to the seat beside the women, extends his hand.

'Krishna Guru Singh.'

'Sara,' says Sara, shaking it. 'This is Maxine.'

'Is this your usual party piece?' she asks.

Maxine is American with the mid-Atlantic lilt of Americans who have lived in London for years, the smooth faintly stunned features of good surgery, the one-off jacket and skirt of haute couture, 25k in diamonds studding her ears, a snake smile that could mean its opposite.

Krishna shakes her hand and leans forward with a reassuring smile.

'You know, I only just thought of it.'

'Spontaneity can be very attractive,' she remarks.

'That depends on what you happen to be doing spontaneously,' he says. 'Combusting, for example, has never been considered attractive.'

'Oh, I don't know, there are a few people I'd be happy to see burn.'

'Unhappily married?' he asks her.

There's no reply. He places his hand on his chest.

'I'm sorry...'

'She's not,' says Sara.

'How about you, Sara, are you married?'

'You're very forward,' she responds with a voice like the tinkle of a chandelier.

'You don't spend £80 on a bottle of champagne if you're shy,' he says.

'It must be nice to have so much money to splash around,' adds Maxine.

'You don't exactly look like a pair of untouchables.'

'We didn't spend £80 on our drinks.'

'Neither did I. I get thirsty,' he confides and nods towards the Australian, 'and he gets low.'

'And likes to get high?' says Maxine.

Ozzie refills the glasses, the bottle cranking in and out of the ice patently phallic. Sara squirms in her seat. She could give Maxine a decade. There are lines fanning Sara's eyes, but the whites are bright, the pupils have a twinkle; she was still good looking, the last autumnal blaze of it, slender, of course, familiar in some strange way.

She raises her glass once more.

'Well, well,' she says. 'It's not every day one finds themselves drinking champagne with a drugs baron.'

'That's what makes life so interesting.'

'Perhaps we should sample the merchandise, Sara?' Maxine suggests.

Sara shakes her head and Krishna disguises his vague disappointment.

'I promised to collect Gordon from Heathrow,' she glances at Krishna, 'my husband,' she adds and turns to Maxine. 'You have the first...taste.'

'Test the quality,' her friend responds.

'I didn't know you were an authority on cocaine, Maxine?'

'Are we talking about cocaine?'

'Are we hell.'

They clink glasses. This is why they come to *Dick's*. You never know who you're going to meet there.

......scene 33

Silvia's lips are full, fleshy, naturally red. They shape words like they're made of metal and she chops them out of her mouth like horseshoe nails, spits of hot iron.

'They drive us from our farms. They drive us from our lands. They rape and kill your sisters. They kill your father.'

Miro looks up. In his head he's in the black hills of Pristina, a quarter moon, a blaze of stars. He can't see the farmhouse hidden below, but he can hear the screams.

He lights a cigarette.

'I kill my father.'

Silvia lowers her voice.

'Now you kill the one who take your gun.'

'I look...'

Silvia holds up her hand.

'Lech is right. Is Tokarev. Slav gun. When they know, they come for us,' she says. 'You go. You don't come back till you find your gun.'

He stares into his mother's eyes. They don't waver. They stare back, cold and unfathomable. She knew his father was in that farmhouse. She loved her husband. She wanted to protect him, not from the agony, but the humiliation. There is something shameful about being tortured. It scars the mind as well as the body. It never leaves you.

Miro wants to tell her he understands, that he's always understood, but the words get stuck in his throat. There's sweat on his back, a pain in his chest, in his head. It's the smack clawing his nerve ends. His body wants more. That's how it gets you. Miro's fighting it. He knows pain. Pain's not a problem. He stabs out his cigarette and shuffles back his chair.

The restaurant is almost empty. The workers have gone back to work, the slivovitz has borne the remaining drunks into nostalgia; they don't want to leave, they want to be back in the past with the people pinned on the cork board.

You can hear the drone of Teo and Kresimir chatting as they stack pans in the kitchen, the music turned low, the big clock ticking, Slobodan Milosevic staring grimly from the wall.

Lech covers the baklava, places the stand on the shelf below the counter and gives the glass top a polish. He had a shot at the A&E at St Mary's and the dressing they put on makes a white cross on his face. The swelling around his eyes is plum colour, but the painkillers are doing their job. His mind is clear, clearer than it's been for a long time.

Miro paces between the tables. He looks at Lech as if he doesn't quite recognize him.

'They fix it gut, eh?' he says.

'Yeah, Miro, they fix.'

'Iz gut?'

Miro pauses a moment, like he wants to say something else, but doesn't. He grabs his bike helmet.

As he passes the table of drunks one of them shouts in his own tongue Only unity can save the Serbs, the cry from the streets of Belgrade. Miro raises his fist in acknowledgement, confirming in some strange way that Lech has come to the right decision.

He watches through the doorway as Miro fires the Harley and carves into the traffic with the brute self-assurance Lech is tempted to ridicule as well as envy, as one envies the rich their wealth while mocking their pretensions.

......*scene 34*

It's not easy being an intelligent man without power. Without money. It's not easy working as a waiter, a cleaner, a drudge, his dreams turned to dust, shattered, like his glasses, like the bones across the bridge of his nose, like the fragile familiarity that has kept him here at Silvia's in Charlotte Street.

Lech Jovanovic was the only one from the village, from all the villages, to leave the pig shit behind for university, a scholarship, his room in the hall of residence looking out over the towers and spires of old Belgrade. This was where he belonged, among people with new ideas, students from across the country who would shape and build the future. There was music in the cafés at night, a bold new version of The Merry Widow at the National Theatre, the smell of his starched white coat a daily reminder that he had left his muddy work boots and dungarees forever.

He had gone to university to learn how to be a veterinary surgeon, that's the extent of your imagination when you grow up on a farm. He switched to the medical faculty when he saw that the course allowed for an exchange at Queen's College, Cambridge. Cambridge, England. It was the Promised Land. They watched English football on television. They followed the life and death of Princess Diana. They admired Tony Blair. In Belgrade they didn't dream of going to Paris and Rome and Frankfurt. They wanted to go to England.

Now he was here at Silvia's with the accordion music and drunks drinking to national unity. Lech wasn't a Nationalist. When he was growing up, no one was a Nationalist. Country people didn't have time for anything but work, they worked from dawn till dusk, and when they walked home from church Sunday morning they didn't talk politics or God, they talked about cold hard cash, the price of fuel, the price of grain, the value of their land and their livestock, the cost of CD players and American jeans their daughters wanted so they'd look like everyone else.

No one he knew ever hammered the table with his fist and reeled off the list of historic injustices inflicted on the Serbs. History's a whore. You pay the price and make it do whatever you want. The vision of a Greater Serbia was just words, slogans that come out of the politicians' mouths one day and the peasants are parroting the next. It makes you feel important when you talk politics instead of pigs. Old men start polishing their medals and remember the good old days that were never good.

It was all a lie.

They knew nothing.

And Lech knows they knew nothing because he knew nothing.

The scholarship arrived by post in the summer of 1998 like a missive from the moon and stars. Nothing quite so wonderful had ever happened to his family before. They started treating him as if he were special, as if he already had his education behind him and was now the fount of all knowledge. Even neighbours came to ask whether they should invest in a new horse or build a barn, or emigrate to Canada? They didn't take his advice, country people always know best, that wasn't the point; the point was to come and inspect this man among them who was going off to the big city to study at university.

As the leaves were beginning to turn gold in the autumn, Lech removed the wedding dress and old photos from the leather suitcase that had sat under the iron bed in his parents' room for as long as he could recall. His mother had brought her possessions in the case when she left Pristina to marry his father and it would be travelling back down the same winding track carrying his clothes and books. It was said in his family that his mother was the smart one, and his father was smart to have married her. His father had had no education after the age of twelve, perhaps that's why he believed in its value and power, he believed education, not cries for Serbian unity, was the way to freedom.

His elder brother Borislav that summer had been flexing his muscles and saying Lech shouldn't be wasting his time working. He should be wasting his time reading. Boris, he joked, was Serbian for Boxer, the carthorse in Animal Farm, the fact that he had read Orwell's novel when it became available in Serbian contradicting the assertion.

When it was time to leave, Boris carried the suitcase and swung it into the boot of the rusty old yellow Skoda, the noise waking Lupe, the Alsatian asleep under the big oak by the gate. The dog ran around the car, faster and faster, the boys following, the girls looking vaguely bored in their blue jeans. The rare family outings always began this way but today there was a new twist. Boris took Lech by the shoulders. He looked long and deep into his eyes. He kissed his two cheeks, and that kiss Lech would remember for the rest of his life.

Boris was staying to look after the farm. The boys were rounded up and pushed through the car windows. Boris pummelled the roof with his big fist, and off they set through the colonnades of spruce that lined the road winding down from the hills to the bus station. Lech sat in the back between Ana and Mileva, teenagers, sullen sometimes, smiling at other, girls were a mystery to Lech, even his sisters. Stevan was seven, strong like Boris. He was sitting on his mother's lap and was almost as big as her. Jovan, a week from his third birthday, perched on Lech's knee unsure what all the fuss was about.

When they arrived at the terminal people were already climbing on the bus to Pristina. From there Lech would get the train to Belgrade. His mother gave him a box with sandwiches and apple cakes. Father pushed an envelope in his pocket; Lech would find a crisp sheaf of dinars when he opened the envelope on the train and though it seemed like a fortune the money would have to be stretched with the big city prices. Father stood back to look at his son, then took Lech in a bear hug, kissing his cheeks, as his brother had done, something Lech couldn't recall his father ever having done before. It wasn't that kind of family, your emotions weren't something you talked about and displayed, it was just there like the air you breathed, like the sea to the fish. You only appreciate who people are and what they mean to you when they're no longer there.

They stood, shuffling their feet, unsure what to say. Everything had been said. Lech told Ana to work hard at school. She was good at drawing. She should keep it up. Become an artist or an architect. Ana was fourteen, dreamy and intense, she wore glasses like him and as a small girl had painted scenes from Star Wars on the bedroom wall and made little niches and ledges where she stood the plastic figures she'd been collecting.

Mileva, a year older, had been named after Mileva Maric, Albert Einstein's Serbian wife; Mileva had helped write The Theory of Relativity whether people remembered that or not. It was a big responsibility to have a name like that. Lech was teasing, it was an old joke, and Mileva just smiled. She was as tall as him, poised and reserved with dark eyes and coppery brown curls that danced with glints of light. Lech took her in an embrace and it was odd feeling her breasts pushing into his chest. It seemed like yesterday that his sisters were children. They were young women now in jeans and tee-shirts, with pictures of English pop stars cut from magazines and taped to the wall where the Jedi knights had once roamed through space.

He kissed his mother. There was a faint smile on her lips and that look in her eyes that was expressive but unreadable. Mileva had her mother's eyes, so did Silvia Stanislav; brown as toasted almonds, almond-shaped, a reminder of the ebb and flow of conquest, the Mongols, Alexander, the Turks.

Serbian unity was the shape and colour of women's eyes.

Stevan helped his father load the suitcase. He'd already claimed Lech's bed in the small room below the eaves and wanted to show he was grown up now, he deserved it.

The bus started, filling the air with fumes. It was time to go. He was anxious to go. To start his new life. Lech took his seat half way down the near side and looked back through the window, Mother and Father, Stevan, Ana and Mileva with little Jovan holding her hand, his family lined up as if posing for a photograph, and it is this picture he sees at night when he closes his eyes and by some trick of his imagination he glimpses Boris behind them, big and muscular, Boxer from Animal Farm.

......scene 35

Six months had gone by. Time is measured in historic events, in great leaps. The Christian era. The Communist era. The rise and fall of the British Empire.

Lech measures time in those six months.

He went skiing at Christmas with a gang of medical students and didn't set off home to visit his family until the Easter break. There was a party to celebrate the end of the semester and the direct train to Pristina was pushing out of the suburbs while he was still rising from his bed with a sore head the following day.

By the time he left the main gates at the university, the sky was streaked in orange, the air dry and brittle as if snow were about to fall. The streets were empty, and only when he saw the yellow brick station from the edge of Sava Square did he realise that everyone had the same idea as him, they all wanted to get out of Belgrade and they wanted to go that same night. Long queues snaked back from the station's baroque entrance, men in box jackets, women in big cardigans and pleated skirts, militiamen carrying rifles.

Lech didn't bother lining up for a ticket. He fought his way through the crowd and squeezed into a carriage that was already filled to the roof. People had climbed on the overhead racks, they were squatting in the aisles, in the toilets. Strangers who would normally have read the newspapers and kept their own counsel were talking loudly, raising their fists, repeating rumours, the oil of revolution, and it was oddly hypnotic being there on that train among those people, a feeling in the air that great events were about to happen.

Lech sat on his rucksack at the end of a row of seats occupied by three young militiamen. The train was delayed an hour. Nothing new in Serbia. The trains were famous for being late, you'd be late for your own funeral if you were taking a Serbian train, that's what they said. And when the train finally pulled out of the old station that had been bombed and rebuilt through two world wars there was an air of victory as if trains are a sign of civilization, that's all's well in the world when the trains are running. Even when they're running late.

One of the militiamen removed the bayonet strapped to his leg to peel an apple. He took another from his pack and threw it to Lech, leaning back and tossing it like you'd toss a grenade.

'Here. Good Serb apples,' he said.

'Thanks, man.'

He seemed to be waiting for Lech to punch the air or come back with a war cry.

Lech took a bite. 'Tastes like home,' he said instead.

'Where's home?'

'In the hills outside Drenica.'

There was silence. Silence from the militiamen. Silence from the people sitting nearby. They studied his clothes, dark jeans, a black anorak with fur around the hood, a plain white tee-shirt giving nothing away.

Was he one of them?

There were more Albanians than Serbs in Drenica, Moslems, Bosniaks, Roma. You'd have to wander down from the hills to Pristina before you could sit down in a café and have a drink with a fellow Serbian.

Lech was playing with them and didn't take it too far.

'Lech Jovanovic,' he said, extending his hand. 'I'm a medical student at the university.'

They shook hands. They blew out their cheeks. They opened a bottle of plum brandy guaranteed to rot your teeth and the best thing for a hangover. Doctor's orders. He took a swig and passed the bottle back. He was one of them. They called him Dok. They told him their names, Ivico, Boris, like his elder brother, and Rambo, the apple eater, big as an ox with muscles bursting from his torn shirt and no sense of irony. Serbs and Albanians had been killing each other for the last twelve months, they'd been killing each other for the last four centuries, and the

Americans had a peace plan that was already in motion as he sat on the train from Belgrade to Pristina. His fate was fixed like the beats of a drama, a Greek tragedy. All he had to do was play his part.

The train rattled through tunnels drilled through solid rock, over bridges spanning gorges and rivers. The ice ages had carved Serbia from ranges of volcanoes and deep whispering valleys. You could see the landscape in the people's faces, rugged, uncultured, inscrutable, silent people who that night had found their tongues.

They passed bottles and slapped neighbours on the back. Only unity can save the Serbs, they roared, throats oiled, voices growing louder and turning to cries of anger and surprise when the lights suddenly died. The train slowed to walking pace. The darkness turned the window beside the militiamen into a black screen. The noise in the carriage faded to silence and it was like sitting in a movie theatre waiting for the drama to begin.

They didn't see the bomb falling in the distance. They saw a pale silvery blue cloud lit orange from below rise mushroom-shaped into the air. Lech pressed forward and watched as another explosion erupted, and another, the sound muted through the glass. You see cities being bombed on television. It's unreal. Incomprehensible. It never makes any sense. It made no sense to Lech as the buildings all around them turned to flame and rubble as cruise missiles stitched a path across the landscape.

This was the American peace plan. This is what NATO would describe as humanitarian bombing.

A thousand planes in European skies as the millennium was coming to an end. It made no sense. There had been atrocities on both sides. He had seen the result of those atrocities working shifts as a volunteer in the hospital.

Was the bombing of Serbia the solution?

Smart bombs are never smart. They hit hospitals and schools. They kill the weak and the old, women and children.

NATO had been threatening to bomb Serbia since he arrived at university in the autumn. He didn't believe it was ever going to happen, and didn't trust his own eyes even as the train ground to a halt and he watched the blitz intensify through the carriage window.

The bombing campaign was designed to break the will of the Serbian militia. But the militiamen that night were safely hunkered down in bunkers and basements biding their time. As the smoke thickened through the narrow streets of the poor quarters in cities across the land they would seek revenge, not on the NATO pilots taking off from Italian bases and flying their jets at 35,000 feet. They would take revenge on the Albanians who had yet to flee across the border.

Serb fighters and Serb citizens ransacked Albanian shops and Albanian cafés. They burned the mosques. They demolished the newspaper offices of Kosovo Sot, as if by destroying the presses you could you censor the news. You can't stop the news. The news is like the tide. It just keeps coming, and from that ocean of words the truth emerges, burning itself into your memory as indelibly as the crossed flags tattooed on Rambo's arms, the death mask side by side with the red, blue and white tricolour of Serbia.

The rail tracks had been hit on the outskirts of Paracin and he clambered out of the carriage behind the militiamen with their hunting knives and loaded rifles. Was he as angry as them? Did he blame the Americans and their NATO allies for bombing Serbia? Or did he blame the enemy within, the old enemy they'd been living with for four centuries? On the last night of the semester when he drank cheap wine with his friends in the medical faculty he would, like them, have blamed the Americans, the Russians, the politicians, history.

Now his throat was filled with cries of unity, revenge, hatred.

Kill the Albanians. Kill the fuckers. Kill them all.

They marched through the smoke and cordite fumes into Paracin, a broken, depressed city, squalid houses on the outskirts, Soviet style cement blocks in the centre. Fire sirens wailed. Flames leapt into the air. You could feel the heat through your clothes. It burnt your throat and tasted of sulphur. A green sheen lay over the world. The noise. The chaos. The anarchy. Serbs shouted liberty as they carted televisions from smashed shops. People had black streaks on their faces, madness in their eyes. They talk of vampires in Paracin. He felt like a vampire, his scorched throat thirsting for blood.

They watched an old man in a long smock and white crocheted cap hurry by on a bicycle, his legs moving in an arthritic but concentrated motion, and Lech thought, even then he thought: why is he wearing that white cap that shows clearly at night and reveals so blatantly what he is?

'There's one,' Rambo cried.

'Kill the fuckers. Kill them all.'

Like a pack of wolves they followed, Ivico and Boris with their schoolboy faces, Lech with his rucksack full of text books.

The old man reached the crest of the hill and pedalled faster, gaining on them on the descent. He reached his house and bolted the door just as they arrived at the broken fence surrounding the property. They paused to catch their breath.

The house was square, one storey with a flat roof and shuttered windows. Ivico starting hammering the shutters with his rifle butt. Rambo gave the door a kick. It rattled in its frame. He took a few paces back, ran at the door and it splintered under his weight like matchwood. Rambo rolled into the passage in a tangle of muscles and tattoos. The boys cheered, and he cheered. There is something intoxicating about smashing things, looting shops, it appeals to something deep and animal, the desire to conquer and rule.

If there had been a moment when he could have redrawn his contract with fate the moment passed as Lech crossed the threshold into that house behind Rambo, Ivico and Boris. The passage was unlit. There were doors on either side. Rambo and Ivico booted them open one after the other. There was a rhythm, a pattern, like the cruise missiles falling over Serbia.

Men are prey to patterns, and sometimes at night when car doors slam in Charlotte Street it is like an echo that awakes Lech from a dream where doors are being battered open, and inside the rooms the walls aren't walls but photographs of his family standing at the bus station, his parents, the boys, Ana, Mileva, her dark eyes full of secrets, Boris mysteriously behind them. He remembers his brother's kiss on his cheeks. No kiss from a woman has the long memory of that kiss. The women have been paid for and paid women don't kiss their clients.

Lech tries to imagine what it must be like to be a father unable to protect his family; what it must be like to be a woman about to be raped and beaten; what it must be like to be a small child watching these horrors. The terrors that family in that shabby house in Paracin suffered that night is something Lech tries to imagine and can't imagine. The family was helpless, victims of events bigger than them, beyond their control. They stood against the wall in a room lit by a single bulb listening to strangers' boots approaching down the corridor, four young men with rifles and hunting knives, breaking down doors and screaming oaths.

He awakes from these nightmares in a cold sweat and lays there immobile like a stone carving until the morning light presses through the curtained windows. It could have been different. Those three young fighters respected him. He was a doctor. He was going to be a doctor. Doctors have a special responsibility. You become a doctor to cure people, save people.

Lech presses his eyes shut in the shadowy room in Charlotte Street and draws a picture of himself standing in front of Rambo. He stares into his eyes until the fog of madness passes. Enough is enough, he says. These people aren't the enemy. Maybe the Kosovo Liberation Army is the enemy. Maybe the politicians in Belgrade in their suits and ties are the enemy. We won't build a new Serbia harming these people.

He didn't say these things. He didn't think these things.

There was an air of relief as the last door was booted open, the feeling the police must get when they have tracked and cornered their suspects. On the far side of a kitchen with an iron range and a scrubbed table the old man stood tall, arms spread as if trying to hide his family behind him, his wife, two small children, and two older girls, teenagers in headscarfs and long skirts.

The old man removed his crocheted cap and held it to his chest.

Maybe he wasn't so old. He just seemed old because his face was worn and his clothes were ragged.

He bowed his head and then looked up.

'We have done nothing. Please.'

There was a stillness, quick as a heart beat. Then, everything seemed to happen at once. Time is out of kilter. Fractured. When you try to piece the events back together nothing fits. You can't remember what happened first, and how it went from one thing to the next.

You're sure Rambo said something.

The old man said something back.

Then the old man was on the floor.

Rambo had struck him sideways across his face with his rifle butt. Blood splashed across the wall. There was blood everywhere. So much blood. It was hard to know whether the man was dead or alive. The old woman screamed and fell on top of her husband. The girls cried out in high chiming voices that announced their presence, a reminder to those young Serbs that they were the prize.

Ivico tore the headscarf from the tallest of the two girls. She ran at him, hammering at him with her fists. Boris slapped her so hard the blow sent her sprawling across the floor and probably broke her cheek bone.

Her mother knew what was going to happen. Of course she knew. She rocked backwards and forwards on her knees, hands held in prayer. She was wailing and pleading at the top of her voice. One of the two small children was crying hysterically. The other just stood staring with big dead eyes. Rambo went for the other girl. She was barely more than a child, thirteen or fourteen, small, shrinking into herself in terror.

They had no need of their rifles now. They had no need of their knives. They tore the clothes off the girls with their bare hands and on the kitchen floor with the old woman weeping and the children clinging to her skirts they spread their legs and fucked them, taking turns, changing from one to the next, and after they'd fucked them, Rambo pissed on their naked bodies. The others joined in, and he joined in, and while they humiliated that family of Albanians in Paracin that cold spring night, other Albanians as if by osmosis were gathering in mobs around the villages of Drenica. They raped and killed the Serbs, they burned their farms and fled across the frontier into exile.

......*scene 36*

Lech stands on the pavement watching as Miro skims through the traffic and vanishes in the haze. He steps back inside the restaurant and waves to Sylvia, pointing at the dressing on his face. She nods and waves back. She'll deal with the drunks and set the tables for the evening.

He taps his pockets. He's got his mobile phone and six numbers in his contacts. What kind of a life is that?

Lech sets off for the gardens in Russell Square. The sun beats down on his head. They were told that it always rains in London. Now it's always hot. He sits on a bench with high bushes behind him and watches a couple kissing, the girl ebony, the boy pale, their faces pressing together like two keys on a piano. The painkillers are wearing off, but that's good. He's got to keep his mind clear, look into the future. The past is an echo. You escape by getting away from it, by moving on, moving away.

He kicks at the pigeons swirling about his feet. He likes pigeons. They're survivors. Lech has survived. Now it's time to go home. Back to university. It isn't going to be easy starting again. But he'll make it. He's going to be a doctor. He's going to help people. Put something back into this life. Get the nightmares out of his head. Ten years have gone by. Ten years. He isn't so young any more. He'll have to pay his way, and he isn't going to wait tables and clean up other people's shit. He needs a stake.

Lech has a scrap of paper in his pocket. On it is a number he stabs into the mobile phone. He speaks to a woman who gives him another number. It takes four calls before he finds who he's looking for.

......scene 37

Half term. A while ago.

Bella should be studying for her A levels but isn't. She just wants to lie on the sheepskin rug in her room watching the clouds changing into faces, animals, swirling and reforming. She can't even be bothered to get dressed.

The door bursts open. Daze, hormonal as always. That's the thing with fourteen year olds. They scream and get excited for like nothing.

'Come, Bells, come. Sime's got a new poem.'

'I've heard it.'

'You haven't heard this one.'

Yawn.

'Bella, just come, or I'll sit on you.'

Bella drags herself off the floor and pads along the hall to Daisy's room, a frenzied array of dolls in Victorian dresses, uplift bras, a locked diary keeping count of endangered species and melting ice caps, her French homework spread out on an unmade bed inspired by Tracy Emin and watched over by signed head shots of Cillian Murphy, Orlando Bloom and Casey Affleck. A girl at school is a member of just about every fan club in the world and runs a business selling the glossy prints she gets for free. She'll end up marrying an MP or being one.

Bella isn't sure why Daisy has acquired these photographs, especially as they never get to see any movies, and would be surprised if Bella told her that if you shuffled the features from these three stars and put them together you would have a good photofit of Simon.

Simon is every girl's dream of a brother. He never gets angry. He joins in with your games. He even lets you dress him up in Bella's clothes when the bores as Bella calls them are out at a dinner party or, worse, hosting one in the conservatory with the swaying date palms, the circular Indian table with ivory inlay (old ivory, naturally) and the twelve director's chairs with yellow cushions and Roman numerals on the backs numbering I to XII like the digits on a clock. So amusing. There are framed covers from Father's books and a red oak Boston upright on which Father beats out honky tonk for the agents and publishers and people who critique and promote books. Father is famous and doesn't want anyone to forget it.

He's upstairs right now – *should that be write now?* – the door bolted against the world; you must not under any circumstances disturb Daddy when he's writing. It's Daddy's writing that pays the bills.

Don't you know how lucky you are?

'This better be good, Daze,' Bella says and yawns.

Simon is standing in the bay window beside the Hollywood portraits like an actor about to go on stage.

'She's here,' says Daisy.

Bella gives Daze a *doh* look and folds her arms.

'Come on then, Simes,' she says, 'Let's get it over with.'

'Well, if you insist.'

Simon gives himself a little shake and takes a deep breath.

Down down, sinking down
Sinking down through a hole in the ground
Sinking down there's no way up
Until the monster comes and gobbles you up
Down down into the deep dark sea
Down down to eternity –

There's a double rap on the door. It's like a bomb exploding. Father's head appears and Simon freezes like a bird shot in flight.

'A word, if you please.'

Simon scurries out like a rat. He looks terrified. Bella doesn't know why, even now, she still doesn't know why. Why doesn't he just tell him to fuck off? Fuck off back to your writing. Leave me a alone.

Why doesn't Simon run away?

Father's head pops back around the woodwork.

'Put some clothes on, Bella, you're not a child.'

She's wearing knickers and a little top.

'Whatever.'

'Do it. And do it now.'

She doesn't answer. And she has no intention of getting dressed until she feels like getting dressed. I mean, why? For Daisy. For Simon? Father is just so brilliant he can't get it through his brain that she has nothing to hide from Simon, no mysteries, no secrets. She is Simon. Simon is her. She feels what he feels and right now she feels like killing her father.

'Not again,' she says with a sigh.

Daisy feels it, too. Not as strongly. But she feels it.

'He always picks on him,' she says.

'He should stand up for himself.'

'Some people can do that and some people can't,' says Daisy. 'You can. I can. Simon's just...just Simon.'

Bella gazes at her sister. Daze is like the Dalai Lama. She's wise. She cares about dying whales. They are alike in many ways. They look alike. They look like their father. Dark hair. Green eyes. Simon's more like Mummy. Blonde, fey, dreamy, blue eyes sheened in unshed tears.

'Come on.'

Bella leads Daisy up the stairs to the third floor where the attic has been converted into an office, a long open space with a pointed ceiling and about a million books arranged in genres on the shelves. A few of the books, seven to be exact, stand face on so you can see the covers, *Unvanishing Footsteps,* Father's Spanish Civil War novel; *A Green Hill Far Away,* his fictionalised story of the Knights Templar; *The Few,* his bomber command book that was turned into a movie, *et cetera*.

A rowing machine and a stationary bicycle stand on one side of the peak and an L-shaped desk with his computer is on the other. Father doesn't want to get RSI or a bad neck. He stops every two hours and pedals or rows for 20 minutes. He takes 18 months to research his books and compile an outline, 12 months to write the manuscript, 1,000 words a day not counting holidays and those times when he reaches the quarter finals at the Queens Tennis Club annual tournament and has to do some intensive training. He's never won but the trophy in the conservatory shows he did come second once.

The door is open a crack and Bella watches as her father in his dark blue track suit prowls like a caged bear around the attic slapping Simon's report card. Simon just stands there, head bowed like a servant in some costume drama.

'Biology, C. Physics, D. Maths, D. You know your problem, boy, you don't want to work. You've had it too easy. Prancing around. Everything that comes to you in this life comes from hard work. It comes from your own toil, and it starts with education.'

'I am trying, Daddy. Really...'

'Bloody poetry. Where's that going to get you? You're a disgrace, that's all I can say...'

Father crosses the room in two strides and uses the shameful report card to slap Simon across the face, first one cheek, then the other, the full force of his forehand smash behind the anthology of shoddy results.

Daisy grips Bella's arm, stopping her from entering, and Bella slopes off to the bathroom to shave her legs and consider her long thin body that has grown suddenly so shapely, so feminine, so like the Madonna in the chapel at the Convent of St Sebastian the Holy Martyr.

That was then.

......*scene 38*

This is now.

It's late afternoon, the red drapes are drawn, candle flames reflect in the gilt mirrors and light the features of Napoleon on his pedestal. Bella wears black plastic thigh boots with spiky heels, a network of leather straps that crisscross the marble cupolas of her breasts, a black thong that shapes the curvature of her bottom, and a devil mask that covers the top half of her face, the curly horns repeated in the shape of the eye-sockets framing green eyes that dance with light.

As Guy said that day three months ago when he appeared in the living room with a tray of caviar wearing a chef's hat: you should always dress for the occasion.

In her right hand, Bella holds a chain on the end of which there is a dog's collar containing the neck of Henry Fox, quiz show host. The chain connects to the leather harness restraining Henry's genitals. He crawls on all fours and, as he pulls away, the chain tightens and Henry howls with each wave of pain and pleasure.

'You dirty dog. You filthy animal. What are you?'

'A dirty filthy animal.'

Henry edges around the coffee table where the burning candles send shadows chasing over the mezzotint nudes and Dalí's Metamorphosis of Narcissus. He crawls towards the corner, raises his ass and squeals with delight as Bella forces the spire-high heel of her boot into the pallid flesh.

'You dirty naughty boy.'

'I'm dirty. I'm naughty. I have to be punished.'

'I can't hear you.'

Henry wails in the high-pitched voice of a child. 'I'm a filthy little animal.'

'A dirty disgusting filthy little animal.'

'A dirty disgusting little animal,' he cries and she digs her heels in deeper.

'Filthy animal. Filthy like shit,' she says and instantly regrets it.

'Yes. Shit. Shit. Shit. Shit on me. Shit. Shit. Shit on me. I'm shit. Shit on me. Please. Please shit on me.'

This isn't going to happen. Bella has on occasions summoned up a jet of pee to please herself more than the client, aiming the stream on bare torsos and into gaping mouth. But shitting is just too yuck to contemplate.

She pulls the chain and prods his scrawny backside. 'You haven't been good enough,' she says. 'You are a bad, bad boy and I'm am going to punish you like you've never been punished before.'

Bella releases the chain, grabs one of the brass candlesticks and, as Henry looks back, she drips a bead of scorching wax on one of his nipples. He closes his eyes, straightens his back, gasps in pain and cries out for more.

'No. No. No,' he cries.

'Yes. Yes. Yes,' she says, switching from one nipple to the next.

'Oh no.'

Drip.

'Oh, yes,'

Drip.

'Oh no.'

Drip.

'Oh, yesssssssssssssssssssssssss.'

As Bella moves the candle back to the table, she doesn't notice the tear of hot wax falling into Henry's yawning mouth.

'Ou...............ch! Agh......... Ouch. Ouch.

Henry screams.

Bella pulls on the chain.

Henry screams even more.

'What's the matter, you little shit?' she shouts.

'Agh.'

Henry's tongue lolls dog-like from his mouth and he tries with pawing fingers to pick off the hot wax.

'Come on, answer me.'

'Agh, oo bitch. Luk ot 'uve done.'

Bella presses her teeth shut and her lips shut. She's trying to stay in character. Her shoulders are beginning to shake.

'You burned my mouth,' says Henry in his normal voice.

A smile like cracking ice splits Bella's lips. The smile widens and Bella can't help letting go with a tiny laugh.

Henry stands. 'What are you laughing at?'

'I'm not.'

'You're laughing.'

'I'm not laughing,' she says and bursts out laughing.

'You little bitch. I paid five hundred quid for this.'

Bella backs away thinking: five hundred quid.

'Little bitch. I want my money back.'

She's not laughing now. 'You'll have to talk to Guy about that.'

'I'm talking to you.'

'It's nothing to do with me. This is a Guy thing.'

'I beg your pardon. It isn't Guy administering the proceedings.'

'Maybe he should. Sounds like you'd have a better time.'

'You little...'

And there's the slap. An open palm across her cheek. Like the report card in Father's hand across Simon's cheek.

Why do they do that? What makes them think they can get away with it? Because they can't. They won't.

Bella is stunned for a fraction of a second.

It's long enough for Henry to get in another slap across the other cheek. Henry likes this. He's beginning to get his money's worth.

Henry goes for a third.

Bella ducks, the plastic thigh boots squeaking as she races around the coffee table, across the hall and into the bedroom.

Henry is close behind, nipples burning, chain rattling.

Bella throws open the torture garden. She bends to seize a weapon, and Henry gets in a couple of good spanks across the domes of her white bottom, slap, slap...and he gets in one more as she turns brandishing a leather bound pole with a circle of wire on one end. She strikes him across the chest.

Henry backs away, yowling, and Bella moves towards him using the circle of wire to try and snag the harness supporting his old man balls.

'Come on then. You want to play,' she cries.

'You bitch. You whore. You – '

'You hit me, you bastard.'

'You hit me. You burned my tongue.'

'You loved it.'

She swings the pole around like a cheerleader, circling Henry, prodding at him with the blunt end and, when she reaches the door, she backs out of the bedroom and across the hall to the bathroom.

'Get dressed and get out.'

'Wait. Wait. It's okay. Really. It's okay.'

'I said get out.'

'No. No. don't go. Please...'

Bella enters the bathroom and locks the door leaving Henry Fox, quiz show host, in the dog's collar, with a bruised chest, a burnt tongue and the fetish gear arrayed behind him like the Home page on an internet porn site.

......*scene 39*

Guy adores poker. He lives for caviar. But he adores poker. With his two pair, jacks and sevens, he sticks a fiver in the pot.

He glances back at Dixie Dean.

'Schoolgirls?'

'Got it all worked out. Ganna pick up a camera. Just need the girls, dun I?'

Kosta adds a fiver, and raises the stake another £20.

Wheezing at his side, the Albanian they call Mental looks at his cards like he's never seen them before then tosses them across the table with an oath that turns Kosta's grim features into a short-lived smile. Mental is a monster, a dirigible, an NHS liability in waiting, a face like a balloon, fingers so fat the gold rings that decorate them would slip off Alya's wrists.

Qerim, the fifth player, doesn't smile. Ever. Qerim looks as if he comes from somewhere further east or further south than Albania, dark-skinned, hawk-nosed, the long scar that must have been poorly stitched running like the *Nike* logo across his face and twisting his lips into a permanent diagonal, an oblique like a backslash on the computer.

'A twenty pound,' he mumbles, and slides a note across the table.

'No, fuck it,' says Dixie, and folds.

Dixie's hand has been professionally bandaged at St Mary's A&E. He was there at the same time as Lech Janović. They actually sat next to each other on the same bench clutching matching foam cups from *Starbucks* and two numbers in sequence from the ticket machine, Dixie with 187, Lech holding 188. Dixie doesn't know Lech. Lech doesn't know Dixie. The coincidence means nothing, but illustrates that the A in A&E is something of a misnomer.

Kosta snaps his fingers and Alya glides like a ghost across the floor to refill the glasses with the sticky sweet brandy they're drinking.

She fades back into the shadows like someone who isn't there, although someone smart might observe that Alya is nursing a vague resentment on top of the all-consuming bitterness she bears like a stigmata, like the scar across Qerim's face. She's usually at this time doing odd jobs, shopping at *Harrods*, jogging with Madalena, serving Kusmi Earl Grey tea after servicing a Cabinet Minister. There's a rumour that two girls, or even three, have done a runner at the same time and Alya has suddenly been brought back to the club as a servant, a slave. Her job is fucking not polishing counters and serving drinks. She's not a waitress, she's an asset, a natural resource.

Dixie glances again at Guy Bradwell. 'You can get 'old of girls, that's you're fing innit.'

Guy's concentrating on his cards, stacks them neatly, drums his fingertips and is about to fold when the game is disturbed by Yilly bowling down the stairs wearing a faint smile, his hands palms outwards in the way of a man who has just performed a feat of magic.

Kosta places his glass on his cards – *like someone's going to sneak a peep at his hand,* and joins Yilly in the centre of the small dance floor. They speak their own language and move as if they are performing some strange Kiwi jig, a long story, a lot of gestures, mobile phones, stabbing digits, slitting throats, Albanian charades. The men then stride purposefully across the club to the back room, leaving the door open. Guy sees Kosta open the wall safe and withdraw two fat stacks of notes, red ones by the look of it, fifties.

Yilly tucks the money away, gets two kisses from Kosta, and follows his boss out of the room. He climbs the stairs. Kosta sits, slugs back his brandy. He's a happy bunny. He looks at Guy's cash. Guy's been doing okay. There must be six or seven hundred in the pile. There's a funny thing with poker, when you're feeling good, feeling confident, the cards come.

'How's business, Mr Guy?' he asks.

'You know, Kosta, up and down.'

Mental makes a thrusting gesture that almost knocks the table flying.

'Up and down. Up and down.'

'You funny man,' says Kosta.

'Hysterical,' says Guy, and slides two blue sheets into the pool. 'I'll see that twenty and raise twenty,' he says.

......*scene 40*

A red BMW, roof down, stands below the blue screen of a scorched neon sky in the drive outside a white house called *The White House* in Hampstead. Nice pad. Mock art deco, circa 1950. Stucco walls. Curved balconies. Metal frame windows. Mature garden. £4.75 million in a cooling market.

Inside. White walls. Pale wood floors. Spotless surfaces. Space. The art consists of white abstracts, the understated feeling of movement mirrored in the fish tank dominating one wall, the sound of bubbles whispering to the surface, the gilded shoals of tropical fish captured in a swaying undulating sea lit by pale green light.

A silver steel coffee table stands in the centre of the room facing a large open hearth and edged on three sides by pale green sofas. The centre of the table is graced by a Grayson Perry urn featuring likenesses of oiks, tarts and weirdoes. There are bowls with an assortment of dates and figs, biblical food, and the three long-stemmed crystal glasses hold a Ribera del Duero Reserva Fiel, a medium price range red considered by some to be the best wine for the money in Spain today.

Trilby leafs through an art book of oiled male nudes and Jordan watches Martin as he concentrates on two small mounds of powder, one white, one brown, chopping each in turn with the ornamental knife withdrawn for the purpose from his lapel. A packet of Marlboro Lights stands on the table, top open, and a fag is stuck Pete Docherty style in the corner of Martin's lips.

He's warming to his subject.

'Speedballs.'

'Which is?'

'Which are. Have you ever taken acid?'

'Course,' Jordan answers.

'Course? In fact you haven't. What you have taken is a mixture of amphetamines and strychnine on the corner of blotting paper, no doubt decorated with a skull and crossbones or a fucking Smiley. Do you know what strychnine is?'

'Poison, innit.'

'So you did learn something at comprehensive school. Strychnine kills you by stopping your heart. What do amphetamines do? They speed up your heart. The mixture counteracts itself, producing a high which, while not necessarily unpleasant, has fuck-all to do with acid.'

'So why do they call it acid, then?'

'Because braindeads like you, no offence, can't tell the difference.'

Trilby refills the glasses.

'Flick your ash.'

Martin glances down, sees an inch of ash perched perilously on the end of his cigarette. He takes the fag out of his mouth, but instead of depositing it in an empty dish, he flicks the ash on the wood floor.

Jordan tries to take this in, slugging down wine, sparking up a Marlboro. He thinks: I shouldn't be here. But why shouldn't I be here? You can hold opposite thoughts in your head at the same time. I mean, what have I got to lose? I haven't paid for the drugs, the drink, the smokes. This bloke in the white suit's a complete cunt. But so what? Plenty of cunts about.

'Whose house is this?' he asks.

Martin doesn’t answer. He doesn't like questions. Trilby flicks the pages of the book. Martin concentrates on the piles of powder, chopping away. The house to Jordan doesn't look like any house he's ever seen before. It's more like a gallery or a museum. Not for living in. More like appearing in. It's not relaxed. You wouldn't lay back with a can and put your feet up. There's no telly for a start. A living room always has a telly.

'As I was saying,' Martin says, 'LSD you can't get hold of. Home grown's so weak it's only any good for retards with terminal diseases. We don't do Qualudes. Ketamine's for poofs and losers. Crack's for niggers. Poppers are for cunts without A levels. And if you don't count MDMA, which is rubbish – '

'Unless it's cut with Viagra,' adds Trilby.

' - all we have are the originals - '

' - smack smack and Uncle Charlie.'

'And thanks to our special friends the Americans in Afghanistan, and our special friends the Americans in Colombia, the supply has never been better.'

'Even if the quality isn't,' Trilby remarks.

'So, occasionally, if the stars are in alignment, and you stumble upon a gram of Bolivia's finest, you take it pure, out of respect. Like old brandy. Or a young girl. Most of the time, though, it's been stepped on by every slimeball from Bogata to Bayswater. So you mix.'

'Like vodka and tonic,' says Trilby.

'Heavy on the smack if you want to relax.'

'Heavy on the sherbet if you don't.'

Martin sits back, gesturing to the two grainy white/brown lines on the table.

'And that,' he says, 'in case you want to do an article for the school magazine, is a speedball.'

'Isn't it dangerous?' Jordan asks him.

'Course it's fucking dangerous,' he answers. 'John Lennon did speedballs. River Phoenix did speedballs. Do you think they'd have gone near the stuff if it wasn't dangerous?'

Trilby removes from her bag a fine silver snorting pipe and hoovers up a line.

Martin leans forward, plugging one nostril, and snorts the whole line up the other.

'Agh, Mary Mother Full of Waste!'

He snorts air, licks his lips. There is a moment of stillness, then Martin's head starts to quiver, his nostrils flare, his shoulders hunch, then he relaxes, smiles and lights another cigarette.

Jordan watches, fascinated.

'You can do your own,' Martin tells him.

'I might just do some coke.'

'Might you now. And why's that?'

'You know, I'm just –'

'A little faggot? Go on then, have some. Just a little bit though, we don't want you to become an addict before you go home to your mum. Sure you wouldn't prefer a glass of Ribena? Or a live yoghurt?'

'All right. For fuck sake. I'll do it.'

'That's what I like: man who knows his own mind.'

Trilby is already mixing. Martin stands, mania taking over.

'Music,' he says, crossing to the stereo and staring at the tower of CDs. 'CDs! That's how the rich stay rich. They don't spend any fucking money on new music.'

He kicks the stack.

'We'll let the fates decide.'

The stack topples like a dynamited tower block and hundreds of CDs skim across the carpet.

Jordan's eyes are spinning out of his head.

Martin slips on his shades and makes a big show of crawling like a blind man around the floor, searching among the CDs. He choses one and places it in the CD tray. The volume is deafening. The music five years out of date. Martin marches around the room, looking for trouble.

On the wall there is a series of eight black and white photographs of Greta May modelling. Martin unhooks one of the frames, licks and kisses the glass, his tongue worming around her pouty mouth. Finally, face twisted in contempt, he throws the frame across the room like a Frisbee. He enjoys this and does the same with the rest, almost hitting Jordan.

'Hey, careful, man.'

The music has become overpowering. Martin turns it off and throws the CD across the room.

'So Twentieth Century Fucks.'

He looks among the other CDs, grinding his cigarette out on the pale wood floor as he does so.

Trilby has finished her preparations.

'Okay?'

Jordan nods. Martin puts on some rock-n-roll and plays air guitar, kicking at the furniture, totally out of control.

'Just relax,' Trilby says. 'Let it happen.'

'Like when you're taking it up the ass,' says Martin.

Jordan snorts a line.

He starts to twitch. His breath is rapid, shallow. The colour drains from his face. Trilby watches like a zoo visitor. The tropical fish make bubbles. Martin pauses. Jordan, like the fish, tries to shape words.

'I think... Where's the...'

He rushes across the room, out the door and up the stairs.

Martin points at the ceiling and makes a swirling gesture with his finger.

……scene 41

Like life, poker's got two rules: ride your luck and cut your losses. Stick to the rules. You won't make a fortune. But you won't end up getting pissed on from a great height.

That's the thing with two pairs. Two pairs feels better than it is. It's like a promise from a junkie.

Yilly's interruption has changed the air. It's got lighter. Kosta's chugging back brandy, cracking jokes that make Mental wobble like whale blubber. He kisses Dixie on his two cheeks and that says without saying the past is past, the broken hand will heal, the merchandise is coming.

'You, I like.'

'Fanks Kosta.'

'You gut.'

Dixie Dean sits back with a stupid grin on his face, his eyes straying from the table to the stage where two girls are going through their paces. Twins. Albanian blondes in black leather shorts, black bras, boots and military caps. *If only he had a camera.*

Qerim's dealing.

'You give me three cards,' says Kosta.

Qerim's got a poker face. It never changes. He deals and tucks the dead cards at the bottom of the pack.

Kosta slowly spreads the cards behind his large fingers. Guy reads his eyes and it's like reading a book in Albanian. The draw tells him Kosta's sitting on a pair and is looking to make three of a kind. Guy takes one card. That tells Kosta he most likely has two pair or a flush. Either way, he's looking for one card for a full house.

There's a difference in these two hands. Guy drawing one card gets one chance. In taking three, Kosta gets a range: three of a kind, four of a kind, two pair that's bigger then Guy's two pair, a long shot full house: three of a kind and two pair.

Kosta covers Guy's £40. Qerim takes three cards and stays in for one more round.

Guy goes for the bluff. He ups the stake with four blues and Kosta pays the £80 to see his cards.

Guy fans out the jacks and sevens.

One at a time, for drama, Kosta turns over three tens.

No big deal. Guy is back where he started. But he forgets rule two. His luck has run dry and, hand by hand, so does his money. So does the £500 Kosta slides across the table, give him a chance to get his money back. So does the next £500.

Mental wobbles off to the bogs. The game's over for the day. Kosta shouts at Alya.

'You, music.'

She turns on some disco from the eighties and the Albanian girls goose step their long legs around the brass pole. Kosta draws Guy to the edge of the dance floor as if these pagan girls with their febrile eyes and mutant carnality will ease the pain. He places an arm around Guy.

'Seven days. Iz okay, No problem,' Kosta says, squeezing Guy's shoulder.

'It's a lot in a week. I mean, you know me.'

'Iz no problem. Get your girl with plenty of – '

'Nyacky nyacky,' shouts Mental, thrusting his big thighs as he wanders back across the club.

'She does what she wants,' says Guy, and Kosta holds up his huge hand.

'She need this. They like,' he says. 'All the same. Romanian. Albanian. English. This they like.'

He points at the girls on the stage, shows his big palm, then folds it into a fist.

'You give. They give.'

Guy watches the dancers. His shirt's sticking to his back. Even with the sour smell of the club and the girls sweating nectar as they kick their long legs, he can smell his own sweat, unstrung and wasted. He feels hollow like an empty bottle, an empty room, a vacant space.

'A grand's a lot in a week.'

Kosta grabs Guy by his ears and pulls his face so close their noses are touching. Behind him, the twins imitate the same action.

'I come from the mountains. You don't fuck me. I fuck you.'

Guy's got his back to the stage and doesn't see the Albanian girls miming Kosta's words, one bent over, the other thrusting at her in a faux fuck.

'All right, Kosta. I'll get it.'

Kosta turns Guy back towards the stage where one of the twins acts out slitting the throat of the other.

'They new. Gut, eh?'

'Yeah, great.'

Guy turns away. Kosta follows him up the narrow cement stairs.

It's like leaving the molten core of Hades. The sky is pastel blue, uniform, a hint of orange outlining buildings that are beginning to lose definition. It's warm still, that silky warmth that grips the air after long hot days.

They stand on the cracked pavement next to the shots of nude girls in the glass panels beside the door. Kosta goes back inside to switch on the lights, illuminating the girls, illuminating the blue neon sign: *Kosta's*. He glances up and down the road as if looking for lost goats in the mountains.

'I like,' says Kosta. 'Good country. You do anything. In my country...' he shrugs, he can't find the words. 'This place, iz gut.'

'A grand's a lot in a week, Kosta.'

Kosta gestures the throat slitting routine, then shrugs again.

'You got other assets, Mr Guy.'

Guy looks up at the giant. 'Yeah, like what?'

'You can sell the girl.'

'What?'
'You bring girl. We talk.'

......*scene 42*

Bubbles glide over the rim of Bella's bath and burst on the black and white tiles. Her cheeks are stinging, more the left cheek from Henry's right hand. The slap wasn't hard enough to bruise, but she's waggling her jaw to make it feel more comfortable.

She is lying with her ears below the surface of the water thinking about Simon. They are eighteen now and she remembers when they were little and Simon used to hide what he called his pinky between his legs and pretend he was a girl. Bella kept in a drawer full of buttons and broken things the arm from a dismembered doll, and when she tucked the little hand between her legs it made the perfect pinky.

Until the age of nine their bodies were the same. Then everything started to swell and ripen. Simon grew shoulders and big feet. Her bottom became round. Little buds like pink flowers popped up on her chest. She should have been a boy, and still surprises herself when she turns sometimes to the mirror and sees a girl of the sort men covet in creepy ways that once made her feel uncomfortable and is now just boring. Men are weird. Men want to abuse the thing they desire, or be abused by it. That's why she was drawn to Guy. Why she is intrigued by Trilby.

When she was growing up, Bella could out-swim any boy in the club pool. She beat all comers in the open tennis challenge and won to Father's mixed pleasure and irritation the junior cup three years running. Fleetingly proud of his first born, frustrated by the always five minutes late second, Father only see himself in any family photo.

Bella's tennis trophies with her name etched on silver disks on the bases gather dust in the junk room with the dust of childhood, a museum of finger paintings, tricycles, Beanie Babies, the Teddy bears with missing eyes. The time for toys ended early at the Channon house and those soft packages that gave such pleasure to press and guess what was inside were replaced by the unmistakeable oblong bricks containing Philip Pullman, Harry Potter, improve your chess, Bach's Brandenburg Concertos. Simon continued to squeeze the parcels wrapping those sensible hardbacks and would throw out guesses. A tennis racquet? New skis? Red leather boots with moons and stars?

Bella could read a book in a day. Simon lingered over every word, running his finger across the page, lips moving, his mind floating on magic carpets. He was Balthasar in the nativity play and spent the autumn term from September till Christmas in solitary dress rehearsals. He loved colours and fabrics, velvet and silk. He dressed in his own lyrical way. He was, as Father liked to say, his mother's son; he had inherited her flair and extravagance. Mummy has a passion for ruffles and frills and believes as she believes in the Eucharist that you should never wear brown shoes with a black suit.

Dressing up is a family fetish. Father costumes himself as a famous writer, espadrilles with a good suit, a pork pie hat he tilts to the back of his head to play honky tonk. Mummy is distant, ethereal, tutored at home in a crumbling manor house with two sisters, she was a step up the ladder for her clever husband and, two decades on, seven best-sellers on the shelves, it is mother who must have had her eye surreptitiously on the main prize. She has a room dedicated to an omnibus of haute couture and keeps her two hundred pairs of shoes in the boxes with photographs on the outside.

Bella played the tomboy but was born knowing how to walk in heels. It was a short step from Marlene Dietrich to black plastic thigh boots and the devil mask with curly horns, and the thing with a mask is you hide the real you, you become the character, Romeo, a black slave in *Androcles and the Lion*, the dominatrix laying the whip cautiously but not too cautiously across Guy's back.

'Isn't it fun?'

She nodded and did it again.

Within a week she was disciplining a stranger.

Bella is aware that there is something oedipal about spanking old men with silvering hair and flabby flesh, but views the interlude as if from the deck of a ship leaving land, a time that's passing, a part of growing up. She didn't go home that day after the funeral because she wanted to punish her father and you don't have to be Sigmund Freud to work out that that's just what she's been doing ever since.

She gazes down at her toes slippered in bubbles. She lowers her head below the surface of the water and remembers Simon's last poem

...down, down, sinking down, sinking down through a hole in the ground.

She should have known what was going through his mind. She did know. She just didn't know where it was going. There were lots of clues, pieces of a puzzle, data to be sifted and filed. She needed a Rosetta stone to clarify the evidence, make a plan. She should have packed Simon's clothes, packed her own clothes, and they should have run away, gone abroad. They could have dressed as angels and played tambourines as they busked their way from bar to bar around the Mediterranean. The best ideas always come too late. While Father was disciplining Simon that day in the attic, she didn't think about what was happening, she did what she always did on these occasions, she ran a bath, filled it with bubbles and lay there waiting.

There was a knock. A timid knock. Then a hard knock.

'It's me,' he whispered.

She stepped out of the water and let him in.

Bella took Simon in her arms. His cheeks were red. He sobbed as she held him, his body pulsing against her. He was a child. Her child. She ran through the clasps on his Tibetan shirt, pulled at the cord on his puja pants, her wet fingers working as if with their own anonymous purpose. He shed his clothes and when they stepped back into the bath she was touched by the memory of floating together in the amniotic ocean where life began.

She added hot water. The steam swirled about them, and through the steam she could see her own features framed in pale sandy hair. She went up on her knees to wash the tears from his face. He cupped her breasts in his palms. He wasn't feeling her. He was feeling himself. What he should have been. His erection bobbed out of the water between them and she curled pinky into her hand.

It didn't feel strange. It felt completely natural. Bella was holding herself. They kissed. It was a long time since they had kissed on the lips and that kiss was sweeter than any kiss would ever be. She squeezed pinky harder, pulled the loose skin over the head and back again, up and down, faster and faster until his body stiffened and his essence pumped warmly into her hand. They looked down at the foamy white island stretched over her palm. She raised her fingers to her lips and on her tongue she tasted the mysterious depths of his being.

Down down, sinking down
Sinking down through a hole in the ground
Sinking down there's no way up
Until the monster comes and gobbles you up
Down down into the deep dark sea
Down down to eternity –

......scene 43

There's a tap on the door.

Déjà vu.

'It's only me.'

Bella steps out of the bath and unlocks the door. She steps back into the hot water as Guy enters.

'He hit me,' she says.

'What? Hit you? The bastard. Works on the telly and thinks he rules the world...'

'I'm not doing it any more.'

'Sweetie, it happens. You'll be alright.'

'You're not listening, Guy – '

'One bad john – '

'I'm going to do something else.'

'Like what?'

She doesn't reply. Guy's somewhere else. He's not listening. He clears a space on the steamy mirror and looks back at her in the reflection. There's a nerve on his neck vibrating as if a tiny insect burrows beneath the surface of the skin.

'Guy – '

'I mean, they do expect a bit of enthusiasm,' he says. 'We're in the service industry.'

'I thought it was just supposed to be fun. That's what you said.'

He turns away from his reflection, shaking his head. 'Bella, come on. You don't pay two hundred quid for some little tart who doesn't know what she's doing.'

'Oh, fuck off, Guy.'

'I beg your pardon?'

'Get out of my bathroom.'

'Your bathroom? This is my bathroom. And my flat. And you owe me rent.'

'I've paid, and paid, and paid. And I told you, I'm not doing it. You can't make me.'

'You want me to show you just what I can make you do?'

'You're just like all of them.'

Bella doesn't cry very often. But she cries now. Real tears. This could be Simon crying that day in the bathroom at home. She keeps getting these flashes from the past, it could be because it's their birthday, it could be that the past is moving away, she's leaving it behind.

'Oh, there you go, playing the water baby. And who cares?' Guy says. 'It doesn't work. I've seen it all and I've done it all.'

Bella doesn't respond. She covers her face with a face cloth.

Guy's weighing up tactics. He can feel the fear in him like a virus. He can see in his mind's eye Kosta Ali Pasha slitting his throat with his finger, he can see the Albanian twins in their garrotting routine. He goes down on his knees beside the bath.

'Bella, I owe someone money, a lot of money,' he explains. 'Once we pay it, we'll go away. To Paris. Or Morocco. I've got a friend with a villa.'

She lowers the face cloth, shakes her head. 'No.'

'Bella, I need a grand, I need it now.'

'Make your own money.'

'It'll take too long. I'm really fucked. Please, Bella. Please. These guys are really heavy. They don't come round and break a few bones. They're snuffing people.'

'No.'

Guy starts crying. 'Please. Please. Be a sweetheart. You're my special girl. There's no one like you. You understand me.'

'Guy. No. It's over.'

'It can't be, it can't – '

'It is.'

He stands, the tic on his neck the peak of a volcano, his body stiff with anger as he lashes out, his right hand drawn back like a tennis racquet.

Bella moves out of the way of his forehand smash and he half plunges into the bath.

As Guy stands, Bella's already on her feet and hits him over the head with a jar of bath salts that splits and covers his hair in pink crystals.

'Don't you dare.'

'You fucking cow.'

He reels into the corner of the bathroom, clutching his head, but comes back with his fists clenched and punches her in the stomach.

Bella falls back into the water and Guy leaps on her, holding her down, forcing her head below the water. She kicks her legs and hits him across the side of his head. He doesn't let her up. She struggles for breath. He's too strong for her. It's like when he jerked the tag off the Prada bag, he's possessed with some demoniac force.

At the last moment, he releases her and she rises gasping for breath.

'Can't make you?' Guy says.

Bella lashes out at him with both fists, but the breath's gone from her and he forces her once more below the water. He holds her there, the strangler's hands around her throat.

She stops kicking.

Bubbles rise to the surface.

She's dead.

Bella's dead.

Guy moves away, dries himself on a towel, and combs the pink crystals from his quiff of bronze hair.

Bella emerges from the water, choking, barely alive.

'I'm going out. I'm going to find a john. And I'm going to bring him back. You don't like it, you can take the easy way out.'

As he says this, he grips his throat with his left hand, holds his right hand above his head and jerks it upwards.

......*scene 44*

A line of shadow moves like a slow tide across the wall. The room is vast. It contains the biggest bed Jordan has ever seen, and there are sofas and chairs like it's a lounge as well as a bedroom. The mirrors conceal doors, you just press them and they spring open to reveal dresses in every design and style, every texture and hue, dark suits, pastel suits, silk and satin tops in shades of pink and ivory, jogging clothes, jumpers in neat precise piles like in a shop.

It's hard to take in. His body feels as if it's made of that soft cheese that melts on the plate and he's slipped into a chair that seems to be sucking him down. His eyes have lost the wide angle and he sees everything as if through a tunnel, the big bed in a wooden frame swathed in netting like a boat at sea, huge pillows, changing and reforming like clouds, everything crisp and white. Trilby has changed into a red dress made of feathers and sits at the dressing table painting her lips the same shade of red.

Martin opens one drawer after the other, removes jewellery, watches, knickknacks, and places them in a shoulder bag.

Jordan is content sitting there being sucked down into the soft chair. The light around the windows is silvery. It's like being in a film. The room is a set. He can't quite work out what Martin's doing and as he speaks the words as they leave his mouth sound slow like a recording.

'What you doing?'

Martin pauses. 'You speaking to me?'

'Yeah, like, like what you doing?'

'Stealing,' Martin says.

Jordan runs the word through his head. Stealing. Stealing. He's done plenty of that in his time, from shops, the offie, from his mum's purse.

'Stealing?'

'Do we speak the same language?'

Martin closes a drawer and opens another. Jordan's thinking: do we speak the same language? *I mean, I only speak one language. There isn't any point speaking nuffin' else.*

'You're having a laugh, ancha?'

'What?'

'I mean, from your own family?' Jordan says

'I beg your pardon?'

'Like, you know, stealing your own stuff.'

Martin points a finger gun at his temple. 'Doh!' he says.

Jordan's parched throat turns to sand. He tries to push himself out of the chair and can't make it. His eyes are two mirrors that have been smashed and he looks out at a fragmented world, a collage.

'I don't...You mean...oh fuck. I'm out of here.'

He tries again to escape from the down padding. No luck.

Trilby has finished her makeup and swings round on the swivel chair. She stands. She wants to be admired.

'Nice,' says Martin, and turns back to Jordan. 'Listen shit-for-brains, what's your problem?'

Jordan tries to focus. 'You're burgling someone's house. That's my problem. What if they come back?'

'Ah ha! Now let's get this straight. You worried about the morality of this, or you worried about getting caught?'

Jordan's found his voice. Not his voice. A voice.

'I'm worried about the fact that I'm burgling someone's house,' he says.

'But you're not. I am.'

'But...I'm here, an' I...I'm an accomplice.'

'Only if we get caught.'

'And we never get caught,' adds Trilby.

Jordan turns and looks at Trilby. With the soft light of evening behind her it's like looking at a film star walking the red carpet at the Oscars. He can't recall ever seeing anyone so...amazing. Except the girl.

What was her name?

'What?' he says.

'We never get caught,' Trilby says again.

'So, what do you want to do?' adds Martin. 'You want to leave? Then what? You go to the police?'

'Course not.'

'That makes you an accomplice anyway. You have knowledge of the crime, but you do nothing about it.'

'Yeah, but – '

'No buts, Jordan. I thought you were going to be fun. That's what you promised. Isn't that what he promised?'

'That's right, baby,' Trilby replies. 'Lots of fun.'

'So, you little pigeon fucker, it seems to me you have two choices. You stay, enjoy yourself, and nothing will happen. Or, you go, you tell the Filth, and by the time they get here, we will be long gone. But I will remember. I will find you. And I will rip your fucking liver out.'

Jordan can't get his head round this. He wants to stand up but it's too much effort. The speedball's bouncing around his head like it's a pool table, brain cells clacking.

'So, what's it to be?' says Martin.

'Whose 'ouse is it, anyway?'

Martin pauses. He doesn't like direct questions. He makes an exception.

'Look at this place. Where'd you get this sort of money from? Working? Excuse me. The owner is an MP.'

'A Member of Parliament.'

'No...a Military Policeman...doh! He's a man whose job is telling lies with a fucking great grin on his gob. He robs old people of decent pensions, keeps them half dead in hospital corridors. Puts eighty kids in a class. He steals their education. He stole your education. He's a cunt. What is he Jordan?'

'A cunt.'

'How come you're called Jordan, anyway? What does it mean? Where does it come from? You a river? A country? You stepped out of the bible? Bit fucking pretentious if you ask me.'

'Look, I won't say anything.'

'You want to go?'

'I'm not like you – '

'You want to be.'

'I don't.'

'I think you do. The piece of shit who lives here, the misery he causes. We punish him for it. We deprive him of the wages of sin, the backhanders of corruption and theft. We take it and spend it living life.'

'On drugs you mean.'

'Drugs, cars, music, clothes.'

'Anything,' says Trilby. 'Money lets you to be who you really are.'

Her voice to Jordan sounds like treacle being poured over ice cream, rich and golden, sweet and dark. He watches as Martin passes her one of his snuff boxes. She takes a pinch of coke, leans over the dressing table and chops it into three lines on a hand mirror. She takes a line. Martin takes his on the back of his hand and snorts. Trilby crosses the room, feathers ruffling, and gives Jordan her pipe. Jordan hesitates, then snorts up the last line from the mirror.

His body goes into spasm. He grows still. His glazed eyed come back into focus. The computer whine in his head grows silent.

'Better?' she asks.

He nods. He's not sure. But he nods.

'We can do anything,' Martin says. 'Anything.'

Trilby does a twirl in the red feathers. She takes Jordan's hand and seems surprisingly strong as she pulls him out of the chair. She runs her hand through his hair and kisses the tip of his nose. Then his lips. Just gently. Not opening her mouth or anything. It feels nice. His brow's sweaty. He can feel wet under his arms, down his back. His breath comes in short gasps.

He's not sure what she's up to now. But he's up for it. In for a penny. She gazes into his eyes and he gazes back at her as she shuffles the dress from her shoulders, down to her waist, over her bottom. She's wearing silky white knickers and a white bra like in an underwear ad. She steps out of her white heels and their eyes meet. They are the same height.

'It's your turn,' she says.

Trilby unzips his jeans, pulls the Che Guevara tee-shirt over his head, runs her finger round the circle containing a big capital A tattooed on his left arm. Jordan's trembling, sweating, his eyes pinpricks that see everything as if in a camera obscura, a dark chamber of shifting shadows. He did promise to be fun, didn't he? It's fun to dress up. He unlaces his trainers. He steps into the feathered dress. Trilby pulls the zip up his back. She sits him in the chair.

'Close your eyes,' she says, and its nice sitting there with the late sun warm through the window, big brushes and small brushes dusting his face in powders and creams, a pencil running around the eyes.

'No peeping,' says Trilby.

He feels something being fitted to his head and imagines it's a hat.

'No peeping,' she says again, urging him to his feet.

A hand runs up his legs and removes his boxers. He steps into a pair of shoes he knows are high heels because they make his feet slope at an odd angle, and a thought flashes across his mind: *where did they find high heels my size?* Then the thought's gone as he wobbles unsteadily at Trilby's guidance across the room.

'Open your eyes.'

Trilby is behind him hooking a gold chain around his neck. He stares into the mirror, mesmerised, unsure if it is really him in the reflection and knows it must be as his red lips fall open.

'Wow.'

His eyes sparkle. They are rimmed in black, highlighted in pink. Long chestnut hair rolls about his shoulders. He looks a bit like the girl. Bella. That was her name. Bella.

'You're beautiful.'

'I'm beautiful,' he says.

Trilby takes his hand and leads him to the big bed.

'Close your eyes.'

Her voice is soft, dark as a spell. He kicks off the shoes, slides beneath the netting and lies back on the snow bank of white linen. With eyes closed it feels as if he has left his body and is floating above looking down, not at himself, but at Bella with her chestnut curls spread about the pillows. He isn't sweating now. He feels relaxed. The brown does that. The coke keeps you on the level. The brown makes everything easy, effortless. If he had his guitar now he'd be able to play *Stairway to Heaven* all the way through.

He doesn't see Trilby remove the bra containing silicone pads, the white pants containing an erection. He feels her slither across the sheets. She runs the red dress up his legs. She takes his cock in her mouth and he feels his body grow lighter. He could be a feather from the red dress falling, falling, floating through the air.

He doesn't see Martin watching. He doesn't know Martin likes to watch, and keeps watching as Trilby draws him deeper and deeper into her velvety mouth, deeper and deeper until at the point of disappearing he lets go with all life's stress and frustration, all anxiety and doubt. She keeps sucking at him, drawing out every seed of rage and discontent, and when he's drained he feels completely relaxed as her firm gentle hands roll him over on to his stomach.

She parts the cheeks of his bottom and releases his semen into the crack. It's warm and sticky, a trickle runs between his legs. It feels weird but not so weird, unexpected, but not totally unexpected, when Trilby nudges her way through his cheeks into the heart of his body. He lets it happen. He buries his head in the pillows, knees spread, back arching. This is what it must be like being a girl being fucked.

Trilby's fucking him, pressing him down into the big soft bed, drilling deeper and deeper like she's searching for something lost and precious.

Then she comes, vanishing into his backside just as he had vanished into her mouth, and really Jordan isn't sure what's happening, who he is, where he is, why he got lost after buying new guitar strings and how one wrong turn always leads to another.

……scene 45

Martin leaves the room and enters the study at the far end of the upper hall. He scrolls down the contacts on his machine. He gazes out of the window. Orange light seeps across the horizon. Two rings and the phone answers.

'Me. Hi, where are you?'

'Covent Garden,' she answers.

'I knew it. Serendipity. I was thinking of you. Listen, there's a great place, the Coffee Mill. You must try it. '

'Okay – '

'Try the hazelnut mocha. Greta. Greta, you still there…'

He presses the red key, slides the phone back in his pocket and starts with the desk. He opens the middle drawer, cheque books, bank statements. Boring. Down the left side. Nothing. Nothing. A Patek Philippe in it's box. He tosses it in the shoulder bag. Down the right. Nothing. Nothing.

Something.

In the bottom right drawer he finds a gun metal blue money box. A large one. Almost as big as the drawer. He removes it and stands it on the desk.

Where were those keys?

Yes. Top right. Loads of keys, house keys, cars keys, old keys, bent keys, male keys that no longer have wives to poke at. Why do people keep all this junk? He shuffles from key to key. Finally the lock turns.

He lifts back the lid. He expects a surprise. And gets a surprise.

That's the second one today.

His mouth's dry, drug parched. He remembers seeing downstairs a bottle of old brandy. He'll have a shot to celebrate. He leans forward. Then leans back again. His eyes are glowing. Red tinged. Lit by the dying sun. Martin tips out the valuables in the shoulder bag, stores the money box in the vacant space and adds a few choice pieces, the Patek Philippe, a ruby and diamond ring, some gold chains.

He studies his reflection in the darkening windows, opens his jacket, readjusts the gun, buttons the jacket and stands with his spine erect. Luck comes in threes. He's owed one.

Trilby rolls Jordan over. He looks up into her eyes. At her boyish chest.

'You're beautiful,' she says.

He can't get his head round this. He can. Perhaps he just doesn't want to.

'You fucked me.'

'Yes.'

'But, but I'm not like that.'

'Everyone's like that.'

He goes to speak, but there's a rap on the door.

'Time. Ten minutes,' says Martin.

......*scene 46*

What the young don't know is that when you get old you don't feel old. When you step out of a taxi at a restaurant or a store or the hairdressers you feel the same as you've always felt. If you happen to catch a glimpse of yourself in the taxi window or a shop window it's always a surprise. Every time. You never get over it. The you that you are, that you've always been, slips slowly from its skin and some stranger starts to appear in the glass, appear in your bed, wear your clothes.

The first thing to go is the face. The eyelids sag, the lips shrink, the flesh droops, the light fades. It feels like you're being punished for something you haven't done. You are falsely imprisoned in a decaying body that belongs to someone else, someone who hasn't spent thirty years loyal to Jane Fonda, speed walking, swimming, drinking little, eating nothing, taking massages, regular sex, multi-vitamins, glucosamine, HRT, omega 3 complex, prozac. Bruises linger. The turned ankle doesn't heal overnight. You can't unscrew the top of the soya milk, or read the small print on the Nurofen box, or bend from the waist to pick up the dropped glove you drop more often.

Do you give up? Do you heck. Maxine has been married four times, marriage to her is a calling, an art form; she reminds new husbands straight off the bat that at heart she remains a Palmer and can trace her family tree back to the timbers and masts of the

Mayflower. The Palmers fought Indians, the Crown, the Spanish, Confederates, the Japanese, Democrat taxes. They made America and Maxine makes herself.

Maxine has amber eyes that glow in the dark, cat's eyes men always say, and when she had the eye-brow tuck and bag purge it wasn't to turn her into something that she wasn't but to change her back into what she had always been. Her ears are sea urchins escaping from gold ear-rings shaped as shells, her collagen lips full, soft, downy and kissable. She has always liked her nose, faintly retrousse, well-proportioned and set between ample cheekbones with moulded implants that tauten the skin and form a frame for the face every bit as important as the frame that reflects the portrait. She keeps her spine rigid, chakras stretched. Even when alone, a beautiful woman stands tall, shoulders back, every hair and fold of fabric in place. You have to maintain standards. You have to believe in something, and there's nothing more important to believe in than you.

Her last sortie with surgery was the neck lift in Paris, a two hour op to tighten the marbling effect, you don't want to be taken for the Thanksgiving turkey, and though she has been known to spend £480 on a tube of face cream, Maxine has come to believe that creams are the opposite of answered prayers, a triumph of optimism over experience. Her skin is firm rather than soft, and the stretch marks silvered into her waist by Nicholas have paled to translucent threads as imperceptible as ectoplasm. Motherhood in the time before equitable distribution in California was the price she paid to ensure a just settlement when she freed herself from Ronald, her first husband.

When Maxine lies flat, her tummy dips between the curving rise of her hipbones. She is lying flat at this moment, heart racing, one arm flung over the side of the bed, the street lamps on the sidewalk casting a sepia glow across the room with its zebra-skin on one wall, a portrait of William, her second husband, the English one, on another.

She is wrapped in a sheet like a pasha, slices of her toned body revealed against the white silk, a creamed right leg, a polished hipbone, her left breast exposed like a figure in a temple frieze, the neat dome shaped by the scalpel. Maxine did not suckle Nicholas and believes her forty-five year old son's short-comings are due to a deficiency of good Palmer genes and has nothing to do with the fact that he was brought up by a stream of nannies, or that from the age of seven, when she moved to New York, he rarely saw his father in Los Angeles, that the best schools and an allowance that could buy friends wasn't enough to buy what he apparently craved. We are the master of our own ship. We sink or survive by our own deeds and desires.

Warm semen seeps from her vagina, luscious, untamed, the tang of the stable rising from under the sheet. Is she worried about Aids, sexually transmitted diseases? Life's too short for that. She wants to feel hot male come in her body and on her body. That's what keeps you young.

She looks up at William staring down from the painting. His eyes are the colour of the sky under which he stands. In an otherwise generous smile she cherishes the mischievous turn of his lips, the fissures scored into weathered cheeks. He is dressed for the bush, eyes amused, strong hands that stilled her as he kissed her neck, blunt, forceful kisses that sent snakes of fire through her body, his warm tongue slithering into the well of her sea creature ear. He would peel away her clothes, as he peeled a ripe mango, cutting it with the tip of his Ghurkha knife, stripping back segments like orange flames.

The knife is crescent-shaped, the filigreed handle studded with coral and turquoise, a gift from a maharajah. It lays beside her on the bedside table in a leather sheath trimmed with silver, stained with sweat. She holds it to her face. His smell has gone, stolen by time; in the end, time takes everything, even the curve of your bottom.

The past lay about her in a conspiracy of objet d'art that reminds her of warm days when they made love beneath the mosquito netting, the unseen hands of servants stirring the sticky air with the soft murmur of bamboo fans, the chime of cymbals escaping the Hindu temple perched above the riverbank like a giant white cat. There is nothing like sex in the afternoon.

Maxine looks away from the painting of William to the boy sitting beside the window in the mahogany chair pulling on his boots. He could be a temple attendant, a Brahmin. He has the dark glossy eyes, the sensitive mouth, the smooth brown skin.

Krishna Guru Singh.

She likes his name, it tastes of passion and his taste remains on her lips.

He stands, tucks in his shirt. Pushes his arms in his jacket, looks boyish as he looks back at her.

She sweeps a stray curl from her eyes.

'That, darling, was absolutely – '

'Don't tell me,' he says, 'tell a friend.'

She allows a smile to flicker over her lips.

She likes men with a sense of humour and really can't be bothered with those bores who try to impress by talking politics and market prices. Women want to be amused.

The boy stands there, hovering, being polite.

'How was it for you?' she asks. She knows she shouldn't. She knows they lie. She can't help herself.

'You're amazing.'

'Am I?'

He nods.

Her features rearrange themselves in the faintly surprised look of a young woman still unsure of her gift.

'I mean it,' he says.

'I'm sure you do. Now, I think you deserve a little present. How much do you deserve?'

'Well, that's discretionary.'

'Three hundred?'

'Not that discretionary.'

Again the fleeting smile.

Maxine rarely smiles. It doesn't show her at her best, but she can't help liking this boy, and she doesn't want to haggle with the natives. William taught her that.

'Five hundred. But on one condition.'

He sits on the side of the bed and looks into her amber eyes.

'That's fair enough,' he replies.

'Only if I can see you again.'

Maxine takes a purse from her bedside table and counts out £500. Worth every cent.

He tucks the money in his top pocket, the whites of his eyes radiant in the dim room.

She raises her head and he leans forward to kiss her collagen lips.

'Krishna, can I ask you something?'

'Course you can.'

'You rather liked my friend, didn't you?'

He raises his shoulders. 'Yes, she's nice,' he says.

'You liked her more, I mean?'

He runs his finger over her carved cheekbone. 'Not at all,' he tells her. 'You're fabulous.'

She knows it isn't true. She knows that he knows what she knows, but it doesn't matter. She can feel his warm sperm sticky on her thighs. That's what matters.

Krishna turns to blow her a kiss as he leaves the room.

He descends the stairs, his tread muffled by the carpet, and she listens as Aurora , her Colombian, turns the double locks on the main door and lets him out.

Maxine runs a finger between her legs and moistens her lips.

She knows Sara is driving Gordon back from Heathrow but life's too short to wait, to wait for anything. She grabs her cell phone.

......scene 47

Sara believes the law about not speaking on your mobile while driving is ridiculous. People smoke. Look at maps. Eat. Vehicles come equipped with coffee holders. If you can't drive with one hand and hold your phone with the other you really shouldn't be driving in the first place.

MAXINE comes up on the screen.

'Well?' Sara asks.

'He should wear a crown of thorns. He fucks like a God.'

'Did he find your...kundalini?'

'My dear, I haven't even tried walking yet.'

'Lunch tomorrow?'

'You bet.'

'Have to go, I'm driving.'

Sara slips the phone in the pocket under the dash and shunts down the filter road on to the M4. During the day the sun glare masks the carbon rising from the city, but through the long orange sunset the mist over the buildings in the distance creates an impressionistic landscape that would lift the spirits if you were sitting in the park not in traffic.

Gordon's at her side in a foul mood.

'Maxine,' she says. 'She's found God.'

'Americans!'

'I thought you liked Americans?'

'Who said I didn't?'

'Darling...'

'Sorry.' She hears his sigh. 'It's the bloody Europeans that get my goat.'

'You knew that when you took the job.'

'That doesn't make it any less tedious. Six months grubbing about in agriculture before I can even get a shot at the treasury.'

'You'll get there.'

'Don't have any doubt about that.'

She doesn't.

Gordon is shrewd, resourceful, dashing in his dark suits and trademark ties; one featuring Duchamp's *Nude Descending a Staircase* made the *Daily Mail's* gossip pages when he took it from his neck to sell at a charity auction attended by Kate Moss and Ronnie Wood. Gordon is famed for fucking every ambitious new secretary and PA that enters the Commons before rivals get a whiff of fresh blood, the fusion of flaws and qualities that Sara once admired in her husband being the same flaws and qualities that, to her own dismay, find her cruising the champagne bars of Knightsbridge with Maxine Fox.

She indicates to change lanes, not that it makes a scrap of difference, both lanes are a snarled asphyxiating miasma, the bus lane empty as always. She waits for Gordon to comment.

'We're in the most important bloody capital in the world, three lanes and one of them you can't use. Who comes up with this nonsense?'

'You're in Government.'

'Cod quotas and fishing permits. I don't even like fish.'

'Poor darling.'

......scene 48

It's amazing how much damage someone bombed on speedballs can do when they put their mind to it.

Broken chairs, CDs in and out of their cases, the Greta May photographs in shattered frames, art books, a 12th century Tibetan *thanka*, and a collection of full and nearly full Scottish malts are piled up on the coffee table in the centre of the living room, the walls denuded of their complex abstracts and the devil masks from Indonesia.

On a surviving side table stand three balloon glasses containing generous measures of Hennessy Paradis cognac.

'Agh, there you are.'

In their own clothes, Trilby and Jordan descend the stairs and enter the room.

Jordan can't speak with his mouth dropping open. His lips move like the fish in the aquarium but nothing comes out. His eyes scan the room like he's at the aftermath of a city bombing.

Trilby takes a brandy from Martin. He holds a glass for Jordan, but the boy shakes his head like he's being handed a fizzing grenade.

'You – '

'Jordan – '

'You user. You – '

'Shush. Listen and learn. Here is a tip you will remember for the rest of your life: always stay for the extra drink.'

Jordan won't take the glass and Martin pours the brandy over the debris stacked on the table. He adds the rest from the bottle. Jordan can't take this in. It's like in his brain there are two or three or four versions of himself all looking out at a world where reality has morphed into a video game.

Trilby raises her glass.

'A toast,' Martin says.

'To the rest of our lives,' says Trilby.

Jordan stares again at the trashed room, then back at Martin.

'But why?'

'Why what?

'I mean, why?'

'Why? Why? The whole world wants to know why. There is no why. There just is.'

Jordan looks about the room.

'I mean, look. Look. Look what you've done. You're just a cunt.' He looks at Trilby. 'You an' all.'

'Careful,' says Martin and, for some reason, an impulse, ESP perhaps, he unbuttons his jacket.

It is at that same moment that Gordon bursts into the room. He's a big man. He rowed at Oxford.

'What the hell?'

Sara follows on his heels. Gordon had told her to stay in the car when they saw the red BMW squatting on the drive, but Sara has a mind of her own.

She stares at Martin, puzzled for a moment, then it strikes her...

'I know you,' she screams, pointing. 'You're that little toe rag who hangs around my daughter.'

'You've met you're fucking match, boy,' Gordon chimes in, crossing the room. 'You think you're going to get away with this – '

He's made two steps but before he completes the third, Martin has the gun out of his waistband.

Gordon's too revved up to notice and has a few more words waiting in his windpipe. 'You don't know what you're dealing with – '

'Don't I?'

Martin flicks the safety and fires a single round that enters Gordon's forehead and turns his skull to mush.

He's done it.

He's actually done it.

Gun club at public school has paid off. He gives a high, hysterical laugh, and turns to Sara. Once you've started, you don't stop. You can't stop. You don't want to stop. You're on skis at the top of an incline. Try to stop and you'll break something.

Sara is frozen to the spot. Martin paces towards her, steps over Gordon, arm at full stretch, and shoots Sara May point blank, the slug entering her throat, exiting through the back of her neck and striking the giant fish tank, cracking the glass with a zipping sound like the screech of car tyres.

Martin only becomes fully aware of what he has done after he has done it. He gives another high-pitched whoop and drops the gun.

It falls at Trilby's feet. She bends immediately, scoops the gun from the floor and drops it in her bag.

Jordan's got that same feeling he had earlier, that he's in a movie, or a video game, a world of whip pans and jump cuts.

'Jesus Christ. Jesus fucking Christ - '

He's hyperventilating, face leached of colour like a photographic negative. He leans forward and throws up all over the pile of debris. His voice rattles the glass in the chandelier.

' – you shot 'em. You fuckin' killed 'em. You're a fuckin' killer. I'm dead. I'm fuckin' dead.'

Trilby is the still point in the eye of the hurricane. She takes the cigarette lighter from the side table.

'Jordan – '

'Fuckin' killer.'

' – Jordan. Shut up.'

'They're fuckin dead.'

'Shut up.'

The boy won't stop.

'What am I doing here? He killed 'em. He fuckin' killed 'em.'

Trilby slaps his face, one good hard slap. She's a strong bitch.

'Shut up,' she says, and he shuts up.

What with all the shouting, no one notices the fish tank. The weight of what must be close to a ton of water against the crack has patiently pressed the glass back and shoals of brilliantly coloured tropical fish, guppies, puffers, angelfish, knifefish, Siamese tigers, rainbow fish reflecting Gordon's signature ties burst like strange birds from the shattering glass, fly briefly across the room and land in death dances across the pale wood floors.

As the water drains through the floorboards, Trilby flicks the wheel on the lighter and, just like the brandy poured over mother's Christmas pudding, the brandy tipped over the bonfire turns to blue flames that race over the white canvases, the priceless, irreplaceable Tibetan *thanka*, the black and white model shots of Greta May, the glossed paper turning to ash, the ash rising on the updraft of heat and settling in burning black stars over the pale green sofas, Greta's dead mother in green Armani, her father in the marine blue tie decorated with golden galleons.

'Martin. Bag. Time to go.'

Martin awakes as if from a dream. He slides his Raybans behind his ears, grabs the shoulder bag as if it is a child and he's a fireman escaping the fire gathering in swirling red and orange tongues about the wreckage, boiling the Scottish malts until the bottles explode like Molotov cocktails. The glass table supporting the inferno disintegrates and the flaming ruins spreads across the floor cooking the fish still flapping around their feet.

Act 3

The Time on the Clock is Now

......*scene 49*

It's a funeral procession from Knightsbridge to NoHo, 30 minutes to cover two miles, meter clicking, radio on Five Live. At least it's private in the back of a cab. Good place to check your texts. There's a theme, a code, and when you break it those texts all have the same message: *where's my fucking drugs?*

It costs a score when Krishna steps out at *Beautiful You*, the tattoo place on Chitt Street.

Chitt Street.

Who'd believe it.

In through the open door below the hand-painted sign, down a corridor strewn with takeaway flyers and estate agents' magazines, and he's back in the torture chamber with the neon fizzing and a view through iron bars of the dustbins from the Somali restaurant upstairs.

Why aren't there any blinds, for chrissake?

The place smells of spider's nests and sweat, the walls look as if they've been illustrated by Hieronymus Bosch, demons, devils, gargoyles, dragons and daggers, Celtic rings, rings of barbed wire, white supremacy symbols, crucifixes.

Winston's washing his tools.

'Yo wassup?'

Krishna points at the ring in his eyebrow.

'Can you take it out?'

'Out, man? Just put fucker in.'

'It's the girlfriend, don't like it, does she?'

Winston leans forward with a warning finger. 'You don't lissen to bitches, man. You fire da bitch and da next bitch say, hey you, pretty boy, you need some bling on your face.'

'Yeah, right.'

'Then, you come back and say, hey, Winston, I gotta new bitch, where's dat ring?'

'Contrary, right?'

'Don't let bitches wear dem trousers, man.' Winston dries his hands on a grubby towel. 'Tenner.'

Krishna snaps a ten from his wallet. He sits beneath the glare of the desk lamp, head tilted over the back of a chair, the day's events spooling through his mind like scenes cut into a sequence in an editing suite: Kosta Ali Pasha smashing Dixie Dean's hand. Alya giving him the evil. Martin sticking a gun in his throat, *twice*. Fucking an old woman starfished on the bed like the zebra hide stretched on the wall. Sitting here with surgical spirit burning his tear ducts as Winston separates the ring with pliers and eases it through the hole in his eyebrow.

'Here, man.'

'Keep it.'

'It's 18 carat.'

'Then don't look a gift horse in the mouth.'

'I wouldn't do dat, man, face like this, I scare da horse.'

Krishna stands, licks his finger and runs it over the wound. Never has nothing felt so good.

'Bye, Winston, you take care.'

'I do dat, man. And you take care of dat bitch.'

Krishna bowls down Chitt Street. Night's falling. The blue dome of the sky is moving through the spectrum from pastel to navy. Things are clearer in the dark. He's got a dozen clients waiting for product. He'll supply one last time and tell them he's out of it.

He summons up Baba's face and hears his voice singing the same old song; Baba's Hanuman, the monkey on his shoulder, haughty and wise. *There comes a time when you put childish pleasures behind you.* He's said that like a million times, like a chant, like a mantra, and it's done what mantra's are supposed to do, it's reached him. He's not going to go back to the LSE. He's not cut out for law. Trade's his schtick. If you can deal drugs without getting your throat slit by the Jamaicans, the East Europeans, the Chinese, the new Pakistani gangs operating out of the Midlands, if you can swim in those waters and keep the punters happy, you can apply the same set of principles to anything. Books. Films. Fashion. Software. India's a gold rush. He'll find his future in his past.

......*scene 50*

The sign at *Kosta's* is lit up, the blue neon making the world seem lightless. Krishna descends the stairs into the dense sweaty air, into the wall of sound, shrieking music, chatter, laughter, the ping of glasses. There's a girl on stage in a black top and shorts working her body up and down the pole, head flung back, breasts gyrating, long legs in black boots.

The editors and production assistants from Wardour Street come straight from work to catch some flesh for the journey home. There's the usual bunch of older guys up from the sticks, groups of two or three, safety in numbers. They've been in and out of the strip joints and girlie bars all afternoon and pitched up at *Kosta's* where the heat and noise and the press of bodies makes them feel good and the drink makes them feel daring. Hindus don't have one God. They have thousands. Same with Hell. It's multi-layered and down in the dank dark bottom that's where you'll find *Kosta's.*

Alya, Madalena, the Brazilian, and the Albanian, twin of the girl up on the dais dancing, weave through the throng. They'll climb up on stage and strip for twenty quid. You can pull up a chair and scope out their shaved pussies gleaming with sweat. If you want a fuck it's a ton for ten minutes. The girls say they're students working through school, good girls, there in the bar next to naked because there's nothing wrong with taking off your clothes, and if she likes you, and she certainly seems to, it will be fun to have some fifty-six year old delivery driver with his gut spilling over his jeans crushing you into the black leather sofa in the back room.

Krishna's surprised to see the acrobat girl from *Interface* at the far end of the bar with Kosta Ali Pasha. She's dressed in white with white blonde hair, a splash of paint on a dark canvas. Krishna knows Natalya Alexeyeva in the way you imagine you know people when you see them day in day out. She's smiling. He's never seen her smile before. Girls from Eastern Europe don't seem to find much to smile about.

Mental's squeezed in behind the bar. Krishna gets a beer, pays his fiver, and as he moves through the crowd he notices Guy Bradwell, dwarfed beside Kosta, a glass in his hand, a grin on his face.

'Ah, my friend,' says Kosta. He puts his great arm around Krishna. 'This is Natalya. She dancer.'

'Yeah, I've seen her.'

Kosta acts surprised, angry even.

'You see. Guy, he see. Why I don't see? Why you keep her from me?'

He turns to Natalya and throws up his big hands like he's surrounded by fools.

Krishna drinks his beer. He glances at Kosta, at Guy, at Natalya, and it's like London's some village where everyone knows everyone, everyone knows everyone's business, and he knows that the girl at that moment, even if she doesn't know it herself, is standing at the top of a high building, one false step and she'll plunge over the edge. He looks round at Alya. The life on her face is painted on, and behind her blue eyes there's nothing, a void. He looks again at Natalya. She is filled with hope, with optimism.

He leans closer to Kosta.

'Can I have a word?' he says, and Kosta holds up his big hand.

'Iz no problem. Tomorrow.'

......*scene 51*

Starbucks. Oxford Street. Do they have Starbucks in Belgrade? Sure they do. The whole world's changed in ten years. Starbucks, McDonald's, Gap. It's one big America now. Serbian. Albanian. Croat. Romanian. Russian. What does it mean? What did it ever mean? The past has gone. You can't live in the past. Lech remembers his father saying the time on the clock is now. They got up at sunrise and worked till the sun went down over the hills. When something has to be done now is the time to do it.

Yilly appears in the doorway holding a supermarket bag. He looks from table to table. The white dressing on Lech's smashed face is like an X marking the spot. Yilly lines up, a big man sweating in a black suit behind kids in shorts and tee-shirts, girls in short skirts, tits on show like medals.

Opposite the counter is a stand with shakers of chocolate powder, vanilla, cinnamon, napkins, straws, plastic spoons. Everything's been thought out.

Yilly sits with a big coffee and carrot cake. He eats as they talk.

'You have something?' he says.

'Yes. I have something.'

'Something that belongs to us?'

Lech nods.

Yilly eats.

'You give back?'

'I owe them nothing. You get one life – '

'I don't think about your life.'

He eats.

'You have the money?' Lech asks.

'I have it.' Yilly sips coffee, specks of chocolate dotting his top lip.

'Half now, as we agreed,' says Lech. 'Half tonight. You come at twelve. Is quiet.'

Yilly finishes the cake. Sups from the coffee cup. He places the supermarket bag on the table and keeps his big fist wrapped around the handles before Lech can take it.

'How you know?'

Lech thinks for a moment. What the hell. 'We watch. In Khandahar, Kabul, Tehran, Istanbul. We watch all along the way to England.'

'Lot of people watching. Lot of dead Serbs when we find them.'

He releases the bag. Lech takes it, rests it on his knees. Inside there is £50,000, 10 blocks of £5,000 in £50 notes wrapped in rubber bands.

He looks up. Yilly's on his way out, talking on his mobile. 50K. He could leave now. Right now. Disappear. He's got his British passport. His phone. He doesn't need anything else. Just go. Get the train out of St Pancras. He'll be in Paris before they know he's gone. If he can cross the Serbs, he can cross the Albanians. Fuck 'em all.

......*scene 52*

The BMW flies, the road inexplicably empty, the scene in the rear-view mirror backlit by blue flames climbing into the sky. The gun's in her bag, under the seat. Alive. Pulsing. Martin's at her side clutching something precious, and you don't have to be in Mensa to work out what it is. The boy's in the back, glassy eyes staring at nothing.

She looks at her hands on the steering wheel. Thomas's hands. He takes over when she's driving, and she can't work out why she drives intuitively as Thomas and thinks intuitively as Trilby. She's two people out of sync. She fucks boys as a girl because the high wire is life, but her body truly blossoms joined with the soft skin, pliable limbs, the moist warm openings of girls, and it makes her sad sometimes that she'll never know what it's really like being a girl.

Trilby needs space. She needs to think. You don't shoot people, not rich people, and get away with it.She's got to separate Martin from the gun, then work out where to go from there. This is a game of chess, one wrong move and you're dead.

She pulls up along the street from *Kosta's*, drawn by instinct, by the pattern of stars appearing in the night sky.

'I'm outta here...'

That's Jordan, half out of the car before Trilby can drag him back in.

'What's going on?'

That's Martin.

She keeps the motor running. 'Where'd you get the gun?' she asks.

'What?'

She speaks through gritted teeth, an angry hiss. 'The gun, Martin. The gun. Where'd you get it?'

'What the fuck's it got to do with you?'

'I'm going to get rid of it.'

'No you're not. Give it to me. Now. Right now. Give it over.'

He's clenching his fists, shaking, sweating. Trilby stares into his eyes, faces him down.

'I said I'm going to get rid of it.'

'What - '

'It's the only way.'

She reaches for the shoulder bag he's clutching and he pulls it away from her.

'What's in the bag, Martin?'

'Leave off. None of your fucking business.'

'You shoot people, everything's my business.'

'Fuck you.'

'Give me some money, I may need it?'

Martin thinks about this before pulling out a fat wedge of fifties and peeling off £100.

'That do you?'

'For now.'

Jordan's watching, eyes filmed in wet layers lit by the street lamps. He can't believe he's been fucked up the ass. People shot. Fucking fish flapping all over the place. The drugs are swishing through his bloodstream. He can hear *Stairway to Heaven* on the soundtrack.

Trilby jerks the gear stick into first.

'Look after the boy, Martin,' she says.

'You telling me what to do?'

'What's in the bag?'

'Fuck you.'

There's a beat.

'Where will you be?' she asks.

He glances at the neon sign. 'Like there's a lot of choice,' he answers.

Martin steps out of the front passenger seat, pauses, like he's going to change his mind. Things are slipping away. He's got to keep a grasp. Keep hold of the bag. Jordan gets out of the back of the car and throws up.

'You're disgusting, you know that...'

Trilby catches the disorientated look in Martin's eyes as she lets out the clutch. He's moving back to the car, but it's too late. She zips through the gears, slows for the speed limit, and zigzags through the back doubles to Covent Garden where she lives on a fourth floor walk up on Mercer Street.

……*scene 53*

As she climbs the last flight of stairs, Trilby sees a pair of sneakers huddled under bare legs, a denim skirt, a shock of dark hair, a white hand clutching a pink mobile phone. The hard lines on her face soften.

'Why aren't I surprised to see you?'

Bella looks up at her with the big green eyes of a lost kitten.

'You said you'd tell me the future.'

'You know something, I think it's here.'

She takes Bella's hand and hauls her to her feet.

The flat's warm, girlie, lots of lace, clothes thrown on chairs, lamps with big yellow shades, a poster from the movie *Blue Velvet* above a blue velvet sofa.

Trilby inspects the bruise on Bella's cheek.

'Now, would you like a nice cup of tea?'

Bella nods. 'Yes, please.'

There's nothing like good manners.

They drink tea from pink spotted white cups. Bella kicks off her sneakers and sits with her legs under her on the blue sofa. She fidgets restlessly like a boat tethered to the quay, anxious to be moving. Bella has a sense that time's racing, that she's wasted time and it's time to catch up.

'Who hit you?'

'That's nothing. Guy twied to dwown me. I hate him,' she says. 'I hate all of them.'

Tears well into Bella's eyes. Her shoulders start shaking. Trilby saves the cup before the tea spills, places it on the table. She sits at her side, takes her hands.

'It's my birthday today. Our birthday.' Bella's voice is a whisper. Trilby waits for more. 'Simon. My bwother. It's his birthday as well.'

'Where is he?'

'Daddy hit him, and...'

Now the tears come in big sobs that erupt through her body in waves like the aftershocks of an earthquake. Trilby takes her in her arms and the girl weeps, rocking backwards and forwards, the air catching in her throat, her pain, months of pain, passing by osmosis between them until Trilby's eyes grow moist. Bella sobs until the tears run dry. She clings to Trilby, exhausted, her words murmured into her neck.

'Simon tied a towel around his neck and hung himself in the shower at school.'

'I'm so, so sorry, Bella...'

'I don't know why,' she says. 'I do know why but I don't know why.'

'Some times there isn't a why, there just is – '

Bella pulls away and looks into Trilby's eyes. 'I hate Guy. I hate him. He's just a user. They just want to use you. Or hit you. Or fuck you – '

Trilby's taps the side of her head.

'They can't fuck you here.'

'You sure about that?'

'Yes, Bella, really sure. Take control. You choose to be a victim. Or you choose to be whatever you want to be.'

'Is that why – '

'Don't ask.'

'I'm sorry – '

'Don't be. Didn't someone say never explain, never complain and never apologise?'

'My father, pwobably.'

A fresh cloud passes over Bella's features, a look of anger, too, and confusion, and determination.

Trilby stands. Pours more tea. She brushes her hand through Bella's hair, a masculine gesture. Bella likes it.

'I want to do something and I don't know what,' Bella says.

'Sure you do.'

'I want to be like you.'

'Not much chance of that, honey.'

Bella grins; tears and smiles.

Trilby leans downs and kisses her on the lips. She then takes her bag and crosses the room to the chest of drawers where a collection of snow domes are laid out on the top, views of Paris, Amsterdam, an explorer riding a camel around the Giza pyramids, the scenes replicated in the gilt mirror above. She glances at Bella in the reflection.

'Where'd Guy go?'

'Where else? He thinks he's some big pimp all of a sudden. He doesn't understand: I do what I want.'

'There, you see, you do know.'

Trilby keeps her back to Bella as she slips the gun from the bag, locks it in the top drawer of the dresser, puts the key back in the bag and snaps it shut. She's not exactly sure why she's leaving the weapon behind, why she doesn't just clean off the prints and drop it in the river. That's what Thomas would do. But Trilby thinks with her guts.

She gives one of the domes a shake and places it on the table next to the sofa. Inside the glass sphere an old car from the 1920s carries a couple away from the Eiffel Tower, the road ahead growing deep in falling snow.

'Bella, I've got to go – '

'Go?'

'I've got to go and work a few miracles. Cure the sick? Save the whales. Save myself. Why don't you stay here?'

Bella's a child again. 'Can I?' she asks

'For as long as you like.'

'Great, I'll go and get my things?'

'Course, a girl needs her things.'

Trilby goes back to the dresser, opens another drawer, roots around and finds a spare key.

'Here.'

She places the key on the dresser and throws Bella a kiss as she leaves.

Bella returns the Paris snow dome to its place on the dresser. She counts them. There are fourteen and she shakes them, one after the other until they are all snowing at the same time. She tries the top drawer and wonders what Trilby could possibly have locked inside.

......*scene 54*

Now he's yawned his guts into the gutter his eyes are seeing things more clearly. The synapses in the grey matter are sending impulses over the neurotransmitters to receptor sites where they are processed into thought.

'You killed those people. You fuckin' killed 'em.'

Martin looks back at Jordan. How did he come to be standing here, with this kid, the car gone, the gun gone?

His fucking car.

His fucking gun.

He needs a drink. The drugs leave you dazed and paranoid. He needs to top up, be cool, think. He stares at the kid.

'Are you stating the obvious?'

'What?'

'This is what it must be like having children. That's why we get sent away to boarding school,' he says. 'Listen, boy, and learn: two things you can't change, the inevitable and the past.'

'You can't just kill innocent people.'

'Innocent. You fucking moron. No one's innocent.'

'Look, stop keep fuckin' callin' me a moron, right.'

Martin can feel the void in his waistband. What the fuck was he thinking letting Trilby take the gun. That's the second time he's let it out of his sight, first Krishna, now Trilby. And this is supposed to be his lucky day.

It *is* his lucky day.

He squeezes the leather strap on the shoulder bag and urges Jordan down the road towards the bar.

'Come on.'

'What? Where you going?'

Jordan lopes along at his side, the gold chain around his neck forming a halo over the head of Che Guevara, jeans falling down around his ass. What the fuck was he thinking taking this little cunt to Greta's in the first place? He should have shot him while he had the chance. You fire off a speedball and the inhibitions vanish. The high hits gravity and you freefall into an infinity of doubts and rationalisations.

'We need to get some things straight.'

'Nuffin' to get straight, you killed them fuckin' people.'

'Didn't you just say that?'

Little cunt. He needs to keep him close till Trilby gets back. She'll know what to do.

They pass *Kosta's* and turn into the passage leading to a stretch of sludge where barges once carried hides from the tanneries. Locals would remember the horse post that prevented vehicles entering, but it got knocked down or dug up, an orange cone stands in its place, and a black Mercedes is parked outside the club's rear entrance. At the end of the passage, a streetlamp stands against a low wall, the cobbles lit by the light filtered through the grimy rhomboids of glass. They say in London you are never more then six feet from a rat. This is where they breed.

Martin produces a packet of Marlboros, lights two and puts one in Jordan's mouth.

'Here...'

'Listen, man, I haven't done anyfin,' Jordan says.

'Haven't done anything? You dressed in their clothes. Look, you're still wearing the fucking chain.'

'Couldn't undo it, could I – '

'You fucked in their bed.'

'No I didn't.'

'Your DNA's all over that house. You can go away for ten years just for being there.'

'But I didn't do anyfin.'

'Who fucking cares? Me? Trilby? The police? The government? This is the Apocalypse. Everyone's got blood on their hands. How many people do you think they killed in Iraq, in Afghanistan? And for what? What have you got that fucking tattoo on your arm for? This is what you've been waiting for. This is anarchy.'

'Yeah, but what if we get caught?'

'Only stupid people get caught. Common people. They rabbit. They show off. They lie. They get a conscience. They're cunts. You're not a cunt, are you?

'You still fuckin killed 'em.'

'They're scum. They're gone.' He snaps his fingers. 'It doesn't matter.'

'You're a real fuckin bastard, you know that?'

'Course I am.'

Jordan smokes the fag. It feels good. Settles the stomach. The synapses are working.

'Is there any more coke?' he asks.

'Jesus. Two hours ago you didn't want anything, now you're River fucking Phoenix.'

'Who?'

Martin closes his eyes as if with a sudden pain and reaches for his snuff box. As he opens the lid, Jordan slaps the container from his hand, showering Martin's face with white powder, then jerks his elbow hard as he can across his cheekbone. He runs off screaming at the top of his voice.

'You cunt. Fucking cuuuuunt.'

Martin reaches for the gun. Fuck it. It's a lesson learned. Never part with your piece.

......*scene 55*

Bella's one more problem she didn't need. Not tonight. But the girl's touched some half-formed instinct. Maternal? Paternal? Life's a mess.

She sets off back to *Kosta's* with Thomas at the wheel but it's Trilby who turns off Tottenham Court Road at Goodge Street and touches down on the single yellow line opposite *Interface*.

She's going to find Guy Bradwell, warn him off, but as she steps from the car a hand of iron seizes her wrist.

'You. I know you.'

Trilby tilts her head to one side. Rolls her shoulders. Smiles. TVs expect the random fist in their face every time they step out. They have to know all the moves.

'Sure you do,' she says.

She flutters her black lashes. Looks for an exit. The guy's dressed like a cowboy in Cuban boots and a leather coat too heavy for the warm night. She notices behind him a buffed up bike, all chrome and shiny paintwork, a black helmet on the back rest like a skull on a pole in *Apocalypse Now*.

The big cowboy keeps a lock on her wrist and drags her across the street to the bar. They stand at the entrance gazing round at the crowd, leathered queens, trannies, girls in skinny tops, dealers and punters, dancers in fetish gear swaying to dark rhythms. Frenchie holds up his hands like a barman in a Western, playing the part, and Trilby spots Guy getting cosy at the bar with some aging hunk of muscle with cropped silver hair.

'Iz here?'

'Who, honey?'

'The man in the white clothes?'

Now she gets it. It's like a coin dropping in a photo booth. Lights flash, wheels turn, his face comes into focus, a spread of white teeth, the V of two fingers pointing to his eyes.

I see everything.

Interface. That morning. A lifetime ago, the cowboy looming over their table looking spaced, grinning at Bella.

Now he's looking for Martin. She can guess why.

She unwinds the fingers gripping her wrist.

'He's at *Kosta's*.'

'Kosta's.' He hisses the word through closed teeth. His body stiffens. 'He got something that belongs to me.'

'He's got something that belongs to me, too.'

'We go.'

She thinks about speaking to Guy Bradwell, but it can wait. Bella's safe where she is.

......*scene 56*

Bella's found a long thin screwdriver and she's picking at the locked drawer in Trilby's flat, stroking the steel mechanism like a tongue toying with a decayed tooth, round and round until she finds a lever that she manages to ease back a fraction before the spring snaps and the tool flies from her hand across the floor.

She retrieves the screwdriver, pulls up a chair and starts again. At least she's found the lever. There it is. Easy. Easy. She's gritting her teeth. Holding her breath. Almost there. Then the tightly coiled spring bites again, forcing the screwdriver back through the keyhole.

If at first you don't succeed. She remembers the story of Robert the Bruce after he lost his kingdom watching a spider trying to leap from one rafter to the next so that he could build a web. He tried and failed. He tried and failed. One last go.

Bella takes a firm grip along the edge of the dresser, leans into it with all her weight, and slides the tip of the screwdriver back in the lock. She presses down on the lever and, as the spring presses back, she keeps her hand rigid, holding the pressure against the metal coil. She draws air through her teeth, gives the lever one last heave, and hears a click as the bolt turns.

'Open sesame.'

She slides the drawer open.

Lying on a cushion of Provencal place mats is a gun, chunky, matt silver. She has never seen a gun before. It looks brutish yet beautiful, repellent and tempting. It's heavier than she anticipated and seems to fit as if made for her small hand, odd because unbeknown to her the Tokarev has the same feel in Miro Stanislav's hand. A gun is all things to all men.

She stands back and shoots herself in the mirror.

'Kapow. Kapow.'

A gun.

What's Trilby doing with a gun?

What could she do with a gun?

Find out how it works. That's the first thing. She returns to sit on the blue velvet sofa. She holds the gun with the barrel pointing away from her, just in case. There's a spring mechanism, like the one in the dresser drawer. When she flicks the switch, the clip falls out in her hand. She looks inside. There is space for eight bullets.

Four remain.

She slides the clip back in place.

She puts her sneakers back on, puts the gun in her bag and is about to leave when a thought strikes her.

She piles up the down cushions on the floor in the corner of the room, holds the gun at arm's length and pulls the trigger.

Nothing. Just a dull click.

There's a slide control you can operate with the gun in firing position.

She tries it, fires again.

The explosion is deafening. The slug rips through the down padding, drills into the floor with a thud and Bella is a child in her own snow dome as the white feathers fill the room, swirl about the ceiling and rain over her.

……*scene 57*

Trilby pulls to a stop along the road from *Kosta's* and they step out of the car.

'You, you bring. I wait,' Miro says.

'Okay, honey.'

She turns and he calls her back.

'Hey. No fuck me,' he says.

She shakes her head, although she wouldn't mind.

There's a guy in a black suit with a slashed face standing at the entrance. He doesn't smile as Trilby passes and descends the stairs. The club's packed, clammy bodies pushed together, twin blondes in black tops and shorts slither like coils of smoke about the golden pole, and she remembers Bella saying it was her brother's birthday today as well as her own and it only occurs to her now that they are twins. Were twins. Poor kid.

Trilby spots Krishna with Martin at the end of the bar, Martin like some cheap gangster in his Raybans.

As Trilby presses through the crowd she watches a couple of guys pulling out their wallets, shoving twenties in a girl's hand.

'Took your fucking time, didn't you,' Martin says as she's kissing Krishna's cheeks.

'Try being nice,' she replies.

'Fuck you.'

He lowers the shades and she studies the puffy bruise around his eye with an overwhelming feeling of schadenfreude.

'The little prick elbowed me,' he explains.

'You should have been nice to him.'

'Cunt,' he says. 'Where's my fucking gun?'

'Safe,' she tells him.

'You didn't get rid of it, did you? I want it back. I want it now.'

She doesn't answer. She holds out her hands, she's clean.

Krishna's reading the subtext. The ring in his eyebrow was like a crosswire in an electrical circuit and full power's back on. He knew when Martin left the Gyroscope Building with a manic look in his eyes and a gun shoved down his pants somebody was going to get hurt before the day was done.

What did Martin say?

There are two rules in life. Rule One: There are no Rules. Rule Two: Don't forget Rule One. Rules for a man who doesn't know which rule to break and just wants to break them all.

He glances at Trilby. She's in control. She always is.

'Martin,' she says, 'time to go.'

'Is it now?'

He raises his empty glass. Mental jerks along the narrow space between the bar and the optics panting like Jabathehut.

'Vodka tonic.'

He glances at Krishna, at Trilby, holds up three fingers.

Krishna watches Alya climb up on the low stage. She slowly slips from the two scraps of gold cloth that cover her breasts and shaved mount and all the while she's dancing she stares at him with a look of pure concentrated hatred, a hatred that taints the soul, and he remembers Baba saying a man's word is his bond, there's no way of escaping it, you are either a man with honour, or you're a man with nothing.

......*scene 58*

Bella's dressed in her school uniform. She had wanted to give it to Oxfam, but Guy thought it might come in handy, and Guy was right. Some men want to be spanked by a schoolgirl, others by a mistress, by mummy, a nurse, a nun. They want to be gagged, weed on, beaten like dogs. Kink is a kaleidoscope, endless colours and combinations. To her mind, the men who come to Guy's flat act strong but it is all a façade, they really feel weak and inadequate, they pay to be humiliated and then feel justified humiliating others.

Guy has been brilliant drawing her into his world and making it seem normal. He has found weaknesses in her, as he finds weaknesses in the punters, but when he held her under the water in the bath, like the famous drowning man the last three months of her life flashed before her and it all looked so cheap and gaudy, so vulgar and dull. The air fled from her lungs and it felt as if she were sinking back into the amniotic soup with Simon.

Well, that didn't happen. She's here and she feels oddly relaxed on the sofa in Guy's living-room, the naked girls in a row of prints along the wall, details of nipples, buttocks, the smooth inner surface of thighs lit by the glow of the chandelier. Napoleon's next to her on his plinth, alabaster eyes shaded by her straw hat. The iPod's playing Amy Winehouse, and the gun is in the Prada bag wrapped in a white scarf.

Bella remains stretched out when Guy minces in with a beefy old guy with cropped silver hair.

'Agh, here she is...'

Guy's smile blends approval with satisfaction. The uniform's just *purrfect*, it shows he hasn't lost his touch.

Guy imagines he knows how girls think but he doesn't. Girls go along with things because that's the nature of girls. They are born with the word YES on their tongue, and keep saying YES even when inside they are saying NO. It's all so clear now. It might have something to do with turning eighteen. She's not a girl any more. She's a grown up, and she can read in Guy's eyes the assumption that she's come round, all she'd needed was a slap and the pot of gold at the end of the rainbow would be there for him, flowing and abundant.

That's how much he really knows human psychology.

'Bella, Bobby. Bobby, Bella,' he says.

Bella pulls the pods from her ears. Shame. She was getting into the music.

'Hi, Bella,' says Bobby.

He has an American accent, somewhere from the South, a big chest made for medals, and rheumy blue eyes that study her like a landscape.

She glances back at Guy.

'I just came to say good bye...Guy. Hey, it rhymes.'

'Is there a problem?' Bobby says.

'No. There's no problem. What's going on, sweetie? Not still angry?'

'I'm quite welieved, weally. I'm going home.'

'To your father?' Guy says, half laughing, breathless. What a fruit.

'I waited because you owe me money.'

'Me owe *you* money? After all I've done for you. Given you a roof – '

'Hey, man – '

'It's all right, Bobby. Be cool,' says Guy. 'See, I told you, she is wonderful.'

Bella flutes her brow as she turns to Bobby.

'Bobby, be a good boy, and buzz off,' she says.

But he doesn't move. He can't move. His feet fuse to the floor. His eyes deepen in his head, suck him down, down to his deepest fantasy, the neon singing in the hot Saigon night, the bars, the strippers, the girls, the girls, who can forget the girls.

'Bella – ' says Guy.

'You owe me £500,' she cuts in.

'I beg your pardon?'

'I want it. I want it now.'

Bobby surfaces.

'Excuse me.'

'Excuse me,' says Guy. 'You just hang on a minute.'

Bella stands as Guy crosses the frayed Persian carpet towards her.

He pokes her with his finger, forcing her back against the wall. Bella is unafraid.

'Bella, you are going to be nice to Bobby,' Guy tells her, speaking like she's a child in need of discipline. 'You're going to do what Bobby wants. You're going to do everything Bobby wants.'

'I don't want any trouble,' Bobby inserts.

'There, you see, Guy, no twouble,' says Bella. 'Just your cup of tea.'

Guy raises his hand to hit Bella. Her expression makes him hesitate. His slap barely touches her shoulder as she skips from his reach and retreats across the room.

Bobby likes this. Maybe it's part of the show. Maybe it was always part of the show...

Girls in gold cages, flashing lights, Jimi Hendrix, images hung in his mind like the paper lanterns suspended over the chop suey stands, a buck ride in a pedicab to Rick's at the end of the strip. He remembers that night like it was yesterday, the big colour sergeant from Tennessee taking the girl from the cage, bending her over his knees and drumming her bare flesh to the throb of the music, the wail of the guitars, the wail of the guys chanting beat that ass, beat that ass, clapping in time, the sergeant playing that drum until the last breath was beaten from her body. The guys cheered, the music grew louder, a couple of goons carried the girl from the stage, and sometimes he hears Hendrix in his dreams, he sees through the fog of marijuana the girl from the cage bent over and it's his face across the room, his arm raised, his hand coming down on that little brown ass.

'Come on now,' says Guy. 'There's a good girl. Come and be nice to Bobby.'

'You scum,' she says. 'You disgust me.'

As Guy approaches again, Bella in one kinetic motion flicks the clasp on the bag, removes the package and lets the bag fall to the floor. With a flick of her wrist, the white scarf uncoils like a flag and Bella holds the gun confidently, pointing it at Guy.

Guy's mouth drops. Bobby's lifeless eyes flicker with life.

'Wow, hang on. Where're we at?' he says.

'Bella, what's going on? What's got into you?'

'Give me my money,' she says

He's looking closely at her, at the gun, eyes like snake eyes.

'Bella, look, it's okay. I didn't mean it.'

Guy starts to edge forward. Bobby watches, afraid, intrigued, uncertain.

'Let's just chill, baby,' says Guy.

'Don't move,' Bella tells him.

'Look. It's all right. Just calm down.'

'I said don't move.'

Guy lunges. He catches her by her left arm. The gun's in Bella's right hand. She swings round and shoots out his kneecap point blank, the sound of the explosion echoing about the room as Guy falls screaming to the floor.

Bobby holds up both hands.

'Oh, fuck. No. No. Fuck me. Help me. Bella, help me. Why? Why? Oh, fucking hell.'

'Hey sorry,' Bobby says. 'I shouldn't be here. None of my business.'

'You fucking shot me,' Guy cries. He's holding his shattered knee and rolling about the floor. 'Look,' he says, 'there's blood on the carpet.'

Bobby pipes up again.

'Listen, I...I gave him two hundred and fifty pounds,' he says in a voice that says he probably shouldn't have mentioned it.

'Then you were lucky you didn't see the goods first,' Bella tells him.

Bella takes the wallet from Guy's jacket, removes the £250 and shoves it in the top pocket of her blazer.

'But –'

'Bobby,' says Bella.

'Yeah?'

'Goodbye.'

Bella glances around the flat. Down at Guy. He's clutching his damaged leg, blood everywhere.

'Help me,' he pleads.

Bella finds Guy's mobile in his pocket and gives it to him.

She goes through to the bedroom and reappears with another bag. She wraps the gun in the scarf and places the parcel back in the Prada bag. Bobby watches. He's a big guy. He could grab Bella, take his money from her, but it doesn't occur to him. You're either with the power or with the victim. You can't play both sides of the fence.

'Are you still here?' Bella says.

'Hey, that was something else.'

'Worth every penny?' Bella asks and he can't help nodding in agreement.

'Help me. Please help me. I'm dying,' Guy weeps.

'No you're not,' she says and turns to Bobby.

'Do you want to share a cab?'

'I guess...'

......*scene 59*

As he watches Greta tuck a slither of poppadom between her lips it suddenly occurs to Krishna that he should marry her. The daughter of an MP, they're the same caste, all Europeans are honorary Brahmins. It would make Baba happy. He'd see it as the law of cause and effect in action, his son climbing into bed with the upper classes, his karma visible in the next generation.

Greta sits back, drawing a coil of hair into a clip from which it instantly escapes. She notices his eyes on her.

'What?'

He smiles and shakes his head. 'Nothing,' he says, and she raises her thin shoulders in a shrug.

She is a pleasure to watch, the wells in her collarbones growing deeper with that little shrug, the way her long fingers snap the poppadom and feed crumbs between her lips. Conversations and cutlery had grown still when they arrived at *The Ferryman*, eyes drawn to her fragile perfection, the faceless couples below the swaying palms taking an inventory of her body, its angles and curves, gold curls in blustery eruption, her progress choreographed by the catwalk. A beautiful woman defines the man. Love is narcissistic. Greta May is that obscure object of desire and, straight or stoned, it's curious that naked on the bed like a portrait by Goya, she's about as sensual as a glass of tap water, the promise of packaging over content.

'I was just thinking we ought to get married.'

She sips her Tiger beer.

'Okay,' she says.

She reaches for her cigarettes before rememberlng even she can't smoke at *The Ferryman* any more.

She looks up and smiles.Waiters appear, their steamy trays infusing the air with the spice smells of the bazaar.

Greta's had an *awful* day. She *hates* Angus McTee, little oik. She doesn't want to be the face of *Shameless*.

'It's so demeaning, so deceitful, so corrupt.'

'Poor baby.'

'They want a girl of twelve to sell body cream to grandmas.'

'Advertising. The last lie,' he remarks. 'The last and the biggest. Blair, Cameron. They're nothing more than Ad men.

'Mad Men.'

'Exactly.'

Greta aims the serving spoon at the circle of silver bowls.

'Mmm, delicious,' she says, serving Krishna, eulogising the food without eating any.

It strikes him how similar Greta is to Alya, same hair, same eyes, like moonlight, a wan reflection of the sun. When he gives up dealing he'll never see Alya again. She'll dance at the bar. She'll fuck every man Kosta tells her to fuck, and she'll end up dead with an overdose, or her throat cut. Alya will vanish. She'll be dropped in a landfill, or fed to pigs. No one will know and no one will care. It's what happens. There are more girls with blonde hair and blue eyes arriving on the bus from Bucharest and Budapest.

Krishna stabs a nugget of curried lamb and holds the fork before Greta's lips. Her eyes dance. Her lips open and she seizes the chunk of meat in her teeth. She brushes curls behind her ear, shapes a ball of rice in her fingers and opens her wide jaws to shovel it in. Turmeric marks her cheek.

Krishna dips his napkin in water. As he wipes the yellow stain from the corners of her mouth he's aware of the four men at the next table watching. She's a toy. They'd like one.

Greta has made a display of eating and will eat no more. Eating's not her thing. She pushes the food around her plate as if by doing so it might vanish. The leftovers will go into waste bags, the bags will be raced by trucks to be incinerated in areas where poor people live, the poison will rise into the ozone and carbon trading companies will fly to Borneo to pay naked tribesmen not to cut down the forests.

She looks into Krishna's eyes, studies him, and he waits for her to notice the absence of bling in his face.

'Have you ever thought about doing, you know, something different?' she says.

'About five hundred times a day,' he answers.

'Angus said I'd made the last three. He asked for my number...'

'Doesn't he have your agent's number?'

'What an arse.'

She sips her beer.

'Did you mean that? About getting married.'

'Yeah.'

She smiles and eats another piece of poppadom.

......*scene 60*

An ambulance with its blue light slowly turning stands on the circular drive outside the White House. The house is a blackened shell. Firemen dampen the embers. Forensics in white like poltergeist hover in the plumes of smoke. A team of paramedics are cautiously bandaging the remains of a cremated body to hold it in one piece.

They've already dealt with one corpse. It's lies zipped in a vinyl bag inside the ambulance.

Inspector Patel took a glimpse, not that there was anything human that he recognized. He has to show dead bodies to live witnesses. You have to have a stomach for it and he doesn't.

He moves down the drive taking quick breaths through his teeth. Through the wrought iron gate at the side of the house, the tradesmen's entrance, he can see the rear garden, the neatly cut lawn, long as the first hole where he plays golf at Addington. When he has time. Which is never. The rockeries are edged by cedar fencing and, off in the distance, the view vanishes into mature trees silhouetted against the night sky.

He wanders back into the glare of the police arc lights as Sergeant Marley steps out of the Mercedes clutching a mobile phone.

'I'll call the last few numbers,' he says. 'Might be something.'

Patel watches his sergeant's fingers skip over the keyboard. Two rings and there's a voice on the line.

The Inspector leans closer to listen.

'Yes?' says the voice.

'Oh, hello, I'm sorry to bother you, Madame. My name is Sergeant Marley, I'm a policeman. Are you a friend of Mr and Mrs May?'

'Hey, what is this? Who are you?'

'There's been an accident – '

'An accident! What do you mean? What's going on?'

'There has been a fire, at the house of Mr and Mrs May.'

'A fire. Are you serious?'

'It is serious, I'm afraid, yes.'

'Where did you get my number?'

'There was a mobile phone in the car parked outside the house. Yours was the last number received.'

'Oh, my God, you are serious. Are they all right?'

'We can't be sure at this stage. I would like to take a statement if I may, as soon as it's convenient.'

'Jesus. I had lunch with Sara. Listen, is Gordon there?'

'As I say, we can't be sure at this stage. The Fire Brigade is still here.'

'I don't believe this. You're sure now?'

'It would be very useful if we – '

'Look, you listen a minute, are you at the house?'

'Yes, Madame.'

'You give me twenty minutes, I'll be there.'

'That's very kind – '

……*scene 61*

Maxine had just stepped from the shower wondering what to wear and now she's going to be interviewed by the police it has given her an excuse to début the pale grey Loulou de la Falaise with the sheer blouse from Nicole Farhi and those delectable Yves Saint-Laurent undies.

Mother didn't have money, poor thing, Maxine had to climb that mountain on her own two feet, but one thing she taught her is that a woman should always dress for the occasion. Maxine has refined the advice by making it a policy not to cross state lines, as she puts it, French with French, Italian with Italian, Spanish with Spanish now the Spanish are growing so clever.

Grey is serious, it's what the occasion calls for, the Nicole Farhi is alluring, and you can never go wrong with Yves Saint-Laurent.

Her eyes move along the ranks of carved bottles like sculptures on the glass shelves.

What could have happened to poor Sara? And Gordon?

She chooses Paul Smith Rose, a youthful fragrance she dabs in the hollow between her breasts. They are firm beneath her palms, dappled pink from the shower, alert in the discreetly padded bra she slips over her arms. She steps into her panties and turns back to the mirror.

'Eat your heart out.'

Between the bathroom and the bedroom is a hallway lined on both sides with closets. She yields to temptation, opens the far door and steps into the embrace of her winter furs, arms reaching for her, drawing her into an embrace, the smell of dust and jungles and bloody sunsets claiming her like memories. Her fingers discover between her legs a hint of dampness she savours on the tip of her tongue. She is wet still. Like a virgin. The boy did that.

She steps from the closet into her skirt, the blouse, the jacket, a long row of silver bangles. In William's gaze from the bedroom wall she discerns approval. The memory is a puzzle of irregular pieces that can be laid out and gathered in, then laid again in immeasurable patterns. He was forty when the portrait was painted. He was older than her once and now he's younger.

She jiggles the mirrors, checking her rear view, the tube of bangles like something alive as they wriggle up and down her wrist. Her legs are good. It's so important. She is hot in the grey suit and feels like taking it off, running naked. She did it once on the Promenade d'Anglais and William had been boyishly proud. She blows him a kiss before turning out the light.

......scene 62

When the paramedics finish bandaging the second cadaver it looks like the invisible man, or a pharaoh being zipped into a post-modern sarcophagus ready for some future tomb robber to uncover. Sometimes the pathologist gets more answers from the dead than CID get from the living.

Steve Zimmer from forensics emerges from the ashes and picks his way towards Patel. The black smears on his white jumpsuit make it look like he's dressed as a skeleton for Halloween.

Zimmer carries a ziplock baggie in the tips of his fingers, swinging it as he gets nearer.

'You're going to love this – '

Patel identifies what's in the bag: a compacted pellet of milled steel.

'You're not going to tell me it's from the same fucking gun?'

Zimmer grins. He likes his job. 'Wouldn't like to say, Arthur – '

'Arjun – '

' – more than my job's worth.'

'You know sommink, he's my fucking MP.'

'Didn't know you were a Tory,' says Zimmer.

'All coppers are Tories, ain't that right, Marley?'

'No, Sir.'

Patel shakes his head despondently and stares back at Zimmer. 'We've got a long fucking night, Steve, is it the same gun or not?'

Zimmer throws up his shoulders. 'At first glance, I'd say so. A Tokarev, 33 series, eight live ones in the clip. Hundred and fifty quid in Kings Cross.'

'How come you know all that?'

'Got two shells back at the lab. This time tomorrow I'll know who packed them in the crate for shipping.'

They pause as the paramedics push by with the body bag on a wheeled stretcher, then turn and watch as a metallic grey Porsche roars to a halt at the entrance to the drive.

A woman in clothes matching the car steps out into the sodium glow of the arc lamps. She pushes by the two Bobbies who make little effort at holding her back, hurries, slows, then hurries again towards the house.

She collapses into the arms of Inspector Patel.

'Oh my God – '

'It's all right, lady – '

'Oh no. No. What's happened, what's happened?'

She feels as light in his arms as the bag of shirts he drops off at the laundry once a week.

'It's all right – '

'It's not all right, what's happened here? Who are you?'

'Inspector Patel, Madame. You know the people – '

'They're not *people*, they happen to be my friends – '

The ambulance doors close. The paramedics climb aboard and the vehicle pulls away, the blue light flickering across Maxine's face so that she looks like a new guest just arrived at the all souls' party. Tears pool into the hollow of her cheeks as she hammers Patel's chest.

Steve Zimmer slips the baggie in his pocket and makes his way back into the conflagration.

Patel strokes Maxine's shoulder. She likes this.

'What we really need to do is speak to a member of the family.'

She sniffs and sobs. Sobs and sniffs. She's determined to be useful.

'Yes officer,' she says. 'Of course.'

She stands away, sliding a slim silver iPhone from her bag with the same geometry of movement a woman would show running nylons down her leg, unhooking the clasp on her bra, the act subconsciously erotic.

She squints down the file of names. 'Why do they make these things so small?' she hisses and presses the key. The phone rings three times.

'Greta, it's me, it's Maxine, I'm so, so sorry...'

......scene 63

There are three gum wrappers and a half dozen butts around Miro's boots. Dangerous work being a hitman. You could smoke yourself to death.

A kid all in white ambles by with his girl both carrying bags and coffee cups from *Subway*. Miro knows it's not who he's looking for but swings him round by the wrist to make sure.

'Hey, man...'

There's something gnawing like a rat at Miro's insides and it registers that he hasn't eaten all day.

'You give, I take.'

The kid can't believe he's being mugged for his sandwich.

'You can't do that...'

The hand around his wrist is like a force field, like some powerful electro- magnet, he can feel the flesh burning under the pressure. He can't move, even his feet are stuck, and he watches like a statue as the big guy reaches behind him and pulls a couple of twenties from his back pocket.

'You take,' he says.

The kid does a double take.

'Okay, man.'

He takes the money, but remains locked to the spot: he can see himself in the pub telling the story.

Miro digs into the bag, takes out the chicken salad baguette and lets the bag fall to the floor with the fag butts.

The kid moves away, then comes back, extending his arm.

'Coffee?'

Miro takes the cup and keeps his cold stare across the street on *Kosta's.*

There are a few more fag butts on the ground when Trilby exits the bar with Martin.

Miro grasps around in the corners of his memory, it's unclear, disjointed, a flashback, the whore with red lips and yellow hair...*Your whole life shows in your face, Cowboy, and you should be proud of that*, the Chinese midget, the dude in the white suit pushing by in a hurry.

His head's clear now. Good sandwich. He watches as they make their way towards the car and steps out of the shadows.

'You - '

'Who the fuck are you?'

'Gun. My gun.'

Martin twigs, glances at Trilby.

'Tell him, babe – '

Trilby glances at Miro, shrugging, and as she takes a half step away from Martin an icy sting runs up his spine. He can't believe this. Not now. Not after all he's been through.

'You bitch. You cunt. You...you fucking prick...'

He's stumbling back the way they'd just come, the cowboy gripping his shoulder, Martin gripping the shoulder bag, Trilby's heels ringing on the cobbles as she trots behind them down the passage to the canal.

'Listen, man,' Martin says, 'she's got it.'

Miro's not listening. He's searching Martin, under the arms, down his sides, round his belt, down his legs. He learned all this stuff from the movies.

'This is a fucking set up, man. Are you listening to me. It's a fucking set up.'

'Gun, you fok, vhere is my gun?'

'Fuck me, man, I had it, now she's got it.'

Miro looks back at Trilby. She shakes her head.

'She's fucking got it you stupid cunt...'

Miro's had enough of this. It's been a three-pack day. He seizes Martin's head in the vice of his two big hands, gives his neck a sharp jerk that snaps the spinal cortex, and Martin Campbell Gilchrist feels a slow creeping paralysis move down his arms to his fingers, down his legs to his feet, muscles destabilizing until he crumples like a pillar of salt. His Raybans fall to the floor, and he stares into Trilby's eyes, his lips shaping a single word as the breath of life puffs from his dead body.

'Why?'

There is no why. There just is, Trilby's thinking as she scoops up the shoulder bag.

'Come, baby,' she says. 'I know where to look.'

'Vhere?'

'Come. We go. I show.'

Miro stares at Trilby. If the gun was in that shoulder bag the guy would have handed it over. Fear would have done that. Whatever's in the bag, that's what she was looking for. Now he wants what he's looking for, what's his. He wants to feel the Tokarev back in the waistband of his blue jeans. It would be just as easy to kill her. It goes through his head. But that won't get the gun back. You make choices. You trust no one. Just your own instincts. They stand there in the foggy glow of the Victorian lamppost like a portrait enigmatically titled *A Day in the Life of a Gun.*

Miro picks up Martin's lifeless body in one hand and drops him with a dull thud into the slime of the canal. By daybreak a million rats will have picked him clean.

......scene 64

Bella and Bobby aren't going in the same direction. She steps out of the cab at the Bayswater tube.

'Listen – '

'I never do that,' she says, slams the cab door, and skips off in her tartan skirt down the steps.

It's five stops on the Circle Line to Sloane Square.

The train's almost empty. It's that nowhere time, too late for the office crowd, too early for the clubbers. A couple get out at Notting Hill and as the doors slide shut she hears the sound of sobbing at the far end of the carriage.

She recognizes the Che Guevara tee-shirt, the twin ear-rings, the mop of hair, and goes to take a closer look.

'Are you all right?'

He looks up. He doesn't answer. He sniffs back tears.

By some trick of the light the girl appears to Jordan like an angel. It's like everything's gone supernatural. All day he's been a player in a video game and now he's coming face to face with the Princess in her ice castle, the final act in some fantastic drama. He stares at her.

'Where're you going?' she asks.

'Nowhere. Just round in circles.'

'I did that once,' she tells him.

His face crunches up and two tears roll down his swollen cheeks. 'What the fuck's wrong with people?' he moans.

'Anyone in particular?'

He looks up. 'I'm going to prison,' he says.

'I don't suppose it's got anything to do with Martin?'

'Him. He's a cunt...sorry. He's nothing. Nothing. Just...nothing.'

Bella goes to speak and pauses. She sees her reflection in the window, then it vanishes as the train slows into High Street Kensington. The platform's empty. The train races off. The driver wants to get home

'He made you do something you didn't want to do?' Bella asks.

'I did a lot of things I didn't want to do – '

She cups his cheeks in her palms, stares into his eyes. 'Never do anything you don't want to do,' she tells him.

'It's really bad.'

'Weally, weally bad?'

He nods.

'Are you sorry?'

'Course I am. I'm not like that. I hate him. I wish I could just forget about it.'

'You have to forget about lots of things.'

'I wish I could just go back to this morning. I only came up to buy some guitar strings. I wish I'd just left when I had the chance,' he says. 'I didn't do anything.'

'Then you don't have to worry.'

'These people, they...they really fuck you.'

Bella taps the side of her head. 'They can't fuck you up here.'

He thinks about that.

Gloucester Road.

The hiss of sliding doors. A few on. A few off. Everyone at the centre of their own vacant universe, bad jobs, debt, internet dating, random violence, carbon footprints.

'If you didn't do anything,' Bella says, 'move on. And if you can't move on, go back and make it better. Then move on.'

'I want him to go to prison for what he did. Even if I have to go as well.'

'That'll just wuin your life.'

'It is ruined.'

'The only person who can wuin your life is you. You choose who you are, you choose what you do.'

'Not always.'

South Kensington. The stops are coming quicker. They're racing through time. She could get off here, it's the same distance to home as it is from Sloane Square, but she prefers the walk along the Kings Road. The train pulls away. She takes his hands.

'You choose to feel guilty,' Bella tells him. 'That's all right. You probably should. Doesn't mean you have to go to prison.'

'I want *him* to go to prison.'

'He comes from a wich family, Jordan. He won't go to prison. It's people like you who go to prison.'

'It's not fair.'

'I know. You choose to be a victim,' she adds. 'Or you choose to be whatever you want to be.'

He tries to take all this in.

'You look like an angel,' he says.

'Perhaps I am.'

He wipes away his tears. Smiles. He feels better now.

'Can you do something for me?' he asks.

'If I can?'

'Will you take this off. I can't do it.'

He turns round and Bella releases the spring holding the clasp on the gold chain he's wearing.

He folds it into her hand.

'Will you take it, please?'

'OK.'

She kisses his forehead as the train dashes into Sloane Square.

'My stop,' she says.

She takes her bag, waves, and Jordan watches as she tracks along the platform and disappears.

......*scene 65*

Fire's a metaphor for man, careless, destructive, violent. It's all about greed. That's what the Fire Chief says. It's about not knowing when to stop. Give it some air and it won't stop. Ever. London's as dry as death in the heatwave, a breath of night breeze and drifting embers flicker to life, hover across fallen beams, insulation, charred floorboards, stray picture frames, family treasures.

'Oi, you'd better move yourself,' he shouts at Steve Zimmer, and as the forensics man backs away the Chief directs his finger at a young fireman with a sardonic look about his smoke-weary face.

'There, Jason, there.'

The fireman switches the aim of his jet, the water rising in a rainbow under the arc lamps, their dome of yellow light giving the scene the look of a stage set in a Harold Pinter play.

Maxine has moved on from Inspector Patel and clings to Sergeant Marley. He's younger, better looking. More her type.

A taxi pulls up.

Maxine unwinds herself from Marley and hurries on her heels to Greta, tall, skinny as hell, a little black skirt, a red shirt half open, hair any which way. You can only get away with it when you're twenty-three years old.

She can't believe it's Krishna's paying for the cab. As he turns, Maxine imagines her eyes are playing tricks on her. He moves towards her and the mask of grief stretched over her wide cheekbones turns into something more abstract, like this is a love triangle and for some perverse plot point the characters need to be here at the same place at the same time.

'Darling. Darling Greta,' she cries and takes the girl in her arms.

She peers over Greta's shoulder at Krishna. Her expression remains inert, but in her eyes is the message: don't breathe a fucking word.

Greta pulls away. A man's approaching, Inspector Patel, and he's staring at Krishna, not her. Maxine registers this. It's confusing. She's becoming a bit player.

'What the hell's happened?' Greta cries. 'Where are my parents?'

Greta falls to her knees. She clenches her fists and though she sees what she sees it seems unreal, something you see on television, the smouldering ruins of a school or a hospital in some far away place bombed from 50,000 feet. The house was three floors when she left this morning. Two have gone. Jagged bits of wall along the back stand dangerously above the rest, firemen train jets of water into the morass.

'Sergeant,' says Patel.

Marley goes to help Greta from her knees. The Inspector corners Krishna.

'What are you doing here?'

'She's my, my girlfriend,' he says, then points at Greta as an afterthought.

Patel releases a long sigh. 'Right bloody mess, I can tell you,' he says. 'How's your father?'

'Baba's well.'

'I'm very pleased to hear it. And you, Krishna, what about you?'

'Me? I'm...'

Patel holds up his hand. He stares into Krishna's eyes.

'In a vacuum you are either sucked down into nothing, into samara, or you stand tall like a pillar. Whatever you do, do the right thing.'

Krishna's not sure why the older man is saying this. He can see his father in Arjun Patel's features, they are old friends, they sit on the same advisory bodies, the community small as a village.

'What do you mean?' he says

'Krishna, don't take me for a fool,' Patel answers. 'I know more than I want to know. Now, do as I say.'

'I will.'

'You mean that?'

'Yes, Mr Patel, I do.'

......*scene 66*

It's coming up to midnight and a lot of people are looking at the clock like it's New Year's Eve and some resolution's about to be struck.

It's hard to believe it was only 12 hours ago when Miro Stanislav kicked over his Harley and headed for Goodge Street with his Tokarev primed and ready.

Two shots. Head and Heart.

Now he's sitting in the passenger seat of an open topped car crossing London still looking for his weapon.

......*scene 67*

The Albanian twins at *Kosta's* are performing a military dance, marching like clockwork soldiers, coming to attention. They remove their tops, throw them like they're grenades into the chanting crowd of beer-swilled Englishmen and fire imaginary machine guns, shaking their small firm breasts.

Kosta glances at Yilly.

Midnight.

Time to go.

Qerim joins them. Mental leaves the bar for Alya to serve drinks. It makes a change from fucking.

As Mental takes up a position at the bottom of the stairs like a grounded dirigible, the others file into the backroom, down a flight of steps concealed under a trapdoor to a low cellar still stinking of coal. Kosta opens a long metal case and throws Yilly a Chinese Type 56 assault rifle. He throws another to Qerim. Takes a third and closes the case.

There's another flight of steps that wind up through a narrow service shaft to the cobbled alley and the Mercedes parked beside the club.

......*scene 68*

Bella strolls along the Kings Road and feels oddly at home being back in her own part of London, bright shops, clean streets, nice accents.

......*scene 69*

Feathers frost every surface in Trilby's flat. A brass cap indented with a hammer blow lies buried in the floorboards, the gun that fired the cartridge has gone walkabout, and there's a jumpy Serb coming down from H with sweat on his back and low tolerance to disappointment.

'You fok me.'

'No, it's, him,' Trilby says, pointing back as if at the past, the canal. 'He left it here. Now he's gone.'

Her mind's racing. *Where the fuck has Bella gone? Why the hell did she take the gun?* Trilby looks round at the feathers, at the snow domes on the chest of drawers, at Miro.

'You fok me,' he says again.

'No. Come, I take you. It's OK.'

'No iz OK.'

Miro grabs her wrist and pulls her close, stares into her eyes like he's looking for something he may have overlooked, like in all that blue there's some mystery he can't quite fathom. Trilby stares back. He sees no fear in her eyes. That's the way she's playing it. Show fear and you're dead.

'Honey, we'll find it. I promise.'

He lets her go. Trilby leaves the shoulder bag. It's zipped and buckled, heavy with some treasure and there's been no time to find out what. If she doesn't play it cool with the Serb, she'll never find out.

She locks the door and follows him down the narrow wooden staircase with its threading carpet and the sweet noxious smell of overripe fruit rising up from the wholesalers on the ground floor, worse in summer, worse this year than ever before.

The night's warm, the breeze cool on her bare arms. Miro sits beside her in the car like a lost boy gazing at the buildings, the lights, people going home, people going out, working girls, dealers, pimps, clubbers, players, schizophrenics pushing supermarket trolleys in intricate circles like characters fated by some ancient myth, sheiks with chauffeurs and blonde companions, Nigerian warriors in oversized uniforms checking the resident parking bays, cop cars with blazing blue lights threading through the traffic with takeaway pizza, runaway girls sleeping rough for the first time. London rocks 24/7. There's no city like it, not anywhere.

......*scene 70*

The colour's blanched from Guy's face. He's tied a towel around his shattered kneecap and the blood has clotted in a burgundy patch. He's sobbing gently, drawing comfort from crying, the tears drying in smears on his cheeks.

When the door buzzes in the street below, he pulls himself across the carpet but can't stand to hit the switch on the entry-phone. It buzzes again and again. There's a brief silence broken by feet on the stairs and in his paranoia he imagines it's Kosta Ali Pasha come for the grand he owes him.

It's not. It could be worse. The door to the flat bursts open and the big cowboy from some other lifetime erupts into the living-room with Trilby.

They all speak at the same time.

'Help me. Help me.'

'Vhere iz my gun?'

'Where's Bella?

'That little bitch,' says Guy.

'Gun. Gun.'

'It's not here. Help me, Trilby, please. I'm fucking broke – '

'I vant my gun – '

Miro's clenching his fists. Flames stretch over his cheeks.

'It's OK.' Trilby turns from Miro back to Guy. 'I'll call an ambulance.'

'Are you crazy? My father will kill me. I can get that doctor, you know the one, but I need a hundred pounds. Please...'

Trilby takes £100 from her purse. She holds it just out of Guy's reach.

'Where's Bella?'

'I don't know. I don't know. She shot me and then pissed off.'

'I knew it was your lucky day,' Trilby says, and Guy doesn't understand. 'She didn't kill you,' she adds.

Miro's trying to follow this but he's distracted by the gallery of naked girls and fat-assed men around the walls, the marble busts, the candelabra, Dalí's painting of *The Metamorphosis of Narcissus*, a rock emerging from water and transforming into a man. It draws Miro into the landscape and takes him back to the hills of Pristina.

'Help me, Trilby. Please.'

The whining's getting under Miro's skin. He turns away from the painting and glares at Trilby.

'Gun? Gun? My gun?'

Trilby shrugs.

'Bella,' says Guy. 'She's got it. She shot me.'

Trilby goes to speak but Miro holds up his hand to stop her.

He looks back at the row of naked girls and his mind spins in a Catherine wheel of flawed memories, a long fizzing flashback: he saw this guy running through the street with the girl, the girl with green eyes, the girl from the bar sitting in a ray of silvery light, the girl he wants to tell things to, he wants to tell her about his sisters, dead now, his father...

'The girl?'

'Bella,' Guy says.

'She do this?'

'Yes, yes,' Guy replies and Miro breaks into a smile.

'Vhere is she?'

'I don't know, man, she just shot me – '

Miro glances at the money in Trilby's hand.

'I kill.'

'He ain't worth it, babe.'

She drops the money in front of Guy.

'I want this girl?'

'I can find her. I'll find her, and I'll find the gun.'

Miro processes this. Trilby can see the light changing his eyes like he's a computer loading. She didn't know how she was going to get out of Guy's place in one piece. Bella's a lifeline.

'I take you somewhere and come back. I find her, I find the gun.'

'You don't fok me.'

'No.'

He takes a long look at Guy.

'Why she do this?'

'I don't know. I don't know.'

He looks back at the naked girls, back at Guy.

'She not OK, I come back.'

......*scene 71*

She is OK. She's standing outside a four-storey house in Carlyle Square and notices that the attic lights burn brightly.

Bella lets herself in with her key. As she closes the door, Mother appears, the long fingers of her left hand reaching for her throat, features tentative, head dropping to one side in a gesture Bella has grown up imitating, the pose of a beautiful woman conscious of its effect. Mother wears a black linen suit and the espadrilles she bought when they stayed the previous summer with friends with a finca outside Granada.

'Bella, it's you...'

Bella drops her bag. After walking the length of the Kings Road it feels like it weighs a ton. Mother glances from the bag back to her daughter.

'Hello, Mummy.'

'You can't imagine how worried I've been – '

Mother sounds like a radio actress from the fifties, breathless, mannerly, vaguely fatigued with inflections Bella adjusts to.

'Didn't Daisy tell you I was all right?'

'With her usual reluctance,' says Mother. 'Where have you been?' You just disappeared. Your father's beside himself.'

'Where is he?'

Mother draws her shoulders up; it's another familiar gesture. 'Finishing a book, the eighth – '

She's about to say more but pauses and Bella suddenly feels sorry for her mother, her looks a fading asset, her power declining in ratio to Father's growing acclaim. Mother at forty-one belongs to another time, another age, another England. It's not family name that matters now, it's celebrity and that vulgar unmentionable stuff: money.

'Where's Daisy?' Bella asks.

'In bed, darling, it's gone midnight. What's wrong with you? You look, I don't know – '

Mother looks again at the bulging bag untidily on the hall tiles, at Bella in her school uniform. A thought strikes her, her pale lips part.

'It's your birthday – '

'Our birthday,' Bella says, and the hand goes back once more to Mother's flushed white throat.

'Bella, I know, I know, I'm so – '

'I'm OK, Mummy. What about you? Are you OK?'

'Bella, what are you saying?'

'Mummy, I'm going to talk to him.'

'He's busy.'

'He's never too busy to talk to his children.'

'Bella – '

'Mummy?'

'Bella, I know...'

Bella smiles briefly. She takes her mother in a rare embrace and Mother accepts the gesture, drawing into her daughter's arms, and Bella is conscious for the first time that she is taller than her now.

'Won't be long,' she whispers, and crosses the hall to the stairs.

Daisy appears at her bedroom door in her night clothes as Bella turns on to the top landing. Bella holds her fingers to her lips and takes Daisy in a big hug.

'I missed you,' she whispers

'I missed you,' says Daisy. 'Hey, you're eighteen, that's cool.'

'Did you get me a present?'

'I'm, like, totally broke.'

Bella kisses her fingertips, plants the kiss on Daisy's lips and feels an odd sort of relief as she climbs the stairs to the attic, the Prada bag over her arm.

......*scene 72*

A black Mercedes slows to a halt outside *Silvia's* restaurant.

Inside it's quiet. The gypsy music's been turned off. A few drunks nurse one last glass of slivovitz.

Silvia puts the baklava back in the glass cabinet. She stands straight and looks at the big clock with the picture of Republic Square in Belgrade. It's ten after midnight and still no sign of Miro.

Teo collects the *Absolut* ashtrays with their malodorous galaxies of ash and crushed filters and carries them through to the kitchen where Kresimir and Lech wash dishes, stack saucepans, speak their own language, smoke. Where they grew up it was illegal not to smoke.

The bruise on Lech's face has spread like a purple stain across his brow, temples and cheeks. He glances at his watch. He's sure it read ten past ten minutes ago and it's still ten past. Time's frozen. Petrified. He should have taken the 50K he'd got from the Albanians and gone, just gone. This is someone else's war. Nobody wins. Nobody ever wins. The money's zipped in his leather jacket with his passport. He'll be gone tonight. He'll have a hundred grand. He'll start a new life.

The sound of gunfire is surreal, expected but unexpected.

Kresmir drops a plate that smashes into tiny pieces and runs through the open door into the restaurant.

Lech remains watching from the doorway as three big Albanians spray the premises with machine-gun fire, short, quick, deadly bursts that take out Teo, the late night drinkers, Kresimir in mid-step, scattering tables and chairs as he stumbles in a death march towards his mother.

Only Silvia is left alive, untouched. She glances at Lech Jovanovic in the doorway. She knows.

She turns from Lech to face Kosta, one hand on her wide hips, the other sweeping back her black rooted blonde hair in a provocative way that's almost touching.

'Kosta.'

'Silvia.'

Lech calls.

'I'll get the case.'

They wait, studying each other as Lech hurries upstairs, slips his arms into his jacket, and descends two steps at a time carrying the attaché case.

'It's all here.'

Yilly flicks the locks, checks the contents: twenty bags of glittery brown powder from Helmand Province.

Silvia spits on the floor. 'Judas,' she says.

Yilly nods towards Kosta and it is Qerim who squeezes the trigger on his assault rifle, it barks briefly and Lech falls dead. Yilly unearths the 50K from Lech's pocket and Kosta Ali Pasha shrugs with the modesty of a game show winner. He looks back again at Silvia.

'My son will kill you,' she says.

'I know.'

Qerim opens fire.

Silvia falls dead at Kosta's feet. He bends and brushes her hair from her face. He closes her eyes with two fingers and stands gazing about the restaurant as if with an eye on the real estate, his features tinged with a hint of sadness. Silvia Stanislav was a warrior, a survivor; when you kill your enemies a little piece of yourself dies as well.

......*scene 73*

The big Merc slides into the hot night and it's just a moment later when Miro turns the corner and pulls up outside the restaurant on the Harley. Trilby's close behind in the red BMW. Miro drags off his helmet and walks back to the car.

'My place,' he says, and points at the sign: *Silvia's.* 'You come with me.'

'I come back.'

'No, you come,' he says, and grabs her wrist through the open window.

She doesn't flinch. She stares into his eyes. 'I come back,' she says again.

Miro's hesitation is like a computer loading programmes, circuits buzzing and straining, the street lights flickering in his eyes. He tightens the grip on her wrist.

'I won't fok you,' Trilby adds, and Miro grins.

'Maybe,' he says, and releases her. 'You find girl. You find gun. Or I find you.'

'You got it,' Trilby says.

He strolls on Cuban heeled boots towards the restaurant door and Trilby races back to Covent Garden.

......scene 74

Father sits on his kneeling chair before the computer. The machine is positioned in such a way that Bella can see the words like black ants marching across the screen. An angle-poise lamp shines on his papers, the austere glow giving his craggy features a stern, almost fiendish look that softens when he turns it off.

'Bella, Bella, darling. I've been worried sick - '

'You killed my brother.'

The air goes out of his sails. 'You know that's not true, Bella,' he says. 'You have to be strong - '

'Simon wasn't strong.'

'I did what I thought was right. I wanted my son to be...prepared – '

'Didn't work, did it?'

Bella sits in the chair facing the desk. From her bag, she takes out the white bundle and slides her hand inside the folds of the scarf. She glances at the book jackets on the wall.

'The great writer,' she says.

'Bella, what's got into you?'

'At least you'll be remembered.'

He shrugs. He wants to be remembered, in this life and the next one.

'Bella. I love you, you know that, I'll do anything for you. I love Daisy. And I loved Simon.'

'You loved him to death.'

'I never thought –'

'I'm sorry, Daddy.'

Bella stands, the gun in her hand glowing mutely. She moves towards the desk, the sights aimed at her Father's head, hand steady. She's been thinking about this since she found the weapon in Trilby's drawer, although she didn't find it, not exactly: she'd had an inkling, an intuition, that it was going to be there, maybe she caught a glimpse of the gun as Trilby hid it. Whatever. It seemed right. It seemed like it was meant to be. Today. Their birthday.

'You killed my brother.'

'I didn't. I didn't.'

Tears well up in his eyes and the face he pulls is the same face Simon wore that day in the study when Father hit him, the same look of abject terror, of loss and desperation and hopelessness.

She hears Mother behind.

'Bella. Bella. No - '

Bella glances back. Mother presses weakly at the door. Daisy holds on to her.

Bella moves closer, calm, poised.

Father's bladder gives way, the stain spreading over his trousers as he pisses himself.

'No. No. No,' he cries.

Bella leans closer, shouting at the top of her voice.

'BANG!'

Turning, she shoots the computer screen.

The machine explodes in a gleam of brilliant green light, and Father falls unconscious from the kneeling chair to the floor.

......*scene 75*

24/7 licensing laws.

Makes life easier. Patel and Marley are having a quiet pint in a noisy bar full of binge drinkers getting caned, teenagers, dead beats, druggies.

What are you going to do, arrest them all?

Patel's suddenly got an Indian accent, a head full of nostalgia. Marley's heard it all before, but he likes the Inspector. He's a good man. Good at his job.

'I could have played for England, I had a trial, of course, I was excellent, but there used to be a lot of prejudice in the bad old days.'

'What about the good new days, Inspector?'

'They're just around the corner, Sergeant. You just have to know where to be looking.'

His mobile rings; his accents switches to Cockney, the colour drains from his cheeks as he listens.

'You're having a laugh, aren't you?' he says and as he switches off he glances at Marley. 'Told you it was the fuckin' Balkans out there.'

......cut

Miro sits on the floor nursing Silvia in his arms, surrounded by blood and dead bodies, tears streaming down his face, blue lights revolving in the street outside.

......scene 76

Maxine's nursing a glass of sparkling water in the library filled floor to ceiling with books, few of them read, her face shadowed by that weariness that comes when she drinks champagne at lunchtime.

She hears the door open, hears footsteps in the hall, a few words spoken to the maid.

Henry enters with his usual half smile, half apology, half pleased to be home, entirely pleased to be himself: a national treasure it said once in the *Daily Mail*. The quiz show host sweeps back his silver mane, a familiar gesture, and two tears roll down Maxine's cheeks.

'Darling. Darling. What's wrong?' he says.

He goes down on one knee as if to propose, takes her frail hands in his, and Maxine's glad he's home. She doesn't care if Henry's come from a girl, or a boy, whatever it is he does, she's indulgent with him and he is indulgent with her. They're together. That's all that matters.

......*scene 77*

Jordan eats cheese on toast at the breakfast bar. It's not breakfast time. It's just gone a quarter past twelve and Mum was about to put the cat out and go to bed.

'What sort a day d'you 'ave then?'

He blows out his cheeks.

'Memorable,' he says.

'That's nice.'

'You know somink, Mum, I fink I'll go to college.'

Mum smiles and pours her boy a glass of Ribena.

......*scene 78*

Hash makes you feel relaxed, lethargic, a vacuum. It's a natural tranquilliser. Greta May needs it. She takes long draws on the joint and stares with glassy eyes at Krishna. She's in his bed, in his pyjamas.

'Why?' she says. 'Why. I keep running everything through my mind. I mean why? It doesn't make any sense.'

Krishna takes the joint, flicks off the ash, looks at the fiery tip, and gives it back to her.

He doesn't want to tell her what he suspects. Let the police find the facts. That's their job. His job is to look after her. Himself. He runs his finger over the place where the eyebrow ring had been and as he looks down at Greta with her sleepy dead eyes it's the face of Alya that comes again to his mind. He remembers that day when she told him her story and he knew when he promised to help her he never would.

......*scene 79*

Trilby opens the shoulder bag. A pink glow lights her face.

She takes out a bundle of £50 notes, 100 sheets thick: £5,000. She lays the bundle on the table.

As she is taking out another bundle, her mobile rings.

'Hi, babe.'

......***intercut***

Bella in a taxi.

'Trilby – '

'It looks like an angel's been here.'

Trilby grabs some feathers and blows them from her palm.

'Can I still stay?' Bella asks.

'For as long as you like.'

Bella mouths a kiss.

'Mmmmmwah,' she says.

Trilby hangs up.

She continues taking bundles of £50 notes from the bag, one after the other, and stands back looking at the pile as you would a readymade in a gallery titled *Is Marcel Duchamp worth £300,000?*

Her mobile rings again.

......intercut

Krishna looks down at Greta asleep in his bed, his mobile stuck against his ear.

Trilby answers after three rings.

'Krishna. What a surprise...'

......fade

To a black sky studded with stars. The moon's racing towards the horizon. The sun appears, emerging from the east into a chroma blue sky. The light glimmers on the Thames, the roofs of the Houses of Parliament, the glass buildings, the motionless glass pods on the London Eye. Green emeralds sparkle from Hampstead Heath to Blackheath, Battersea Park, Hyde Park, Kensington Gardens like stones from a bracelet flung randomly among the city streets where ten million people rise to another long summer's day filled with potential and the potential for despair.

......*scene 80*

Trilby's behind the wheel of the red BMW, hood down. Only it's not Trilby, it's Thomas in a pale grey suit and white shirt, the Patek Philippe watch on his smooth wrist showing ten after ten.

Krishna's sitting in the back with Bella. She wears a white cotton dress with a lacework front, silver shoes.

......*cut*

Dixie Dean sits in *Kosta's* drinking hot sweet coffee, his bandaged hand resting on the bar like an exhibit.

Alya polishes glasses, stacks them on the glass shelves.

Qerim and Mental sit at the card table, cards still, Mental eating a cheese and ham bagel, Qerim, expressionless, drinks vodka, down in one, filling the glass. Yilly's standing on a chair with a long screwdriver tightening the brass pole joined to the low ceiling.

Kosta's in the back room spooning quinine, milk powder and ant killer into a plastic bowl containing a half kilo of brown, stirring the mixture and weighing the cut into deal-sized baggies. He does the work himself. That's what life's taught him. You have to do everything yourself.

......*cut*

Bella shows Krishna how the gun works like she's some expert, sliding out the clip, pointing at the last bullet in the tank, and sliding the clip back with a reassuring click.

'That's the safety,' she says. She disengages, then flicks the catch back on again. 'Make sure it's off.'

Krishna takes the gun, his damp hand squeezing the hilt, trigger finger stroking the trigger. There's a ganglion of nerves big as a fist in his insides.

Thomas slows to a halt.

'Five minutes and I'm out of here,' he says.

Krishna steps out of the car and sticks the gun down the back of his trousers. He disappears as Thomas backs down the narrow passage towards the Mercedes.

Bella's kneeling on the back seat and can see two blue eyes gleaming from the cobblestones.

'Look, sunglasses,' she says. 'That's just what I need.'

'Quickly,' says Thomas, but she's already skipped over the side of the car and is hurrying down the passage towards the canal.

Thomas opens the passenger doors.

......cut

Krishna bowls into *Kosta's* grinning like he hasn't got a care in the world.

'Hi,' he says.

Qerim and Mental don't bother acknowledging his appearance. Yilly waves a screwdriver at him and goes back to work.

Krishna approaches Dixie.

'Found those girls for the videos yet?' he asks.

'Nah, but I spoke to Guy, didn't I?'

'Don't know, if you say so.'

He moves down the counter towards Alya. He stares into her eyes. She stares back with hatred.

He's been rehearsing this.

'You come in one minute,' he says.

She goes to speak.

'One minute,' he repeats and it's like a light has gone on behind her dead eyes.

Krishna knocks on the office door and strolls in.

Kosta Ali Pasha's sitting at his big desk behind a set of electronic scales.

'Now, you see, I have everything.'

Krishna's sweating. He's thought about this, but now he's there in that small room with that big man, fear has got hold of his spine.

'You have stress?' says Kosta.

'Must be the drugs.'

Kosta leans back, his mouth falling opening in a belly laugh.

At that moment Krishna pulls out the gun, flicks the safety and deposits the last bullet in that yawning chasm.

Kosta goes rigid, staring, then slumps forward, head crashing down with a thump on the alchemy of powders that rise in a cloud and hang motionless on the still air.

Alya enters immediately. She's been right outside. She closes the door and shoots the bolt with cool precise movements. The girl has no fear. Not any more.

'Come,' says Krishna.

Now he's actually done the deed he's terrified, trembling, the sweat freezing over his skin like a glacier.

'Wait.'

Alya pulls open the drawers down the side of the desk, one after the other.

There's pounding at the inner door.

Krishna's waiting, back door open, a triangle of light finding its way over the high walls along each side of the passage.

Alya pulls out files and papers until she finds what she's looking for: a passport and two photographs. She has life in her eyes when she finally rushes out of the room, Krishna behind her.

'In the car,' he shouts.

She dives into the back with Bella, Krishna in the front.

Thomas accelerates out of the passage as Yilly appears from the club entrance, arm stretched, gun in firing position, and as he pulls the trigger the fender on the red BMW clips his thigh and sends him reeling back against the wall, a spray of bullets dotting the brickwork above their heads.

Mental emerges from the club like a giant slug unused to daylight, raising his gun as the red car disappears around the bend.

......cut

Krishna's shaking like a leaf. Bella takes the gun from him. She cleans the prints off with the white scarf.

NoHo. Across Oxford Street. Zigzag through Soho to Shaftesbury Avenue. Right down Charing Cross Road to Trafalgar Square where Krishna steps out of the car and runs across the intersection to the tube. He wants to get back before Greta wakes up.

Thomas keeps the speed down as he threads through the back doubles to the Embankment.

'Okay, now where?' he asks.

'Bucharest?' says Alya.

'OK,' says Bella.

As the car crosses Lambeth Bridge, Bella throws the Tokarev into the river. She pulls the Raybans over her eyes and they glimmer with sunlight. It's going to be another hot one.

......fade out

3654636R00155

Printed in Great Britain
by Amazon.co.uk, Ltd.,
Marston Gate.